SEVEN NIGHT STOPOVER

ZARA COX

Boldwood

First published in 2014 as *Spiral*. This edition published in Great Britain in 2025 by Boldwood Books Ltd.

Cover Design by Head Design Ltd.

Cover Images: Shutterstock

Every effort has been made to obtain the necessary permissions with reference to copyright material, both illustrative and quoted. We apologise for any omissions in this respect and will be pleased to make the appropriate acknowledgements in any future edition.

A CIP catalogue record for this book is available from the British Library.

Paperback ISBN 978-1-83678-917-8

Large Print ISBN 978-1-83678-916-1

Hardback ISBN 978-1-83678-915-4

Ebook ISBN 978-1-83678-918-5

Kindle ISBN 978-1-83678-919-2

Audio CD ISBN 978-1-83678-910-9

MP3 CD ISBN 978-1-83678-911-6

Digital audio download ISBN 978-1-83678-913-0

This book is printed on certified sustainable paper. Boldwood Books is dedicated to putting sustainability at the heart of our business. For more information please visit https://www.boldwoodbooks.com/about-us/sustainability/

Boldwood Books Ltd, 23 Bowerdean Street, London, SW6 3TN

www.boldwoodbooks.com

1

————

Noah King stared back at the grave faces across from his desk with a growing sense of disbelief. For several seconds he was sure they were joking. But then nobody, least of all he, was laughing.

"Let me get this straight. You three are here to stage some sort of fucking *intervention*?"

Gabriel shrugged. Mike folded his arms in a defensive gesture that hadn't changed since the fourth grade. Damon, his oldest friend, rubbed the side of his nose before staring him square in the face. Noah knew he wouldn't like what came next. Not that he liked what they'd just announced.

"Take it easy, man, we're just watching out for you," Damon said.

"By ambushing me in my office? What are you, The Real Housewives of Corporate America?"

Mike laughed, then sobered quickly, his palms out in a "chill, man" gesture when Noah glared at him. "Damon's right. We're worried. You haven't been your-self for a long time now—"

"Yeah, I wonder why," Noah cut across him, his insides clenching with the effort it took just to breathe through the vice around his heart and the anger boiling in his gut.

The three guys—his best friends until exactly five minutes ago—exchanged wary looks.

Gabriel stood and paced a few steps to the window before turning to face him. "Noah, buddy, it's been two years," he said quietly.

"Dammit, I know exactly how long it's been." His tight smile held no mirth. "What I didn't realize was that I was on a goddamn clock."

"I told you he wouldn't make it easy," Mike muttered.

"Yeah, you two should've listened to Mike and killed whatever it is you're cooking up," Noah growled. Bitterness still burned like acid, and he would've given his right arm not to be having this conversation.

"Hey, that wasn't what I said," Mike protested.

"I don't give a fuck what you ladies decided on your way over here. This... whatever *this* is, is over. I have a meeting in ten minutes, so..." He gestured toward the door. None of them moved. Noah's sense of disbelief grew. "Are you kidding me with this bullshit?"

Damon grimaced. "Yeah, we're not leaving, pal. We kinda made a pact."

The back of Noah's neck tightened. "A *pact*? Do you have any idea how very eighties high school sitcom you sound right now?"

"We're not leaving here until you agree to hear us out."

"Then get to the point," he said through teeth clenched hard enough to crack his jaw. "So I can kick your asses out the door and carry on with my day."

"You need to get out from behind that desk, and we don't mean just to go home, crash and return at 6 a.m. We mean, have some sort of life beyond making your next billion."

"What the hell are you talking about? I get out plenty. I've never missed our monthly poker matches."

"You arrive late and are the first to leave," Gabriel said.

Noah exhaled slowly. "Again, I didn't realize I was on a timer."

Mike shook his head. "You can be defensive all you want. Bottom line is, you've given up on living. You play poker with us because you feel obligated. Aside from riding your desk, everything you do these days is an obligation."

His gut clenched harder. "Seriously, watch it, Mike."

Mike glared back. "Fuck, man, you're throwing your life away because of her. You know that by shutting yourself down she's winning, right?"

Noah's breath caught on the jagged anger ripping through him.

"That reverse psychology bullshit hasn't worked on me since we were kids, Mike, and even then it worked like, what, once? Frankly, I'm disappointed you think I'd fall for it."

"Shit, man, we have to try something before you turn into a goddamn zombie."

He collapsed back into his seat and clenched his fists tight to stop himself from going for Mike's throat. Of course, not so deep down he knew the anger that rode him was directed at himself than anyone else. So was the unrelenting tide of anger and confusion that washed over him every time he thought of his ex-fiancé.

Had he pushed her too far in those final months before his life had descended into hell? He'd thought he'd made his feelings and expectations clear enough. Hell, he'd even come straight out and told her what he wanted from her. What he wanted for both of them.

Only, things had gone *spectacularly* wrong.

He scowled at the narrow-eyed, *concerned* faces staring back at him.

Jesus. He didn't want to do this now. *Or ever*. Ashley was *his* past, *his* hell to inhabit for however long he chose.

Whatever his friends wanted didn't matter.

His intercom buzzed. He leapt on it with relief.

"Yes, Maddie?" he asked his PA.

"The clients are here. They're on their way to the conference room."

"Thanks. I'll be right there."

He scraped his chair back pointedly. They made no move to budge. He sighed and speared his fingers through his hair.

"Seriously guys, I'm not doing this—"

He paused as Gabriel reached into his suit pocket, extracted an envelope, and tossed it onto his desk.

Noah picked it up and turned it over. The indigo-colored envelope looked expensive and normally he would've used a little care in opening it. Right now though, he felt no compunction in ripping it open. The contents made him grunt in disbelief.

"No." Hell, this was the last thing he needed. There was a reason he'd been so careful not to put himself in a situation like this... A reason he didn't let the hunger within take over...

"Show some appreciation, man. We shelled out a quarter mil each to get you that ticket—"

"Then get a refund," he snapped at Gabriel, then immediately regretted it. He didn't want to be drawn into a lengthy argument, but the last thing he wanted was to cause offence. The three guys eyeing him with varying degrees of concern were the same who'd stuck by him two years ago. They had his back, whether he liked it or not. And they were stubborn enough to remain put when he wanted them gone. "Shit, I can't do this. I'm keeping seven Japanese businessmen waiting who will consider it an insult if I'm any later than I already am. I'll give you my answer on the next poker night." It'd still be a no, but by then he'd have found a way to refuse without pissing his friends off.

Mike shook his head, the stubborn streak which

had seen him battle through a shattered ACL and shattered dreams to head one of the most successful baseball teams around, in full residence. "No can do. Like I said, we made a fucking *pact*."

Noah hung on to his patience by a very thin thread. "Did you pinky swear too?"

Mike shrugged. "You can snark all you want, as long as you say yes."

He looked down at the invitation. He knew about the Indigo Lounge—the A-class adults-only clubs operated from luxury super jumbo jets. There was no way he'd let himself be talked into taking the trip. For two years, he'd managed to stay away from temptation, to avoid the urge to lose himself... to indulge.

No way.

His hand curled over the thick envelope. "Okay. You win. I'll go."

Shocked faces stared back at him, then Damon's eyes narrowed suspiciously. "You're not jerking our chain? Because if you're humoring us so we'll leave..."

He maintained the poker face that had won him more games than he cared to count. "I said I'd do it. Now, can I get on with the rest of my day, or are you going to break out the tutus and perform the *Nutcracker* for my enjoyment?"

"Fuck," Gabriel huffed. "You've just proven that we

were right to worry about you. Your imagination has strayed very deep into Tim Burton territory." He tugged on his custom-made Armani jacket before turning for the door. "See you at poker on Thursday. And don't even think about coming up with some lame excuse to cancel the IL trip. We may be buddies, but don't think I won't sue your ass if you let my money go to waste."

The other two delivered equally pithy warnings before they exited.

Even before he strode down the hall towards the conference room, Noah had come up with several plausible reasons to turn down the invitation. If worse came to worst, he'd refund them the cost of the ticket with a firm *no thanks*.

Their friendship worked because they each knew when to push hard and when to back off. They'd come close to overstepping today.

It was nothing he wasn't willing to forgive, but by accepting the invitation to the Indigo Lounge, he would be placing himself in a position where his control could be tested. Only Gabriel knew the true extent of what had happened two years ago with Ashley, and he was surprised his friend was advocating this.

So far, he'd resisted the temptation of the Indigo Lounge, had listened, unaffected, as Mike, Gabriel and Damon rhapsodized about the sheer hedonistic pleasures of the luxury outfit.

He'd told himself he was okay with it, that the CFR—*catch-fuck-release*—mantra he'd adopted with regard to his sex life served him well.

So what the fuck if sometimes the mantra rang hollow? Or that the sex barely scratched the deep, clawing hunger he'd locked away under concrete and titanium?

It was the way it needed to be. The only way it *could* be.

Except when midnight rolled around, he was staring at the indigo-colored invitation.

Rising from his desk, he strolled to the window, envelope in hand, and gazed out at the blazing nightlife that pulsed through Miami, the place he'd made his home for the last eighteen months.

February in Miami was a hell of a lot different than February in New York, but once he'd accepted that New York wasn't big enough to contain both him and Ashley, the choice had been easy.

He caressed the envelope. He'd ignored his phone's incessant reminders to confirm his next CFR, this one with an accomplished pianist he'd met at a client luncheon on Monday. Her curvy, petite frame and large blue eyes had tweaked his interest, but even as his mind had clocked her generous attributes, it'd immediately drifted to who would replace her come next week.

The hollow feeling in his gut expanded. It grated to admit his friends were right. Finding risky and cutting-edge opportunities to invest in had become 99 percent of his life, with a marathon sex session with a decent lay who knew the score thrown in once a week.

It didn't even satisfy him anymore that King's Ransom, his venture capitalist business, had made him billions, more money than he would be able to spend in one lifetime. He could make money in his sleep.

That is, if the other 1 percent didn't keep him awake at night.

He glanced at the envelope and drew out the invitation.

Seven Nights. Seven Highs.
An Experience Not for the Faint-Hearted.

He read the brief description, and his pulse began to throb. A heady combination of extreme sports, unique cultural experiences and uninhibited sex.

He allowed the forbidden door to crack open a

cautious inch, granted himself a tiny glimpse into the vault he usually kept slammed shut.

Sucking in a breath, he clawed his fingers through his hair and realized they were trembling.

His ex-therapist would no doubt have informed him that he was at breaking point, that denying his needs was taking a physical toll on him, if he'd still been seeing her. She'd been right about more than a few things. Certainly, she'd been right that the weekly sexual escapades with faceless women would eventually cease to satisfy him. Just as *he'd* been right to warn her he'd never see her again if she kept up the sexy come-ons and he fucked her. She'd kept them up. He'd fucked her on every surface in her office. And then walked away.

Which was a shame because she'd been marginally useful on the rare occasions he needed to unburden. She would've been useful now. Because he was stroking the edge of his endurance. And something had to fucking give.

The inner door creaked wider, and he tensed. But the words hammered relentlessly through his brain.

Seven Nights.

Seven Highs.

Could he do it? Take what he needed and walk

away after? If the cracks were showing enough for his friends to be worried, he was in deep shit.

Seven Nights.

Seven Highs.

He could carry on as he was, ignoring the ache shredding his gut and the need fucking with his brain. Or he could grow some balls and do something about it.

2

Leia Michaels zipped the empty suitcase, put it away and looked around the large luxury cabin on the jumbo A380 she'd boarded half an hour ago. The privacy-loving freak in her had declined the services of her personal valet and unpacked her own clothes.

She was well aware that at some point she would have to let others serve her. The experience wouldn't be the same if she insisted on doing everything for herself, as Warren, her guardian, had warned her.

And considering he'd curbed his objection when she'd splashed out on this insanely extravagant trip, the least she could do was make sure she got her money's worth.

She steeled her spine against the gut-clenching knots she'd come to associate with separation anxiety.

A month ago, she'd turned twenty-three.

Things were about to change, were already changing. Leia had insisted on choosing how she spent her birthday, instead of letting Warren make the choice for her as he'd done since she was seventeen. And although she'd sensed his disappointment when she went ahead and bought herself a ticket on the highly exclusive Indigo Lounge, she couldn't help but think this was some sort of test.

It was one of many tests he'd set for her over the last five years.

In the beginning, she'd failed many of them. But he'd been patient. Nurturing. Gentle even sometimes, when he wasn't pummeling her ass during their sparring matches.

Leia exhaled and smoothed a trembling hand over the side of her head. The six-inch swathe she'd shaved off above her right ear had grown almost a millimeter. She was undecided whether to let it grow back completely or keep it shaved. But that was a decision for another day.

Right now, the only thing she needed to think about was whether to join the champagne reception once they reached cruising altitude, or stay in her suite and decide on which of the *Seven Highs* would be her first. Every self-preserving nerve screeched at her to stay put in her suite.

To stay safe.

She started as her cell rang. Only one person knew her whereabouts. Only one person would call to check up on her so soon.

As usual, mixed feelings of trepidation and elation wrestled within her. She answered the phone. "Warren."

"Are you well, my dear?" His voice, always soft, always modulated, drifted over her senses. A feeling of calm stole over her, like a soothing pat on the back after a long cry.

"Yes, fine thanks."

"Is your adventure everything you dreamed it would be?"

She laughed. "It's barely started."

He paused a beat. "You will be careful, won't you, my dear? You won't forget everything I've taught you?" Although his voice remained soft, she sensed a tiny thread of censure, the same tone she'd heard when she'd told him her plan to take the IL trip.

Her hand tightened over the phone as her trepidation escalated. "No, of course not. I haven't forgotten." Not that she needed the reminder.

Since she'd left the safety of home, Leia's instincts had been on red-hot alert. And she planned to keep it that way.

The intercom next to the door buzzed. "I have to go, Warren."

"Of course. We will speak tomorrow. As we agreed, the board meeting has been rearranged for the day after you return, but there are some papers I need you to sign. I'll email them to you."

"Okay, sounds good."

"I hope you're prepared, Leia. It will be a big change for you."

"I know. But I'll handle it." Stepping into shoes—which had been so violently vacated she was sure there was residual blood and gore in the soles—was one thing she wouldn't be thinking about during this trip.

"But also don't forget you have options. I can make a few suggestions—"

"Do you mind, Warren? I really don't want to talk about that now. And no, I'm not burying my head in the sand. I'd just prefer to deal with it when I get back."

Silence greeted her response. Crap. Warren disliked being interrupted. How could she have forgotten that?

"Very well. As you wish."

"I... Thank you for calling to check up on me."

"Of course. You're precious to me, my dear," he said.

Her heart shuddered at the wealth of meaning behind the simple words. At the subtle changes she'd begun to notice. "Bye."

Slowly, she hung up and breathed deep. Her mind slid toward what she'd labeled *The Next Step,* but she pulled herself back. There would be more than enough time to think about it later.

The buzzer sounded again. Smoothing her hand over her black leather pants, she went over and answered it. Bjorn, her personal valet, smiled.

"Miss Michaels, the pilot has just announced that we're at cruising altitude. Would you care to be escorted to the Ozone Bar for cocktails?"

"Umm, sure. But I can find my own way there, thanks."

"Are you sure? It's really no bother," he insisted.

You need to let go a little. Face your fears.

"On second thoughts, I'd love be escorted."

"Great, I'll be right outside when you're ready."

Since she'd dressed before unpacking, there was nothing left to do but slip her feet into the black Louboutin heels that she'd splurged out on a week ago in anticipation of her trip, open the door, and step into the corridor.

"This way, Miss Michaels." Bjorn, blond and buff with a smile that lit up the whole plane, stepped forward and shut the door for her.

"Thanks."

Leia waited for the flash of warning, of danger, and breathed a sigh of relief when her senses remained calm.

She walked alongside him, unable to stop her gaze from lingering on his well-toned biceps. The inch-thick guide that had come with her ticket had mentioned the exclusive use of valets *in every way*.

The *sex* part of the guide had made her stomach dive and quiver anxiously, despite her determination to go ahead with the trip. But the clamoring had finally grown too loud to suppress. The need had surpassed the fear.

She realized she was still staring at Bjorn when his smile slowly turned curious... then carnal. He moved closer, and she caught a whiff of expensive aftershave.

"Where's the Ozone Bar?" she asked to divert his attention. Whether or not she would choose to take advantage of what he was offering, it was inappropriate to gawp like a bitch in heat. Even if that was exactly what she felt like lately.

"It's on the lower deck, two floors below. We can take the elevator, or we can take the scenic route." He paused beside a sleek glass elevator, one golden eyebrow raised.

The thought of being confined with him in the small space washed away a layer of the excitement that had suffused her moments ago.

"I prefer the stairs."

His eyes widened slightly at her abrupt tone, and Leia curbed the urge to apologize.

"I always like to get my bearings as quickly as possible when I visit someplace new."

Always have an escape route in mind. Mentally and physically.

She pushed Warren's voice aside and mustered another smile.

Bjorn nodded. "Of course. Great idea. The design of the plane is such that you can avoid certain lounges if you prefer. I'll show you the whole layout before we go to the Ozone Bar, if you like?"

She shook her head. She'd already memorized the layout of the various lounges. "That's fine. I don't need a full tour just yet. Just take me to the bar, please."

"Sure." He gestured for her to go ahead of him at

the top of the wide, low-lit indigo-colored set of stairs that led downward. As she took the first step, her heel caught in the carpet.

Bjorn caught her around the waist. "Easy there."

She tried not to panic at his touch, but her senses flared with enough adrenaline to make her jump.

Again, his eyes widened before a small frown creased his brow. "Are you okay?"

"Yes, thanks. That could've been embarrassing," she said quickly.

"Good thing I was around, huh?" His white grin flashed.

She smiled back and gripped the railing. "Yeah."

"Come on. I think you need a drink." Sensing her skittishness, he didn't make another attempt to touch her, for which she was grateful.

They descended the stairs in silence and walked into The Silk Lounge. Swathes of indigo and cream silk lined the ceiling and fell into privacy-providing curtains, behind which several loungers had been arranged.

Besides a couple stretched out on twin leather studded lounges, there were only a handful of staff. The female bartender caught Bjorn's eye, and he winked at her. Her dimpled smile betrayed familiarity even before she gave him a cute three-fingered wave.

Okay, Bjorn was officially off the menu.

Leia followed him down a short hallway into another large space. The doors on either side of the hallway were shut, but she heard the hum of low voices and laughter.

"We've had a few people choose their initial events so we're busy setting up," Bjorn said. "Have you chosen yours yet?"

Heat twisted through her belly as she recalled the activities in store for the guests. "Not yet."

He smiled and led her down another set of stairs into a darker, indigo-lit lounge. "You want to take your time. That's fine. But don't wait too long. You don't want any experience to pass you by."

Before she could answer, he held open the door to the Ozone Bar.

The scene that met her stole her breath away.

There was no ceiling to the room, only white fluffy clouds. Although she knew it was an illusion, Leia was mesmerized all the same. As she walked further into the room, holographs of naked winged cherubs floated past, darting in and out of the clouds. She was so engrossed she stumbled into Bjorn. This time when he caught her, she didn't pull away. Her senses assured her he was harmless.

"Shit. I'm sorry. You must think I'm the clumsiest woman on earth. And you would probably be right."

He laughed. "The first time I stepped aboard my first IL plane I was blown away too."

She smiled. "How long have you worked here?"

"Just over a year. But it's been a hell of a wild ride so far." They reached the circular bar in the middle of the room, and he nodded to the bartender. "What would you like to drink, Miss Michaels?"

"Champagne. And please, call me—" The remaining words melted in her brain. At first, she wondered whether the effects of the room were messing with her brain activity. Then she realized her mind had reacted *that strongly* to him.

The man whose laser-sharp eyes were fixed on her, trapping her in place from ten feet away. He leaned against the bar, a glass of something on rocks in one hand.

The low lights ringing the edge of the bar lit his face, emphasizing the severe cut of his jaw and his rugged, edgy beauty. His strong throat moved as he swallowed a mouthful of drink. Slowly, he straightened, turned fully toward her.

He was tall and lean, with wavy black hair and a symmetry of well-proportioned muscles that begged to be ogled. A black fitted shirt covered a wide chest and washboard stomach, and an expensive dinner jacket hid the rest.

But his body didn't interest her. Just yet. It was his face Leia couldn't look away from. His face that enthralled her to the point of speechlessness.

"Miss Michaels?"

She tried to shake her head. She may have succeeded. She wasn't sure. Voices buzzed around her. Bjorn may have exchanged puzzled looks with the bartender.

What she was sure of was that she couldn't stop staring at *him*.

And the blatant way he returned her stare told her he didn't intend to do the polite thing and break their connection either. Her mouth dried and each breath felt like a huge chore to just make her lungs work.

God.

A glass appeared in front of her, and she took it. The chill registered against her fingers.

Touch sensation. Present.

Heartbeat. Freight train speed, but present.

Staring zombie-like. Reaching critical point.

He moved. She followed him with her eyes. Electricity lanced her belly and spiraled outward, spreading like cracked lightning before zeroing in hard between her legs.

She desperately sifted through her vocabulary to find the words.

Hungry.

Predatory.

Carnal pleasure beyond reason.

He wanted it all from her.

And Leia was pretty damned sure she wanted to give them all to him.

Right here, right now.

3

Noah wasn't sure which part of the woman standing across the bar captivated him the most.

All he knew was that he was staring, a stunned shudder charging through his body at the combination of assets. Jesus, whoever had put her together had done one helluva job. She wasn't drop-dead gorgeous, but her face was captivating enough, with a touch of rebellion that intrigued him, to put her in a sphere of her own.

Dark reddish-blonde hair had been pulled over to one side of her face in a careless tumbling heap that reached the middle of her back. From this distance, he couldn't see the exact color of her eyes, but her makeup gave them a smoky and hypnotic allure. Long lashes quivered with the need to blink. She denied that need and maintained bold eye contact.

There was something daring yet innocent in the way she stared at him that made his cock stiffen. Or, hell, it may have been because she had one of the most sinful mouths he'd ever seen. Plump, wide, and painted *suck-me* red, it was so damned potently sexy, he forgot his own name for several seconds.

He'd spotted her the moment she'd walked in behind the blond guy who looked like he wanted to devour her whole.

With her attention caught by the spectacular ceiling display of the Ozone Bar, Noah had taken a moment to study her, his drink frozen halfway to his mouth.

Her side crop, shaved in a swathe that exposed the delicate shell of her left ear, had surprised him. There was something bold and declaratory about it, but also sexy, in a way that made Noah, who had never given much thought to such things, stop to appreciate the sexiness of it.

He'd watch her stumble. Watch the valet catch her and crack a joke. Her smile had made liquid go down the wrong way. Noah had barely stopped himself from coughing up his lungs and wheezing like a frickin' hormonal teenager.

He stared some more, a part of him silently terrified that if he blinked, she would disappear.

To think he'd almost given up finding someone to take the edge off his hunger. He'd intended to finish his whiskey and return to his suite. Alone. Because of the six single female guests he'd met in the bar so far, none even came close to tweaking his interest. The thought of settling on a willing female just to get himself off had made bile rise in his gut.

But now...

Jesus, when was the last time he'd felt this excited just *looking* at a woman?

A woman who returned his stare without turning away, as mesmerized with him as he was with her. A look that portrayed nothing but naked interest.

He discarded the glass and approached her.

She raised her glass of champagne a fraction, as if to take a sip. Or it may have been a tiny toast to what was happening between them. It paused just below her lips, drawing his attention again to the fullness of her glossy mouth. The corners tilted upward in a saucy curve that just begged to be tasted, and his breath fractured as he imagined doing just that and a whole lot more.

Need pounded through him as he rounded the

bar. Vaguely, he saw her valet's gaze swing toward him and back to her.

A dark emotion fizzed through his veins at the thought of the other man laying any sort of claim on her. "Excuse us," he said, without taking his eyes from hers.

The blond guy cleared his throat. "Umm, sure. Have a good evening, Miss Michaels."

Irrationally, the thought that this guy knew her name and Noah didn't irritated the hell out of him. Noah compelled her not to look at the other guy. Not to look at anyone but him.

Her lips parted, but no words emerged. His irritation abated a little when the valet took the hint and walked away. Her scent drifted in to Noah, a mixture of crushed lilies and designer perfume. He breathed in deep and felt his pulse thunder.

He closed the gap between them until he could see the color of her eyes.

Grey, with a touch of blue. So wide. So alluring. He'd always thought that only soppy morons confessed to wanting to get lost in a woman's eyes.

Hell, he wanted to *die* in her eyes.

The DJ upped the tempo of the music. She jerked and swallowed, awareness of her surroundings suddenly swimming into her eyes, threatening to break the moment. Her lids started to lower.

The sense of impending loss hit him hard. "Don't look away."

She blinked and shook her head. Swathes of hair fell over her arms, caressing her bare golden skin. "I'm sorry. It's not polite of me to stare like this."

Her voice was low, husky with emotions slamming around inside her. The same emotions that were roaring through his bloodstream. He didn't need to close his eyes to hear that voice, imagine that mouth hovering over his skin, kissing him in places that made his cock throb to life. His brain was firing up scenarios just from the sound of her voice alone. Scenarios that pleased and frightened him at the same time.

"Why not? Stare all you want because I sure as hell am not about to apologize for staring at you."

Her cute nose twitched, and he could've sworn she leaned in a tiny bit closer. Hell, he might have been deluding himself, but he liked to think she did.

"Perhaps I have better manners than you," she said, without looking away.

"I wouldn't wholly disagree with you on that. But as much as it would shame my mother to know I was being rude to a lady, I can't seem to help myself."

Heat rushed into her cheeks, and Noah barely stopped himself from groaning. Her long, dark-painted fingers clutched her glass firmer. He flicked his gaze back to her face. He didn't want to dwell on what damage those nails could do to his back. His butt. He didn't want to think about them leaving marks all over his body. Not just yet.

She continued to watch him with that mixture of intrigue and hunger that made his pulse race. God, did she even know what she was doing? How she was stoking fires he was terrified to let roar to life?

"Well, since there's nothing wrong with just looking..." she murmured.

"And we have each other's permission? Just to be polite, of course," he pressed. Not that he intended to let the lack of it stop him. His senses were intent on visually devouring this woman. The actual devouring would come later.

Her eyes widened a fraction. "Yes, I guess..."

"Well, okay then." Taking his time, he dropped his gaze to her mouth and let it linger. He wanted to savor the journey, imprint each of her features on his excited senses so he could visualize them later. When several images of what he could do to her mouth flashed through his brain in quick succession, Noah deemed it wise to move on.

His gaze slid down to her throat. Her skin glowed like warm silk—as if she spent time in the sun. Would she have tan lines, or did she indulge in the ultimate sun worship?

Move on before you make an idiot of yourself, King.

Her sleeveless white lace top stretched across her breasts, emphasizing the delicious mounds.

Small pert tits.

He filed that observation away, travelled lower and froze.

Dear God, she was wearing leather. Skintight leather that lovingly molded her hips, lean thighs and calves.

His gaze reached her heeled feet and traced a path back up her body. The second run was even better than the first.

Small breasts and leather. Two of his major weaknesses.

The throbbing, which had started in his groin the moment he'd laid eyes on her, roared into a bona fide pounding.

Through the loudspeaker, the pop version of John Legend's "All of Me" filled the room.

Noah looked back up in time to see her conducting a blatant survey of her own. Her gaze travelled from his face to his chest, abs and all the way to his feet. Then back up.

She lingered on his crotch. Her cheeks reddened a little more at the blatant evidence of his arousal, but she didn't move her gaze. That little nose twitched again, and a puff of breath left her lips.

This time, he couldn't stop the rough sound that burst through his throat.

He plucked the glass from her fingers and set it on the counter. His fingers brushed hers in the process, and she jerked.

"You're being rude again."

Noah shrugged. "You didn't seem all that interested in the drink. Besides, it's more cool than chilled right now, and champagne should be enjoyed immediately or the joy goes out of it."

Jesus, was he really standing here discussing the perfect drinking temperature of champagne like some snooty etiquette junkie? His ex had been the one who'd concerned herself with social bullshit like that.

"I'm sure I had another five minutes before it went flat." She looked at the glass but made no move to pick it up.

Legend crooned about *curves* and *edges*. Noah

struggled not to check out her curves just one more time.

"Dance with me," he said abruptly.

What the hell? He hated dancing. Hadn't come remotely close to a dance floor since senior prom. And that had been because he'd wanted to soften Emily Bianchini up a little before he taught that cock-teasing princess a hard fucking—pun intended—lesson in the back of his hired limo.

But short of grabbing her delicate wrist and dragging her off to a dark corner to explore those incredible curves, dancing was his best solution. He couldn't stand this close and not touch. Dancing gave him an excuse to touch. Because he had to put his hands on her... Make sure that his mind wasn't playing tricks on him. That she was real.

She shook her head. "I don't dance. Sorry." The apology was tacked on, almost as an afterthought.

He suppressed a smile. "Neither do I. But if we stand here any longer eyeballing one another, something will catch fire. And at thirty thousand feet, I don't think that's a very good idea."

She laughed. He caught a flash of silver.

Noah was pretty sure his vision blurred for several seconds. His breath whistled through his teeth as his brain computed what he was seeing.

A stud.

She had a fucking tongue piercing. The idea of what that silver stud could do to his cock froze his thought processes, then blitzed anticipated pleasure though his already-roaring bloodstream.

When he refocused, she was staring straight at him, the laughter wiped from her face. Fresh hunger slammed into his gut then clenched tight in a vice as awareness blazed in her eyes.

"Dance," he croaked.

"Yes."

The dance floor was set in a larger circle around the room, making the bar the focal point. Several guests were in the "getting to know each other" phase, some a little further along than others.

One of the women he'd considered a possible candidate, a statuesque redhead with enough experience in her eyes to make any guy contemplate a session between the sheets with her, glanced his way. Her gaze swung to his companion, and she raised an eyebrow at him.

Noah ignored her. She wouldn't have held his interest for more than a few hours.

Whereas the woman whose scent lingered in his nostrils...

He turned abruptly, already starved of the sight of her.

She was right behind him, her gaze seeking and finding his. Elation and deep anticipation roared through him. He stepped closer, ready to take her in his arms.

She raised a hand. "Wait."

The imperious command wasn't what made him freeze. It was the brief panic on her face.

What the hell?

"Are you okay?" he asked.

"I will be. I just... I just need to initiate contact first. Do you mind?"

Shock slammed into him. Followed swiftly by the realization that *a,* he didn't mind, and *b,* she wasn't really asking him but telling him.

He'd need to address that when they entered the bedroom.

He nodded slowly, every atom in his body on edge and intrigued. "Go for it."

She licked her lower lip and stepped close. Propriety would've dictated that she place her hand on his shoulder. Or his waist.

Instead, she splayed her fingers over his belly. His breath hissed as fire exploded from the point of her touch.

He stood rock still and let her fingers drift upward over his chest, between his pecs, and up the side of his neck. He had no idea what was going on here. But hell if he didn't want to stand there and keep living it.

The sensation was tortuous. And exquisitely pleasurable in ways he hadn't experienced for a very long time. If ever.

The song ended and a new equally suggestive song took its place. He grew harder as she continued to explore him. Her fingers grazed his shoulder and one forefinger drifted down the side of his neck.

Fuck.

"Honey, if we're going to dance, we need to get on with it. Before I give in to the urge to eat you alive, right here, right now."

His words plucked her from a dream-state. Eyes turned stormy met his, and Noah barely managed to suppress the impulse to bare his teeth in visible hunger at the need pounding through him.

She nodded and started to sway before him. He remained frozen, unable to take his eyes from her body as she sinuously moved.

Eventually, she noticed he wasn't moving and raised an eyebrow. "Are you going to dance?"

"To do that I have to touch you. I'm going to touch you now."

"Oh. Okay."

Her finger caressed his neck again. He reached for her, his arms curving over her small waist to bring her closer. She felt warm, soft and firm in all the right places. But he wanted more.

"I'm going to pull you closer." Like her, he wasn't asking for permission.

"That's... that's fine."

He tugged her into his body. She exhaled sharply, and her breath washed his neck. This close with her heels on, she came up to his chin. Without them she would be tiny.

The perfect, fuckable handful.

He tilted her face up with a finger. "Tell me your name."

"It's Leia. Leia Michaels."

"I'm Noah King. Is there anything else I need to know about you before we get to the eating alive part? I'm especially interested in any steps I can skip, because I have a feeling I'll need to get there quickly."

4

The rough, implacable demand fired another shot of excitement up her spine. Beneath her fingers, his pulse throbbed sure, steady and fast, although not as fast as hers. Hers had taken a wild turn the moment his voice had collided with his indescribable hotness, and it showed no signs of slowing anytime soon.

Noah King.

His name was manly. Commanding. She heard herself silently repeating it and pressed her lips together. She didn't trust herself not to say it out loud. To test it. To taste it.

Shock jerked through her, and she swayed against him. Or perhaps she just couldn't help it; had lost control of her body just like she'd felt her mind going when she'd set eyes on him.

She wanted to melt into him. To feel more of that incredibly hot body against hers; the unmistakable imprint of his cock heavy against her belly as they moved to the music. Another blush flared up her neck and into her face. His gaze traced it, and a small smile curved his lips.

He leaned down and placed his mouth against her ear. "Anyone tell you you'd be hopeless at poker?" he rasped.

"Poker relies on the ability to hold a bluff through the body's reaction. I prefer games that demand more mental aptitude."

He tensed. "Are you saying you prefer mind games?"

"Not those that deliberately inflict discomfort or pain. I prefer healthy mind games."

Sharp eyes bore into hers, speculation narrowing them. Hell, she should've kept her mouth shut. Now she sounded like some mind control freak.

"You haven't answered my earlier question—what else do I need to know?"

"Oh, right." She scrambled for ways to explain without scaring him away or opening the floodgates for more questions. "I have a small thing about being touched."

Blue eyes that defied coherent description pried her words apart. After several seconds, he said, "I don't think it's as small as you make it out to be."

She hesitated, afraid of driving him away. "All I needed was to be the one to touch you. That's all. I won't need to orientate myself again."

"You mean now you've touched me I can touch you back anytime I want?" There was a mixture of puzzlement and pleasure in his voice. The former made anxiety flare deep within her. The latter sent her pulse soaring even higher.

"Something like that."

His answer was to squeeze her tighter. "That's good to know, Leia Michaels."

She looked up, and he stared down at her. Assessing.

They gave up any pretense of dancing and just swayed to the music. His hand drifted down her back to the waistband of her pants.

The knowledge that his hand was a few scant inches from her ass slowly coiled tension in her stomach.

Whatever she'd imagined when she'd signed herself on this trip had been blown to smithereens in a few short minutes. Clawing hunger sank deeper hooks, sending sparks to her clenching sex.

There was a time when Leia had thought she would never feel this way. Never get over her turbulent past to even contemplate the idea of sex again. So much so that she'd been surprised when the hunger had started a few months after she'd turned twenty-one.

At first, she'd tried to ignore it. When she hadn't succeeded, she'd bought a few self-pleasuring gadgets.

Dr. Hatfield, her therapist, had encouraged her to use them on a regular basis. But even they hadn't kept the need at bay. Now she feared she was a hot, sexually frustrated time bomb.

She'd reached the point where she couldn't close her eyes without dreaming about hot hands on her body. Or a hard cock pounding into her.

Except reality was different. She couldn't just go out and hunt down the first willing male she came across. A part of her was horrified that *this* would have to be the solution to her banishing her demons.

Aside from her very real triggers that could flare up at any time, she was Leia Michaels, heiress to a fortune most people dreamed about...

Warm lips brushed the side of her neck, forcing

reality and sensation through her body. She gasped and shuddered hard.

"Easy, baby. Your finger has been caressing my neck for the last few minutes. I had to take something before I lost my mind."

"Oh. I'm sorry."

"Fuck, don't apologize. In the interest of getting to know one another, I like your fingers on my neck. Your mouth would be even better. But I can wait."

They hit a pocket of turbulence and the plane dropped. Her nails dug into his neck and his eyes darkened dramatically. His lips parted and she caught a glimpse of his wet tongue.

Her nipples puckered into hard, painful nubs, imagining that wetness flicking against her sensitive peaks. Blood roared through her ears as she pictured herself kissing him.

"Do you want to kiss me, Leia?"

The question was forceful, demanding an immediate answer.

She nodded before she could stop herself. "Yes."

"Then do it."

She gasped and looked around. "Right... here?"

"I don't think you want to go anywhere private with me just yet, sweetheart. I won't stop at just kissing you. I'm into a lot of things, but I'm not into voyeurism. So yes, right here. Where you're safe from me tearing your clothes and fucking you until you pass out in front of everyone."

Inappropriate images reeled through her mind, strong enough to make her knees sag. She didn't think it was their surroundings that had the man giving in to his dirty side. She had a feeling Noah King spoke with that raw sexuality and intent wherever he was.

She thought about whom else he might have said those words to, and a sharp feeling joined the alien emotions swirling through her. No, she didn't like that feeling. Not one little bit...

Sure fingers speared into her hair and tugged firmly, redirecting her focus back to him. He wasn't giving her the option to back out. She realized that. Not that she wanted to. She licked her lower lip and he puffed out a breath.

"You can take it as slow as you want. But you need to get on with it. You don't want me to take over, baby."

"Why not?" she asked breathlessly.

"Because I'm a greedy, controlling bastard and I won't be gentle." There was a trace of apology in the response, but not enough to reassure her that he didn't mean every word.

The pulse between her legs hammered like a frenzied drumbeat. Again, Leia wondered why she wasn't running, why her insides continued to fizz with excitement when a guy like him was the last person she needed to be around.

Her stomach hollowed out with another sudden drop followed closely by another. His grip tightened around her, restricting her breathing.

His mouth dropped another fraction, and she could almost feel the firm, warm texture of it on her own.

"Kiss me. Now." He breathed the words over her mouth.

Fresh tingles shot up her spine. She sucked in a breath, started to rise up on her toes.

Ladies and gentlemen, we're going through an area of turbulence. We expect this to last between five to ten minutes. If you're already seated we request you to remain seated with your belt fastened. Otherwise please ask your valet to escort you to the nearest safe area. Thank you.

One corner of Noah's mouth tilted up. "This would be the perfect time to take this somewhere more private. But I don't think I'll make it back to my suite without kissing you."

She tensed. "You assume I want to return to your suite with you."

His laugh was tight and rough. "Sweetheart, you're going to end up there sooner or later. For now, we need a location for you to kiss me without us getting thrown up against the ceiling." He stepped back and linked his fingers with hers.

She missed his body immediately, but she was glad for the momentary reprieve. Although the way his fingers curled around hers and pulled her behind him told her he didn't intend for them to remain parted for very long.

"Shouldn't we find a seat?" she asked.

He looked around and back at her. "All the seats are taken in here. Come with me."

He left the dance floor and headed for the door. The plane dipped again, making her stumble. His fingers tightened around hers.

From the corner of her eye, she saw Bjorn straighten from where he'd been leaning against the bar, watching them.

Noah must have clocked him too. His eyes narrowed a fraction as they zeroed in on him before his gaze swung to her. "You won't be needing him anymore," he said.

"Oh, really? Have you dismissed your hostess too?"

He tugged her in front of him as he reached the

hallway and kept his hand on her waist. "Not yet, but she was never going to be an issue."

She looked over her shoulder and smiled at Bjorn, who lingered in the doorway. "I like my valet. He's sweet." She waved goodbye, and he nodded and went back inside.

Noah's nostrils flared. "Yeah, right."

They hit a large pocket of turbulence, and the plane went into free-fall. She lost her footing and Noah caught her, bracing her against his body with one hand splayed over her stomach. Against her ass, the impressive outline of his cock pressed into her. He flexed his hips. The move was so possessive and hot, desire flared wildly. He held her like that for several seconds, the blaze of lust firing up between them.

Leia scrambled for something to say. Something besides begging him to push his hips deeper into her ass so she would feel even more of his thick cock. "You don't think he's sweet?"

"Baby, as long as he stays far away from you, I don't give a fuck whether your valet is the sweetest guy in the whole fucking world."

Her breath fractured. "You have a dirty mouth, Mr. King."

"I can do even dirtier things with it, but only if you beg repeatedly, preferably from a kneeling position."

His mouth brushed the side of her neck again, and another shiver coursed through her. "Come on, I need to get you secure and safe."

His large hand returned to her waist and urged her down the hallway in the opposite direction of where she'd come earlier with Bjorn. After a few feet, the hallway widened into six separate alcoves, three on either side, each holding a thick fold-up leather seat. He pulled down the nearest one and pushed her into it.

It was only after she sat that Leia noticed the couple in the seat farthest from them.

Her mouth dropped open at the blatant spectacle. The man was seated with his trousers around his ankles and the woman, with her dress bunched up around her waist, was on her knees in front of him. One of his hands was buried in her hair and the other fondled her naked breast as she sucked on his engorged cock. The plane jerked through another series of turbulent air pockets. They both groaned as if the tinge of danger added to their pleasure.

"Leia."

Noah was on his knees in front of her. Even at his diminished height, he still towered over her. She looked up, and her breath caught at his intense expression. "Yes?"

"Eyes on me, baby." There was a ruthless command in his voice that demanded her attention.

The man gave another loud moan, and Leia swallowed.

Noah caught her chin in his hand. "I'm going to secure the belt around your waist. Tell me if it's too tight."

She looked down in surprise and noticed two wide belts hanging from either side of the chair. It wasn't the standard-issue airplane seatbelt. It was made of leather and three times wider but with a release catch in the middle of the buckle-like fastening.

He slipped the ends through their holes and pulled. The belt gripped her in place from below her breasts to the top of her pants. The corset-like effect pushed her breasts out, and her aroused nipples pressed boldly against the material of her top.

With quick movements, he secured the second and third buckles, then looked into her face. "Okay?"

"Yes," she responded, struck all over again by the intensity in his stunning blue eyes and the rugged beauty of his face. "Aren't you going to take a seat?" she asked to cover the fact that she was fighting the need to reach out and touch him again, make sure he was real.

The plane jerked sideways, and she gasped. He

smiled, shook his head and ran his hand down her waist to her hips. "No, baby, I'm staying right here until I collect what you owe me."

"The kiss?"

His hand drifted down her thighs, leaving a trail of fire on her skin. He stared at the movement as if the friction he was creating mesmerized him. He reached her knees and raised his head. "Yes. The kiss. Are you ready?"

Breathless, she nodded. "Yes."

"Good." He hooked his hands behind her knees and gripped her tight. "Open for me, Leia."

5

Noah studied her face to see her reaction to his rough command. He needed to know how well she responded to demands. How far he could push before her walls went up.

Because she had walls. Hell, her body practically screamed their presence. She was here to fight her own demons. There were too many shadows in her eyes for that not to be the case. His every sense screamed at him to go slow.

Which was proving to be a living hell as her sexuality and sexiness called to him from a level he hadn't experienced since the time he'd been introduced to the edgier, more rewarding side of sex on his twenty-first birthday.

He glanced down at the belt holding her in place, and his blood roared through his veins. The memory of her ass pressed against his groin when the plane had bucked around them, added to the fire spreading through him.

He sucked in a controlling breath as her thighs parted in answer to his demand. He waited for the gap to widen enough before he positioned himself between them. He'd have to loosen her seatbelt for the juncture of her thighs to become flush against his desperately hard cock.

Deciding to forgo that pleasure for the moment, he let her stay put. Seeing her pinned against the chair was enough for now. Besides, his hands on her thighs were firing up enough pleasure through him to threaten his steel-hard erection to breaking point.

And they were yet to kiss.

Angling his head toward her, he brought his mouth within brushing distance of hers. "Taste me. Now."

The couple engaged in cunnilingus were getting louder. The guy uttered a filthy instruction, and Leia swallowed, another blush creeping into her cheeks.

That persistent sign of innocence sent a trace of caution through him. He pulled back. "How old are you, Leia?"

One perfectly curved eyebrow lifted at the question. "Won't your mother be even more ashamed to hear you asking a woman her age? How old are *you*?"

His jaw tightened. "My mother's not here, and I'm thirty-one. Answer the question."

She glared at him, her luscious lips pursing. "I'm twenty-three."

Noah closed his eyes and breathed deep.

She was more than old enough to do whatever the hell she wanted with whomever she chose. At the same age, he'd been indulging in ways that would've shocked most people. Ways he'd had to abandon when he'd met Ashley.

But Leia was blushing at what was happening a few feet away, which spelled out her innocence loud and clear. And it wasn't just the blushes that made him pause.

Granted, this place was unique enough to induce a few blushes. But her reaction to touching him earlier and the panic he'd seen in her eyes tweaked a few more alarm bells.

"Why are you here, Leia?"

"Excuse me? Isn't it obvious?"

"I thought it was, but now I'm not so sure."

Her face tightened. "What makes you say that?"

"You blush at the drop of a hat or at the sound of a

simple moan. Your eyes widen every time I say *fuck*. There it is again."

"Maybe I'm not used to hearing men swear as frequently as you do."

"No, baby. That's not it. It's not the word. It's the image it evokes for you. Am I right?"

Her nostrils flared. "I thought we were going to kiss, not dissect my reactions."

"Oh, we are. Very thoroughly. But not just yet."

Her gaze dropped to his mouth, and Noah nearly lost it. "Why not?"

"Because I want you to tell me what you're doing here first."

Stormy grey eyes met his with a mixture of anger and arousal. "What does it matter? I'm here for the same reason you are."

"Oh, sweetheart, I sincerely doubt that."

"Why are you here then? If not to... fuck, then why?" Another fierce blush swept over her face.

The couple grew even louder. Gagging sounds filled the hallway as the guy pushed himself all the way into his partner's mouth. Leia's lashes fluttered, a giveaway that she was nervous. And turned on.

The plane jerked again, and Noah's grip tightened. She sucked in a sharp breath, and he froze.

Hell. Deliberately, he dug his fingers deeper,

enough to cause pain. He watched her face. Waiting for the reaction that would force him to back off.

Her mouth dropped open, her breath fractured and her pupils dilated.

Jesus. No.

Surely she wasn't the one? Not this half-innocent with the tight body that screamed at his senses to make her his in every possible way?

The thought that he could break her and force her beyond her comfort zone surged to the front of his mind, starting an uncomfortable tingling in his hands that made him loosen his grasp.

He could take it slow, start with a kiss and see where it took them. But at what cost?

He had too many demons of his own to fight without taking on someone else's. He looked into her eyes, felt himself begin to drown again and shook himself.

"I'm here to fuck, yes. But I won't be fucking you." He smashed down the regret biting hard inside him and started to rise to his feet.

Long nails dug into his arms. "Wait."

Noah barely stopped from growling at the poker-hot sensation that rolled from his brain to his groin. "You're playing with fire, baby."

"You don't know me. You're making assumptions

based on the fact that I blush easily. Big deal. I'm not a child, so don't treat me like one." Her voice was much stronger than it had been moments ago. Anger and steel blended in the husky depths. But he also heard confusion.

He wanted to tell her it wasn't her. That it was him. He was the one who was fucked up. He was the one who couldn't take another vanilla lay without wanting to roar his frustration to the heavens. He was the one who needed darker, edgier sex to curb the hunger riding him. The one who had to have it before he felt he could breathe again.

"Leia—"

"We connected. I know we did. I didn't imagine it." Her thumbs searched and found his wrists and the hot pulse beating there, and a small, very smug smile curved her lips. "Your pulse is racing almost as fast as mine. You want me. Badly." Her gaze dropped to the hard cock straining behind his zipper; the hard cock demanding attention, which Noah had no choice but to deny.

Her bold stare stayed fixed on the bulge for so long, he imagined he could feel its caress along his rigid length.

"Oh God, that's it, suck me like that. Suck it hard, darling. Oh! Fuck, yes!"

The hoarse shout from two seats away held them still as the guy lost it completely. Leia's nails dug deeper and flames burned through his groin.

"I could do that for you. I can do that *to* you," she whispered, her voice quivering a little.

Christ.

"That's not the problem, sweetheart."

She froze. "Then what the hell is?"

"The problem is once I get a taste of you, I seriously doubt I'll let you walk away anytime soon."

"Okay. I can see how that could be a problem for you."

His mouth twitched. She had sass. He liked that. But not enough for him to overlook a whole load of other warnings.

"But isn't that the point of this trip? Indulge and walk away after seven days?"

He shook his head. "I have specific needs, baby. And I don't have time to train you to cater to them."

"You think I don't like the word *fuck*? What about *asshole*?" she suggested mildly, her eyes dark with anger.

His hands, which he'd never quite managed to pry off her legs, tightened. "Watch it."

She shrugged. "Make me understand. Three minutes ago, you were dying for me to kiss you too. Now you're walking away? Is there a male equivalent of a cock tease? Because you're the definition."

The label rubbed him the wrong way. He'd met a few cock teasers in his time, women who thought they'd string him along to keep him interested for longer. They'd joined his CFR list long before he'd coined the actual term.

The seatbelt light pinged off.

Ladies and gentlemen, we've made it through the small weather disturbance and we hope the turbulence wasn't too rough for you. Please feel free to return to your previous activities.

She glanced down at her belt but made no move to free herself from it. Her eyes returned to his, waiting for his answer.

Noah swallowed and tried to arrange his thoughts. "The things I want to do to you, do with you—"

"Tell me," she demanded.

"No. You think you can handle it, but you can't."

"Wow, you are pretty full of yourself, aren't you?"

Her hands dropped from his arms, her thumbs releasing their pressure against his pulse. He missed them badly.

She pressed the button on her belt and it fell free. She started to get up.

"Wait."

"No. I think you've made your feelings pretty clear."

His throat squeezed, the idea of letting her go suddenly unthinkable. "Look, I didn't mean to string you along. I'm not that kind of guy."

She cleared her throat, and her mouth lifted and fell in a quick smile. "It's fine. I'm not what you want. No hard feelings. Let me go, please."

Words clashed in his head, and emotions crashed through him that he couldn't name.

She started to lean forward, to rise. Her breath washed over his chin, her scent engulfing him. That drowning sensation plunged him deep again.

"Shit."

Cupping her face in his hands, he slanted his mouth over hers before she could get up and walk away. One taste, he told himself. One taste and he'd let her go.

She tasted like fucking heaven. Warm, firm and luscious, her mouth melted beneath his, welcomed him with a sigh that snagged on his senses. Jesus, she tasted like all his favorite things condensed into one delectable package. Soft, intoxicating—

She bit him. Hard.

He jerked back, his pulse tripping over itself in shock. The faint, distinctly acid taste of blood coated his tongue. Reeling, he touched a finger to his mouth. It came away with a spot of bright red.

He stared at her, and she returned his look, grey eyes bold and unwavering.

Certainty crashed through like a clap of thunder.

"Fuck, baby, you just sealed your fate."

Wide eyes dropped to the cut on his lip and flew back to his. She swallowed. "I didn't mean—"

"Yes, you did. You know exactly what you do to me. Which is why I'm keeping you, baby. But don't say I didn't warn you."

6

I'm keeping you...

Leia wasn't sure whether to be shocked or pleased at the outcome of acting out on that crazy instinct. The shock of finally having Noah King's mouth on hers had been beyond explosive.

So she'd bitten him.

She'd bitten him!

She stared that the red spot on his finger and watched, mesmerized as he brought it to his mouth and licked it off.

"God, I'm so sorry. I'm not sure what came over—"

He stopped her words with a forefinger on her mouth. "This time, I'll take care of it. Next time, you lick it off."

She gasped at the vivid imagery, and his finger moved to the side of her mouth. Tracing. Exploring. "I... There won't be a next time."

"Yes, there will," he stated. His tongue snuck out and soothed the tiny cut on his lower lip. Savored it.

The intensely sensual action spiked fire between her legs. Her panties grew damper, her clit throbbing incessantly against the seam of her leather pants. She moved in the seat, desperate to alleviate the discomfort.

His gaze dropped between her legs and darted back to her face. "You'll bite me whenever I tell you to. And I'll bite you right there, between your legs."

"I'm not a biter," she said in a rush.

"You've just proven otherwise. You've made me so hard I can't see straight."

Another blush threatened, but she forced it away through sheer strength of will. She was done blushing in front of this man. Her stupid blushes had nearly made him walk away. The recollection hollowed out her stomach, the way it had ten minutes ago when she feared he would.

His finger traced her lower lip and brought her attention back to him. He watched her with such intensity, his gaze compelling her as his finger slipped into her mouth. The soft pad caressed her lower front teeth as if testing their sharpness. He reached her left incisor and pressed down.

Leia squirmed. "What are you doing?"

"Nothing you're not enjoying."

She shook her head, but the feeling of his finger lazily exploring her mouth was like nothing she'd felt before.

"You want me to stop?"

She moaned.

"Words, baby. Use words." He pressed again, and she saw his pupils dilate. "Tell me what you're thinking. Do you like what I'm doing?"

Such a simple thing, nowhere near indecent or decadent. And yet, it felt so erotic, her pussy clenched and unclenched with sharp, hungry need.

"Yes."

He smiled and removed his finger, but not before he circled her lips with its wet tip. "The first rule is vocalization. Whatever you're feeling, you say it. I don't want to have to guess what's going on in your head. Agreed?"

She nodded jerkily. "Agreed."

He rose and held out his hand. About to let him help her up, she stopped as a movement caught her eye.

The couple had finished and were decently

dressed again. They came toward them, and Leia caught the look of complete satiation on the guy's face. The woman's smile held a smug satisfaction at having pleased her man. Her eyes met Leia's, and her smile widened.

Leia looked away, unsure how to respond to the blatant sexual satisfaction she'd witnessed.

Noah grasped her fingers hard and pulled her to her feet. The movement threw her against his hard body. "Rule number two. Don't get hung up with what other people are doing."

"I was just..."

His fingers caressed her cheek. "It's very easy to get distracted in a place like this. I'll try hard not to be a complete asshole when I catch you staring at another guy or another couple having a good time, but I want your undivided attention. I'll give you mine in return. Completely. Does that work for you?"

"I... Yes." Her heart banged against her ribs, reminding her forcefully that she'd strayed a galaxy out of her comfort zone.

He stared down at her, a slightly concerned look on his face. "It this getting overwhelming for you?"

"A little."

He lowered his head and kissed the side of her mouth. His lips drifted along her cheek to her jaw, then trailed down to her neck. "It's your fault. You bit me, baby. Now I belong to you."

Her laughter emerged like a husky croak. She allowed her hand to caress his shoulder, reacquaint herself with the hard muscle beneath his shirt. The thought that this breathtakingly gorgeous man belonged to her for the next seven days sent a shiver of delight and danger through her. "I think you need to brush up on your vampire movies. That's not quite how it works."

"I make my own rules."

She didn't doubt it. He carried an aura of power and control that anyone would be a fool to dismiss. His alpha-ness blasted from him in huge waves that threatened to drown her.

She breathed him in, his potent scent almost an aphrodisiac all on its own. When she leaned even closer, rising up to brush her lips against his throat, his head tilted to one side. The invitation was too tempting to resist.

The first brush of her lips against his throat brought a groan from him. His arm clamped around her waist, bringing her flush against him one more time.

This time, his hand didn't stop on her waistband.

It drifted to her ass, molding her flesh before using the firm hold to tug her hard against him.

Leia ground her hips into him, desperate to feel his thick powerful length nudge her belly.

"You're dying to be fucked. Aren't you?" he crooned in her ear.

"Yes."

"Soon, baby. I promise. Despite our time constraints, we need a little get-to-know-each-other time." With one last thrust against her, he pulled away. They both groaned.

He meshed his fingers through hers and started back down the corridor.

"Where are we going?"

"To find a drink. One which we will both consume this time. Before we do, I need to tell you the most important thing I require from you, Leia Michaels."

Leia's pulse surged. "What is it?"

His face changed. Took on a rigid, unyielding mask. "I need control. Total and unequivocal. I dictate your pleasure and reward your trust. You have until we finish our drink to tell me if you agree. Until then, you're going to tell me a little bit about yourself. I'll even let you tell me some of the things you like to do in bed. Not everything. I want to find out some things on my own."

She stopped herself from letting panic take over. The sex part and what she liked to do in bed could be covered in ten seconds flat. It was the other things, the other questions about her life, that terrified her.

Besides Warren and Dr. Hatfield, only a handful of people knew the truth. One was dead, having taken her secret with her. The other therapists and medical officials she could trust.

Then there was Warren himself.

How did she explain her relationship with Warren to a complete stranger when lately she'd been grappling with defining it for herself?

She mentally slapped herself. Who said she had to lay bare every single inch over one or two drinks?

Feeling hopelessly rusty and unable to completely stem the panic, Leia swallowed. "There's not really a lot about me you'd find interesting."

He laughed in that deep, raspy voice that sent delicious shivers over her skin. "You don't think so? For starters, I want to know about this." His fingers drifted past her temple, over the shaved swathe above her ear. Although a thin layer had grown back, the area was sensitive enough to make her feel as if he were touching her bare skin. He caught her tiny tremble and devoured the reaction. "Then I want to know about this." One thumb caressed her lower lip until she opened, then he plunged his finger inside to graze over her tongue piercing.

Her breath caught. Of its own accord, her tongue curled around his digit. His eyes darkened, and he removed his finger from her mouth.

"Not yet," he murmured. "Come on."

He resumed walking. Her gaze dropped to his firm and masculine ass. She couldn't help it. Her fingers tingled as she imagined clenching it as he pounded into her. She swallowed a groan.

They reached two lounges that opened on either side of the hallway.

One door was painted black and marked with silver studs that spelled out *DECADENCE*. Four members of staff were carrying a large covered object onto a platform set in the middle of four large divan beds.

"What are they doing?"

Noah pulled her into his side and whispered in her ear. "They're setting up for Fantasy Night."

His mouth caressed her ear, and his hand slid around her waist in a firm hold. One thing she'd noticed about Noah King was that he didn't go for light and whispery. His every move was bold and authoritative in a way that made no bones about what he wanted. What he intended to take.

"You can just watch. Or you can join and indulge in

your fantasies." He pointed to the screens currently rolled up on the ceiling. "Or you can have your own party within the party. There are several ways to enjoy the high of your choice. The fantastic thing about the Indigo Lounge is you can find ways to tailor it to your purpose."

"So you've been on one of these trips before?"

She was surprised when he shook his head. "No, this is my first time."

"Then how do you know what goes on here?"

"I have persistent friends who make it their duty to tell me about each trip they take. Plus, I met the owner, Zach Savage, when he was trying to get the venture off the ground. He gave me the lowdown on his vision for this business. I thought it was a unique and fantastic idea."

She watched the staff carefully place the large object on the floor. One whipped away the shrouding. Leia gasped at the exquisite, intricately designed golden cage. It was oval-shaped and big enough to hold six people.

"Sex in a cage while flying high above the clouds. I guess not a lot of people have that on their bucket list, huh?"

His fingers gripped her waist tighter. When she looked at him, his mouth curved in an enigmatic smile. "You'd be surprised just what pops up on bucket lists."

To the right, the DJ was setting up on an elevated platform at the back of the room. From the ceiling, large strobe lights slowly twirled, casting psychedelic lights over the furniture and the floor.

A delicate shiver floated down Leia's spine. On paper, the Indigo Lounge had seemed like a truly unique experience. Reality offered so much more. And she knew the reality with Noah King would be even more exhilarating.

She rubbed her tongue on the roof of her mouth —a childhood habit she'd never managed to break— and peered deeper into the room.

A studded leather rack table had been erected within another grouping of sofas, complete with re- straints.

In the middle of the third grouping, a four-poster bed stood, complete with black and indigo satin sheets and countless pillows. One member of staff was winding white silk ropes almost innocently around the posts. She looked up and smiled as she laid the end of one rope in the middle of the bed. Leia swallowed against another strange sensation skit- tering beneath her skin.

"Your pulse is racing again." His lips grazed the spot. "Time to have that drink, I think."

They passed another door marked *VICE*. It was completely blacked out, but Leia noticed several oddly shaped goggles hanging by the door. "Are those night-vision goggles?" She brushed her fingers over one.

"Close. These are specially adapted to show heat as well as cold. Want to try them later?"

The temptation to play safe welled up, but she pushed it away. "Maybe."

"We'll add that to your *high* list." Again, that imperious tone, denoting a man used to taking charge.

"How do you know there's enough room for more *highs* on my list?" she challenged, just for the hell of it.

He glanced back. "You wouldn't have chosen yet because there's little point choosing *highs* without a partner."

"Fair point. I just didn't want you assuming."

He laughed and led her into the bar at the farthest end of the plane.

It'd been designed into the tail and appeared triangularly shaped. Aptly named Tail Bar, it was the most ordinary space on the whole plane, if pure luxury at every turn could be classed as ordinary.

Noah led her to the bar and ordered a glass of

champagne for her and a shot of Glen Fiddich on the rocks for himself.

Like most of the seats on the plane, the bar lounges were large enough for two or more.

Choosing a golden velvet one farthest from the bar and the couples gathered around it, he sat and patted the space next to him. "What shall we drink to?"

Several thoughts jumped through her mind, all too vivid to say aloud. In the end, she just pressed her lips together and shrugged.

"Should I be hurt that you can't find a single positive thing to drink to?"

"I have toasts, just not very clean ones."

His deep laugh made her grin. He raised his glass. "To the next seven days, and to however many highs we manage to cram in."

She touched her glass to his. "You think it's going to be more than seven?"

His eyes consumed her. "Baby, seven is the minimum number I plan to reach when it comes to the list of *highs* I intend to achieve with you."

7

Noah watched her cheeks burn and wondered again if he was doing the right thing by setting his sights on such an innocent. Then the bite on his mouth throbbed, and he remembered the sass that had followed, and his pulse pounded all over again. Every nerve inside his body screamed at him to grab her and rush them to the nearest private area, preferably his suite. But he cautioned himself to take it slow.

It was important that he arm himself with everything he needed to know about her before he made another mistake. Another mistake would be unthinkable.

He'd known her for a short time, but he couldn't

imagine causing the woman in front of him any upset. He watched her sip her drink and waited for those fascinating grey eyes to meet his.

"I've only seen hairstyles like that on rock stars. Are you an undercover rock star, Leia Michaels?"

She laughed. "What's the point of being a rock star if you choose to be undercover?"

"Okay, let's cross that off the list. You're a sleep-walker with a penchant for alternative hairdressing?"

Her white, even teeth, which could cause him serious harm—or serious pleasure—glistened in the low light as her smile widened. "Nope."

"Then why?"

He followed her slim fingers as they lifted to the side of her head. She caressed the shaven track slowly, the movement so intimate that his stomach clenched. He watched the smile slowly leave her face, replaced by a pensive, almost haunted look.

Walls.

"It just felt... right."

Noah wanted to push for more, but he held his tongue. He knew all about wanting to keep one's innermost self under lock and key. In a little over six days he would walk away from her and from whatever the week held for them, to return to the life that he showed to the world. He didn't need to pry into hers beyond finding out what would bring them the most pleasure in the time they spend together.

He tried for a smile even though it felt a little skewed. "It's more than right. It's incredibly sexy." Against that rich tumble of hair, that sexy swathe just begged to be caressed.

He took a sip of whiskey and, unable to stop himself, drew closer, crowding her, invading her space. She inhaled sharply but didn't pull away. He liked that. Hell, it turned him on even harder.

Stormy grey eyes darted to his and stayed. Another huge turn-on, her eyes. The expressions flitting through them made him want to keep gazing into the mesmerizing depths and decode her every thought.

"Thank you," she responded politely to his compliment.

He caught a glimpse of that stud again, saw it glint on her tongue.

"Open." He made his command firm.

Her eyes narrowed a fraction, but she complied a second later.

"What stone is that?" he asked.

"A pink diamond."

Jesus. A diamond-studded blowjob. He was sure

he incinerated a few million brain cells just from processing that information.

"Did it hurt? The piercing, I mean."

"Yes. Very much."

His nostrils flared. "Was it worth it?"

A small smile and a sip of champagne before she answered. "At the time, I wondered what the hell I was thinking. But then the pain became secondary. I was already in love with it. And it achieved the results I wanted."

Intriguing. "Which was what?"

"Independence. I was sixteen and hated being ordinary."

"At the risk of sounding clichéd, baby, anyone who thinks you're anywhere near ordinary is a damn fool."

Another blush that spiked another flame straight to his cock. Hell, at this rate, he'd blow his load long before he got anywhere close to what he had in mind for them.

"My mother was horrified. I got an earful about how I'd ruined my body."

"But you didn't give in and take it out?"

Her mouth curved higher. "I was a budding rebel. We came to an agreement. I wouldn't get the lobe full of ear studs I was threatening to buy, if I got to keep this."

"She agreed?"

She nodded. "I guess she figured the stud was less... visible than the ear studs would ever be."

"Where was your dad in all of this?"

The cloud of pain that blanketed her face made him curse silently. "He wasn't around. He died when I was twelve."

He cupped her cheek and relaxed when she turned her face into his touch. "Shit. I'm sorry."

"It's okay." She looked up at him. "Your turn. What was the most rebellious thing you did as a kid? I bet there were plenty."

"You wound me, baby."

"But I'm right." It wasn't a question.

Noah shrugged, enjoying the banter despite the growing urgency of the need bubbling beneath the surface. "I learned to play poker when I was fourteen. I wanted a set of wheels badly and sweet-talked my best friend's older sister into teaching me how to drive before I was legally allowed to. On my sixteenth birthday, I organized a poker tournament in my friend's basement. I made thirteen thousand dollars that night and went out and bought a hot rod the next day. I knew I would be in deep shit when my dad found out, but I also knew he couldn't ground me forever. Plus the car I got—a Chevy 63 Impala—was his personal weakness. He halved my punishment a week later and drove me down to the DMV to get my license after I passed the exam."

One beautifully shaped brow arched. "So you're saying you get your way more often than not?"

He drained his drink and set the glass down. Reaching forward, he slid a hand around her nape, his thumb caressing her smooth-as-silk skin beneath her jaw. "If it's something I really want, I never let it get away."

He leaned in and savored her the way he'd been dying to for the last ten minutes. Her soft mouth opened beneath his, and Noah groaned at the intoxicating taste of her. She tasted of champagne and hot, sexy possibilities.

This time he dove deeper, flicked his tongue against hers and pushed past until he got what he wanted. The first scrape of that diamond against his tongue made his blood surge hotter.

"Fuck, you go straight to my head," he murmured against her mouth.

She made a small, impatient sound and opened her mouth wider. Her fingers curled into his hair, her nails scraping his scalp to drag him even closer. That greedy little move set him on fire.

Reluctantly, he pulled away. "Slow down, baby."

"Why?" she breathed against his mouth.

"Because I don't want the first time I fuck you to be a rushed job. You deserve better than that."

She pulled away and stared at him, wide eyed. "What makes you think you know what I deserve?" The question was a rough, confused demand. One that ripped across his senses.

He frowned. "You want to clue me in on what's going on, sweetheart?"

She stared at him for several more seconds before she shook her head. "Nothing. Nothing's going on. I just... I'm not very savvy as to what—" She stopped and pulled in a long breath.

He caressed her nape until her shoulders lost a little of the tension that had seized her. "I guessed as much, which is why I want to take this slow."

She flicked him another glance, her eyelashes quivering as she lowered them. "You must think I'm a complete nut job."

"Yes, I do."

Her shocked laugh eased a little more of her tension, just as he'd intended. "I guessed right, then. You're no gentleman."

"And you're no lady. You bit me within half an hour of meeting me."

Her gaze dropped to his mouth and the tiny cut,

raw again from their fevered kiss. "You're going to make sure I never forget it, aren't you?"

"That depends."

"On what?"

"On where else on my body you intend to use those perfect, sharp little teeth."

Her mouth dropped open. "I don't!"

"You will if I tell you to. If you agree to what I want, you won't have a choice but to obey me."

"Noah…"

"You whisper my name as if you're about to divulge a dark, dirty secret." He let his hand drift down over her collarbone to rest on the pulse hammering at her throat. "Are you?"

"I—"

"Miss Michaels, sorry to interrupt."

Noah fought the irritation spreading rapidly through him. Teeth set to grit, he looked up at the blond beefcake, but the other guy's gaze was riveted on Leia. "The ground crew in Switzerland would like to know if you'd be interested in the heli-skiing or the glacier climbing."

"What's the rush?" Leia asked.

"There's a snowstorm moving in where we'd originally planned to stage the heli-skiing event, so we need to confirm final numbers before we move it to another venue." The guy took a small step back when Noah continued to glare at him. "I can come back later, if you're not decided yet?"

Satisfied his "hands off" message had gotten across, Noah hid a small smile and glanced at Leia. "Do you ski?"

"Yes, since I was a kid."

Noah turned to the valet. "Put us down for heli-skiing for two." His tight smile left the other man in no doubt that he wouldn't tolerate any further interruptions, and, to his credit, he received a small nod before they were left alone.

"What makes you think I don't want to climb a glacier?"

"There are some new experiences you want to enjoy on this trip. That isn't one of them."

The brow, which had arched with her previous question, rose higher. He wanted to trace the beautiful curve with his fingers, see if her skin was as soft and delicate as it looked.

"You sound very sure about that."

"I am," he answered.

"Do you feel like expanding on that at all or should I just take your word that you know my every wish? If I were to agree to what you're proposing, would you take over my whole life for the next seven days?" Irritation snapped through her voice.

Noah's pulse drummed at her spirit. "Did I tell you what I do for a living, Leia?"

"We hadn't quite reached there yet. And at this rate, I'm not sure we will."

He smiled at her curt response. "I'm a venture capitalist. Which means I gamble astonishing amounts of money on knowing what people desire, sometimes even before they know it themselves. You're irritated that I made the decision for you. But I'm willing to bet you've never climbed a glacier, correct?"

Her nostrils flared. "No, but that's beside the point."

He leaned in closer, drawn to her like a doomed moth to a fucking flame. "I have. The preparation alone can take up to four hours. We have six and a half days before this thing ends. Do you really want to spend another half a day exploring how to climb a glacier? Or would you rather spend that time exploring me?"

Wide eyes met his. "So you're saying you chose for me for my own good?"

"Our time together is short. I took a quick way to resolve an issue. You can be pissed off, but you'll agree it saved time. So what's your answer?"

Her lips slowly parted, and a breath oozed out. "To what?"

"To everything."

She hesitated.

"Don't be afraid, Leia. Say it out loud. Tell me what I want to hear."

"I'd much rather spend the time exploring you."

8

Leia thought Noah would let loose another of those devastating smiles once she confessed the yearning that pounded underneath her skin. Instead, he gave a solemn nod and inhaled a long, steady breath.

"I'm glad to hear that."

She tried and failed not to shiver at the look in his eyes when his gaze collided with hers. She searched frantically for something else to cover the fact that every time he so much as breathed, she had taken to staring at him like a dopey teenage groupie.

"You don't like my valet."

His mouth compressed. "I don't like the hard-on in his eyes when he looks at you. For his own sake, I hope to hell he stays away."

"Or you'll stare laser beams into him every time he comes close to me?"

He shrugged. "I have a lot of weapons in my arsenal should the staring not work."

She laughed. His eyes darkened as his gaze swept over her face.

"Fuck, you're beyond stunning when you laugh." Again, he said it in that intense low voice, which vibrated over her senses like the most beautiful musical instrument. Unable to speak around the volatile emotions swinging through her, she started to lower her gaze. He caught her chin in a firm hold.

"No. Don't look away. You're going to hear me say that a lot. So you might as well get used to it. You. Are. Fucking. Exquisite."

"Noah..."

"Do you know what I think of when you say my name like that?"

She shook her head.

"I think of all the bad, fucking filthy things I want you to do to me with that tongue stud. The things I know you want to do to me."

Fire stormed through her cheeks, the flames rushing through her body all-consuming. It embarrassed the hell out of her that he could produce such feelings in her with the barest effort. It also made her a little irritated.

"You think you know what I want just because we kissed once?"

He regarded her with shrewd knowing eyes that made her want to run and hide. She forced herself to keep her gaze square on his. "I know you're here for a specific reason, but you're unsure as to how to get what you really want. But you want to find and conquer it immediately."

"You reminded me just now that we only have a few short days. What's wrong with going after what I want?"

The look in his eyes told her she'd asked the wrong question. *Hell.* She didn't want him thinking she was some sort of sophisticated bed partner, but neither did she want to put him off with how utterly green she was. Perhaps shutting up was her best option.

"What's your favorite food, Leia?"

"Italian."

He nodded. "Think of it this way. Great sex is like waiting in your favorite restaurant for your favorite dish but with all the time in the world to eat it. The breadbasket is yours to devour the moment it arrives.

But the first course takes a little bit of time to happen. Then, when you have it, you breathe it in, savor every mouthful. When you're done eating, you should feel happy and sated, with each nerve ending alive from the experience, rather than discomfort by indigestion because you gorged."

"A food-sex analogy? Really?"

He shrugged. "I like food. I love sex. I crave control. I tend not to do the first two at the same time, but I can make an exception if you grant me the third."

"So you're not the whipped cream, eating-sushi-off-naked-bodies type?"

Intense blue eyes scoured her face. "No. I prefer that nothing come between my mouth and your body. I want your taste pure and undiluted."

"What if you don't like what you taste?" Leia couldn't believe she'd said the words. But she refused to blush again. Or look away.

"I will." Succinct and confident.

She envied those traits very badly. He intrigued her more by the second. "You seem very sure. What if you're wrong?"

"I'm not. I can smell you, sweetheart. That need clamoring through you right now? That insatiable craving that no amount of reasoning or ignoring or fucking other people can assuage? It rides me too."

Her senses jumped at the hard, rough note in his voice. "And you think you can make it go away?"

He took a sip of his drink before he answered, a look crossing his features that set her hackles rising in alarm. "Hell no. But I can make it a whole lot better. I can make it so you can have a decent night's sleep and not wonder whether you're going to die from it. We can do that for each other."

The intrigue escalated. Made her wonder what kept him awake at night. Whether he had nightmares like she did. Whether he slept with the light on like she'd done since she was seventeen.

"There's just one thing wrong with your assessment of me, Noah King."

He drew closer, not resisting the pull of their magnetism. "Which part did I get wrong?"

"The part about me... fucking other people." She whispered the words, part of her afraid to say them out loud.

* * *

Every atom in Noah's body froze as the impact of her words slammed into him. "Elaborate."

"I don't... I haven't fucked for a very long time."

"Say that again." He leaned closer, his breath non-existent.

"I haven't been involved with anyone in a very long time." Her voice broke and a tremble coursed through her.

His instinct blared a loud warning. But he was too hung up on the idea of her, virtually untouched, needy and ripe for him, to heed it too much.

Turning to face her fully, he caught her chin in his hand. "How long is a long time, Leia?"

Grey eyes, wide and stormy, clashed with his. He had a feeling she wanted to look away, to hide her expression, but she kept his gaze. Somehow she'd trained herself not to back down, not to look away. That turned him on more than he knew was reasonable.

His cock hardened, nudged desperately against his zipper. He needed to calm the fuck down before he did something rash, like bend her over the lounger and fuck her unconscious.

Her tongue slid across her lower lip. Her reflex was purely from nerves, but it made his blood fire to volcanic levels.

"Does it matter?" she asked.

"Only insofar as it would dictate the pace at which we take things."

"Would you care whether you hurt me or not?" Again, there was that curious note that sent bad tingles down his spine.

This time, he heeded them. "Of course I would. I'd never hurt you."

"That's... that's good to know."

He frowned as another tremble raked her. "Hey, are you okay?"

She gave a shaky laugh and jerked her head away, dislodging his hand. "No."

He clenched his fists and braced his arms on his knees, fighting the need to touch her. Deep down, he sensed she wouldn't welcome his touch. She was far too skittish. Which made a part of him wonder what the hell she was doing here. "What's going on, Leia?"

Her breath shuddered out. "The way you say my name..."

She was deflecting, changing the subject. He decided to allow her a little wriggle room. But he was determined to get to the bottom of this mercurial creature who turned him on more than he'd been turned on in a very long time.

"What about it?"

"You say it like you like it."

He smiled. "That's because I do. More than I think is wise, in fact."

"You don't have a Star Wars fetish, do you?"

He laughed. "No, not a Star Wars one."

Her eyes darkened to a stormy grey that told him he'd sparked her interest. She was so easy to read, her every expression clear for him to see. The thought excited him more than he cared to admit.

"But you do have fetishes?" She moistened her lips, and heat throbbed in his groin.

"Don't we all?" he replied.

"Tell me one."

"No."

Surprise lightened her eyes. "And here I thought we were getting to know one another."

"We are. But it's better for you to know what I want when you're in the situation."

One corner of her mouth tilted. He desperately wanted to taste her smile. "You don't strike me as the kind of man who sticks to safe and predictable subjects, Noah King."

"I'm not. Which is why I don't want to scare you off, Leia Michaels. You intrigue me. I intend to take this very carefully because the last thing I want is for you to bolt."

The seductive eyebrow arched higher. "Bolt? I'm made of stronger stuff than you imagine me to be."

"No. You're not. Despite what you want to make

me believe, you're very fragile." He gave in to the urge and smoothed his hand over the shaved swathe at her temple. "Someone broke you, Leia. Some vile, faceless motherfucker that I intend to hunt down and wipe off the face of the earth. And before this week is through, you're going to tell me who that person is."

9

She was running on a plane. For a hysterical moment, Leia wondered if she was screwing up her body's chemistry by running toward the back of a plane that was racing forward at hundreds of miles per hour.

The sound of heavy footsteps behind her propelled her even faster away from the overwhelming force of nature that was Noah King.

"Leia."

She'd been crazy to think she could handle him. Beyond nuts to think the first time she attempted to break out of the fear-lined box she'd allowed herself to be placed in would be with someone like him. But something in his eyes had answered a need in her, had called to the broken part of her that was too damaged to be fixed but needed acknowledging neverthe-less. What she hadn't anticipated was that he'd see right through to the core of her so fast. So precisely.

"Leia!"

She turned blindly down a hallway that looked vaguely familiar. Desperately hoping her radar wasn't completely skewed, she headed up the stairs she prayed would lead her to her suite.

"Dammit. Stop."

No. Way.

He saw too much. Battered the foundations of her walls too easily.

Avoiding confrontation is not a sign of weakness. Know when to walk away from a fight.

She shook her head, for the first time uncomfort-able with Warren's well-mannered voice in her head.

Seeing her door ahead, she sprinted to it and keyed in the security code. Firm hands seized her arms before the light turned green.

"Stop." His voice had softened from the harsh command. But the panic escalating within her didn't abate.

"No. Let me go."

He loosened his hold and turned her to face him, but he didn't free her. "You're upset. Tell me why."

"It doesn't matter. I think I made a mistake."

Sizzling blue eyes narrowed. "Excuse me?"

"I made a mistake thinking you were what I wanted. I was wrong. I'm going to bed now. If I'm in the mood, I'll find someone else to hang out with tomorrow. Or I'll catch a flight back home when we get to Switzerland. Frankly, I think this whole trip was a mistake."

"No, you don't think you made a mistake. What you'd hoped for was to find someone to fuck you into oblivion, no questions asked."

She snorted. "Well, you've just proved you're not the right candidate. So what the hell are you doing here?"

A hard smile lifted one corner of his mouth. "You think now that I've found you, I'm going to stand with my dick in my hand and watch you come on to someone else? You panicked because I saw a little deeper than you wanted me to. But that doesn't change anything. Whether you want to admit it or not, you saw me and you chose me. You can pretend otherwise and walk away. But if you stay, I get to fuck you. Exclusively. And if I think that digging a little deeper into who you are will make the fucking all the better, then I'm sure as hell going to dig."

"You can dig all you want. You'll get nothing more from me than you already have."

He tilted his head slightly, that infuriatingly sexy smile playing over his delicious mouth once again. "Are you sure you want to issue that challenge?"

"I'm pretty sure I want you to take your hands off me and leave me the hell alone."

Cobalt blue eyes lit up with sizzling fire. His hand dropped from her arm, and he pushed the door open before taking hold of her again.

"Do you really want me to go?"

She opened her mouth to speak, but no words emerged. His eyes gleamed.

"Invite me in, Leia," he murmured softly against her lips.

It took all her willpower, but she overcame the screaming need to say yes. "No."

"You want a mindless fuck. I'll give you one. But it'll be nowhere near as satisfactory as it can be if you let me in a little." He leaned in closer, making her feel the hard evidence of the gift he could offer her. A gift she could accept at a cost she couldn't afford to pay.

"Do you take the time to get to know every woman you sleep with? That redhead who was eyeing you at the bar. Would you have taken the time to get to know her before you... you..."

"She ceased to matter the moment I saw you. And she mattered way less *before* I saw you. Trust me, baby, what I have in mind is dirty, filthy fucking that will make you scream your throat hoarse. But to get it you need to invite me in."

Evocative images bombarded her senses, but she shook her head. "I'm not inviting you in, Noah."

Her stomach churned at the calculating gleam that narrowed his eyes. His hands smoothed up and down her arms, waking tiny shivers that made him smile with pure male satisfaction.

He dropped his head until their lips were a whisper apart.

"I'm not fucking you out here in the hallway, baby. Your clothes stay on in public. That's non-negotiable. Another non-negotiable fact is that you're not fucking anyone else on this trip. Everything else I'm willing to negotiate."

"Negotiate your hands off me. Right now. Before my knee negotiates itself between your legs."

Something in her voice must have finally gotten through to him. Eyes narrowing further, he dropped his hands and took a step back.

"Do I frighten you, Leia?" he asked, a tension seizing him that made a twinge of shame suffuse her.

He overwhelmed her. He made her stomach cave in on itself with a hunger that defied reason. He made her clit throb and her pussy clench with desperate greed. But he didn't induce fear in her.

She should know. She knew what real fear looked and felt like.

Compelled to be truthful, she shook her head. "No."

He exhaled, his shoulders relaxing a touch. But the tension didn't completely leave his face or his body. He stared down at her for another handful of seconds before he speared a hand through his hair.

"We seem to be tripping over the right way to do this. What can I say to convince you that I want what you want?" Frustration bit through his voice.

"We can agree to keep this... light."

He stared at her another several minutes. Then his eyes dropped to the pulse beating in her neck, then lower to the agitated rise and fall of her breasts. Even lower still, until even her soles tingled with the look in his eyes.

By the time he raised his gaze to hers, she was ready to abandon all reason and throw herself at him.

"I don't do light, baby. Not when it comes to kissing and not when it comes to sex. It's the deep end or not at all. But I don't want to walk away, so I'll make you a promise."

"Wh-what?"

"Invite me in, and I promise to keep my clothes on until we land."

"What happens after we land?" she asked, noting shamefully that her voice had grown husky and breathless.

He shrugged. "We go skiing."

Acute disappointment scythed through her, but she stopped herself from blurting out a sharp refusal to his proposal.

Leia found herself moving from the wall into the doorway, walking backward as he stalked her into the room. Her heart rate tripled when he nudged the door shut with his foot.

For several seconds, they stared at each other with that insane electricity arcing between them.

Noah breathed in deep, drawing her attention to his massive chest. She'd felt that chest up close, briefly explored the rock-hard muscle beneath his shirt. The knowledge that she was allowing fear to take away the chance to explore him again cut like a knife through her.

And yet, changing her mind again would make her the nut job he no doubt believed her to be.

Whirling around, she entered the small living room adjoining her bedroom. An extensive drinks cabinet stood next to the entertainment center.

"Would you like a drink?" She turned to find he'd followed her, stood mere feet away.

"I don't think another drink is a good idea."

She floundered. "Okay..."

He took pity on her, grabbed the remote on the coffee table, and pressed a button. A large screen slid forward from behind a recessed panel.

He strolled to the wide gold and cream striped sofa and lowered his lithe body into it. Like all the seats on the plane, it was large and comfortable enough to double up as a fuck space. Looking over at her, he patted the space next to him. "Sit down, baby. I won't bite just yet."

Walking on slightly unsteady feet, she sank down next to him.

Immediately, he curved his arm over her shoulder and pulled her close.

The unexpected move upset her balance. She fell against him, and he sucked in a breath when her breast pressed into his side. He nuzzled her cheek lightly before he turned his face back to the screen.

"What are we doing?" she asked.

"We're choosing our location *highs* for the next seven days. Assuming, of course, you still want to spend them with me?"

Swallowing, she nodded.

He shook his head. "Vocalize, baby. I need to hear the words so there's no room for misinterpretation later." The hard, low demand gave no quarter.

"Yes, I want to spend the next seven days with you." The moment she said the words, the last of her doubts fled.

She was here. She was doing this. With a man who could well create a whole new set of problems for her. But she was banking on the pleasure to come far outweighing the risk.

She'd done extensive research on the Indigo Lounge before she'd decided to take the trip. Its owner, Zachary Savage, was single-mindedly scrupulous about safety on his planes. And her own instincts, fine-tuned through a brutal test of fire and grit, weren't screaming the kind of danger she'd learned to stay away from.

She relaxed a little more. He felt it and those intense blue eyes gleamed with satisfaction.

"Good." He flicked the screen on, and the distinct Indigo Lounge logo appeared. He forwarded through the corporate spiel until the list of activities came up. "We've got your first high in the bag—skiing on the black run in Zermatt. Next, a half hour session with a band during a live jazz concert or meeting the conductor after the opera in Vienna?"

"What bands are playing?"

He pressed another button and the names flashed onto the screen.

Excitement spiked through her. "*Omigod*. Definitely the live jazz concert."

He slanted her a narrow-eyed glance. "Something I should know about?"

"*Fused Realms* is one of my favorite bands."

His mouth compressed. "As long as you don't throw your panties at anyone, I'll try not to lose my shit."

Leia wasn't sure whether he was joking or not.

"The masked ball in Prague or the private zero-gravity chamber in Cannes?" He looked at her, his eyes predatory and all-consuming. "Do you like the idea of getting fucked in zero gravity, baby?"

Laughter bubbled up beneath all the crazy hyper-awareness. "I can honestly say it's never occurred to me. Is that even possible?"

"We can certainly give it our very best shot." He clicked the button to add it to their itinerary and moved to the next one.

"If you want, we can add a couple more? Private villa or private boat in Bermuda?"

The rod of tension lanced too quickly for her to disguise it. Those astonishingly perceptive blue eyes started to narrow. Breathing out, she forced her body to relax. "Villa, please. I don't like boats."

"Sea sickness?"

"Something like that." She deliberately kept her tone light and scrambled to banish the ugly images that threatened to flood her mind.

His expression told her he'd noticed her evasion. But he nodded. "Villa it is." He entered the request and glanced back at her, his eyes zeroing in on her mouth. "Shall we leave the rest for later?" he murmured, his head dropping closer.

Reading his intent, her breath evaporated from her lungs. She started to nod and remembered his warning.

"Yes."

He pressed another button and soft R&B wafted through the suite. The beats held enough of a throb to vibrate through her body. Or maybe it was just her heartbeat going into overdrive at the thought of kissing Noah King again.

Whatever.

Anticipation inundated her as his lips touched hers. This kiss was different from the first. For one thing, she hadn't given herself the time to stop freaking out about the electrifying effect of his mouth before she'd bit him.

His tongue traced the outline of her mouth and breached her open lips to graze over her teeth. She barely managed to curb the overwhelming need to bite him again.

What the heck was wrong with her? When had the thought of biting *anyone* become a turn-on? But she'd bitten this man. And he'd bled.

She touched the tip of her tongue to the tiny cut on his lip. His shudder echoed hers.

He broke away and stared at her, his breathing harsh and uneven. Pure, unadulterated lust arced between them, setting off sparks she could almost see dancing in the air.

"God." She realized she'd vocalized the wonder burning inside her.

He nodded once. "You see how this could never be light between us, don't you?"

"Yes," she said huskily.

His hand crept over her nape and gripped her harder as he pressed closer. Sprawling back against the seat, he tugged her over him until she straddled him.

He explored every exposed inch of her. Her neck. Her arms. The small of her back bared by her forward-tilted stance. She gasped with each touch of his warm, rough hands.

Then his hand circled her throat again. That possessive, powerful hold did things to her she couldn't coherently describe. It was a statement of control, of ownership that was also oddly soothing. He pressed gently, until she could feel each heartbeat through his fingers.

Any thought that she would be in control in any way because she was on top evaporated when his other hand curved over her waist, imprisoning her against him.

Slowly, he pulled her down and took her mouth again. But this time he controlled the kiss. He gave her just enough to make her whimper shamelessly. "Please."

He gave in to her plea, deepened the kiss, let her hands wander feverishly over his chest and shoulders. Her fingers speared through his silky dark hair before he pulled his mouth from hers with a deep groan. "Jesus, baby. Kissing you is like standing in a field in the middle of a fucking lightning storm."

She emerged from a sensual haze long enough to notice her strap had slipped off one shoulder... that the upper crests of her breasts were exposed to his hungry gaze.

He traced a finger over her left breast and snagged

it in the corner of her top. She noticed the faint trembling in his hand and her breath caught.

"Take it off."

"I thought our clothes were staying on?"

"I said *my* clothes would stay on. I didn't say yours would. I didn't say I wouldn't spread you over me and let you ride me until I came in my pants like a fucking teenager. And I sure as hell didn't promise not to finger you to orgasm and taste your sweet cunt as you lost your mind. Did I?"

10

The rough, filthy words washed over Leia, and another jagged shudder ripped her from head to toe. Her fingers convulsed on his hard-muscled shoulders, her nails digging deep.

He stared into her eyes as he passed his thumb over her silk-covered nipple, then caught the bud and squeezed hard, wringing a cry from her. "Did I, baby?"

She shook her head jerkily.

He curled his fingers into her hair and pulled back. Sizzling eyes pierced hers. "Vocalize."

"No, you didn't."

"Good. Then do as I say and take your top off."

She couldn't move. What he was doing to her skin was mesmerizing. Paralyzing enough to keep her locked on top of him.

"Leia." The command was rough. Implacable.

"I-I can't move."

Blue eyes, dark and swirling with turbulent emotion, captured hers. "Need help?"

"Yes."

He rose from his reclined position. His hands covered hers on his shoulder, meshed his fingers through hers and lifted her arms over her head.

"Stay." He removed his fingers from hers and grasped the edge of her top.

Leia swallowed. In a few seconds, she would be naked from the waist up.

He'd see.

Every self-preserving instinct screamed at her to stop him before it was too late. He'd told her he intended to dig deeper. Letting him see the evidence of the broken soul she was trying desperately to piece back together would make him demand answers.

Because Noah King wasn't a man who glided blithely through life. He wasn't a man who would ignore the questions right in front of him.

He would see.

He lifted her top a few inches, then stopped. "Hell... baby, you're wound so tight. I'm almost afraid to touch you in case you splinter into a million pieces."

She wanted to slam her hands on his, stop him from uncovering the secrets she desperately needed to hide.

But she couldn't move. Something about him compelled her to stay where she was. Do as she was told because the reward would be indescribable.

"Will you break if I touch you, Leia Michaels?"

She exhaled. Inhaled. Struggled to find a modicum of the balance she'd fought so hard to regain these past five years.

"I won't break," she whispered. Pleaded. "Touch me."

Keeping her gaze trapped, he slowly lifted her top over her head. "Keep your hands up."

Both hands braced on her back now, he lowered his gaze. His eyes widened ever so slightly and he swallowed. "No bra." He looked back up. "Why?"

She fought not to squirm under the heated force of his regard. "Don't need one. My breasts are too small..."

"Your breasts are fucking perfect."

He started to lean forward, his mouth parting. Her nipples puckered, anticipation straining every nerve in her body.

At the last moment, he froze. Leia almost groaned in pain, but another fiercer anxiety washed over her as he tilted his head to the left side of her body. Her skin burned when his eyes zeroed in on the single line of writing marring her ribcage.

Heart racing, she watched his fingers slowly drift over the tattoo. He read the words, absorbed them. Then he looked up at her. The question in his eyes was unmistakable.

She shook her head, pleading silently with him not to ruin the moment.

"Vocalize," he rasped, his voice low and thick with questions.

She swallowed around the lump in her throat. "Don't ask me. Please, Noah. Not right now."

His gaze went back to the words. His fingers hadn't stopped tracing them.

From a broken acorn...

Gripping her waist tight with his left hand, he tilted her sideways.

When she realized his intent, her heart slammed wildly against her ribs. "No."

"Yes."

He kissed her there, right where the words were etched into her skin. His hot mouth anointed the words, before his tongue traced each letter.

When he was done, he trailed his mouth upward, toward his initial goal.

A different emotion slammed into her, every breath craving the impending contact.

His mouth closed over a nipple and she cried out. Shivers of delight coursed through her as his mouth worried the nerve-sensitized bud. He suckled. He grazed, then caught it between his teeth, groaning deep when her whole body convulsed in helpless re-action. She didn't realize her hips were grinding into his erection until hard hands gripped her waist, forcing her down further onto the thick cock outlined bold and heavy through his slacks.

He turned his attention to the other nipple, and liquid heat dampened her panties. Raging need pooled between her legs, her clit swelling and rub-bing urgently against the seam of her pants with each pump of her hips.

"Holy fuck. You're so goddamn hot."

He flicked open the button on her leather pants and pulled down the zipper.

Keeping his eyes on hers, he slid his fingers into her panties and grazed her clit with his middle finger.

She jerked, her mouth dropping open to suck in precious air.

"You like that?"

"Hmmm." His finger stilled. Compelling blue eyes probed hers until she found her voice. "Yes, I like that."

He moved the digit. Toyed with her nerve-engorged flesh.

Leia experienced the melting from her core outward. Molten and all encompassing, pleasure drowned her from that simple touch of his finger on her clit.

Squeezing her eyes shut, she rocked her hips in time to the sensual drumbeat.

"What else do you like, Leia Michaels?" he crooned against her skin, the rough stubble of his jaw creating delicious friction between her breasts.

She wanted that friction elsewhere. Between her thighs. But there was no way she was capable of moving off his lap right now. Besides, she was certain she wouldn't last that long. Not this first time. The pleasure was already too overwhelming.

So she did the next best thing.

Shifting sideways, Leia clamped one hand in his hair and tried to move him to her nipple.

His superior strength thwarted her easily, merciless eyes drilling a refusal into her.

She whimpered. "Please."

"You beg me for more even as you get wetter. Why do you need more, baby?"

She ground harder into him, pain chasing pleasure as the storm built faster and more ferocious inside her. "I want..."

"Tell me."

"I want to come. Now."

"Why?" he demanded, giving her just enough to keep her going but not enough to break the storm.

Her fingers convulsed in his hair, a sob rising in her throat when he whisper-grazed his stubble over her nipple for a bare instant before he pulled away.

"Because it hurts," she moaned.

Electric heat lit his eyes. A thin sheen of sweat broke over his forehead, and his mouth parted as he continued to drink in her reaction to his touch. "I want it to hurt a little more, baby. Can you take it?"

She shook her head, her senses screeching at her not to risk losing so much control.

A look of disappointment settled over his face.

Terrified he would stop, she grabbed him tighter. "I'm willing to try."

He immediately changed the angle of his touch. Two fingers slid on either side of her clit, his knuckles digging into her bones with enough pressure to snap her teeth into a tight clench. "Oh God!"

One hand splayed over her lower back, holding her steady as he teased her with a merciless rubbing that shoved dry sobs into her throat.

"Tell me how you feel, sweetheart."

"I feel... tight, like I'm on a leash. It's... it's tightening and I can't break free..."

Another fleeting pass of his stubble over her nipple. The coil wound tighter.

"Do you want me to set you free, baby?"

Her fingers convulsed in his hair, her nails digging into his scalp. "Yes! Please, God, yes."

"Shit. The more you beg, the wetter you get. You know what that does to me, sweetheart?"

"N... no."

"It makes me want you to beg for hours until I'm drenched."

"No! Please... Noah!"

Strong fingers trapped her clit in a pincer motion between his knuckles. Still rubbing the back of his hand into her sex, he flicked his thumb hard and fast over her plump nub. Just when she thought the torture couldn't get any worse, he squeezed her harder, then drew his jaw roughly over her nipples.

Shocking pain erupted into a shower of pleasure so strong her back bowed under its intensity. From beyond the realms of comprehension, she heard the rip of clothing and the sharp hiss of pain. But she was flying, the extreme rush of her orgasm beyond anything she'd ever experienced.

11

The haze washing across his vision threatened to drown Noah. With each second that passed, he was drawn further into the certainty that she was made for him. That she was the one who could pull him from the dark spiral of cloying hunger.

He opened his eyes and watched her. Her gorgeous lips were parted as she desperately pulled in oxygen. The resulting frantic heaves of her chest brought his attention to her magnificent breasts.

Shit, could he use any more adjectives? The word *perfect* didn't exist for him because as far as he was concerned nothing would ever achieve that status in his eyes.

And yet, witnessing Leia's orgasm, that word

sprang into his mind and grew as he watched the flush spread across her skin, heard her soft moans as her body continued to bow under the extreme power of her release.

His gaze drifted down, over the silky soft skin of her taut belly that spoke of a physical care regime. Bartitsu. She took care of her body. All through her exquisite writhing, her thighs had clamped him hard, gripping him as if she'd never let go.

He welcomed that strength, grew heady with the thought of pushing her to her limit.

Trailing his hand back up her body, his gaze locked on the tattoo and the questions tumbling through his mind froze on one line.

From a broken acorn...

What the hell had happened to her?

The overwhelming need to know drove the last of the haze from his brain. Even though his cock throbbed with an almost life-threatening demand to fuck, he smashed down the need and helped her up.

The globes of her breasts were redder, as were her nipples, from the rough treatment of his jaw. A primitive part of him gloried at marking her this way, but the urge to stamp his possession all over her had him turning his hand to cup her soaked sex.

She jerked upright, her wide eyes clashing with his. "I can't."

"You can and you will. But not right now."

A wave of relief washed over her face. "So does this count as my first high?"

He cracked a smile. "This is a bonus. Call it a trial run before we get down to the double highs of extreme skiing and extreme fucking tomorrow."

She swallowed and gave another little shudder.

Unable to drive the question from his mind, he glanced back at the tattoo.

She tensed. He gripped her harder between her legs, and her breath puffed out.

"I warned you I don't do light, sweetheart. Did you think I was joking?"

Her breath fractured. "No, but I was hoping I wouldn't have to bare my everything to you so soon. You have my body, Noah. Use it. Use me. I won't break. I'm much stronger than you think. But this..." She pointed to her side. "Not yet. Please."

The impulse to probe was strong. But hell, she wasn't the only one with baggage who didn't want it to be examined.

What had happened between them just now had been overwhelming enough, despite the ferocious hunger it'd triggered.

The urge to plunge a finger inside her, test her tightness, rushed through him. He barely managed to stop himself. If he gave in, confirmed just how snug and lush she was, he'd never leave this suite tonight. He contented himself with rubbing her slick heat.

But still... "You've just proven that you can handle the deep end, Leia. And you knew I would need to know more the moment you took your top off."

She shuddered. Whether it was from his harsh demand or from his relentless rubbing, he wasn't entirely sure. "What do you want from me, Noah?"

He looked up, his senses reeling at her mingled vulnerability and beauty. His fingers grazed over her ribcage. "I don't want to wonder about this when I fuck you. I want to see your eyes fill with pleasure and not the shadows I can see in them now. That may be asking too much too soon, but I warned you I was a greedy bastard. I want to make you scream in pleasure that'll make you forget why you're broken. If only for a while."

"Why is that so important to you?"

For all his hard demands, Noah wasn't prepared for that question. Nor was he ready for the words that spilled from his mouth. "Because for the next seven days, you're mine. And I absolutely refuse to share you with ghosts."

* * *

Leia fought not to panic at the hard demand in his voice. She was no longer helpless, no longer the girl who'd cowered in the corner, biting her nails until they bled because she believed the madness in her world was *all* her fault.

Noah King had no right to make demands of her.

Her ghosts were her business, her secrets to keep.

So why was she firmly in his lap? Why wasn't she freeing herself from that compelling, possessive hold and bidding him a firm, curt goodnight that would make Warren proud?

Warren.

What would the man she'd let assume a huge role in her life think of all of this?

Take control. Keep control...

But she'd relinquished it to Noah King.

The fingers between her thighs moved, demanded her attention. A helpless shudder ripped through her, powerful despite the tsunami-proportioned orgasm that had flattened her moments ago.

She looked into steady, hot blue eyes and forced down a swallow.

"I won't lie to you, Noah. The ghosts are real and

present. But they won't be a problem between us. I won't let them."

He opened his mouth, and she placed her fingers on his lips. "Please. Trust me."

His eyes darkened, and he stared at her for several heartbeats before he nodded. "Tell me one thing."

She exhaled. "Okay."

He touched the side of her head, then gently probed her mouth to graze his forefinger over her tongue piercing. "Did these come before or after your ghosts arrived?"

"The piercing was before. The hair was much later. Six months ago."

"And the tattoo?"

"Definitely after. I needed something to hold on to... a reminder that my journey wasn't complete... when the temptation to just give in became over-whelming."

He uttered a single, explosive curse, his eyes burning with anger and determination that shortened her breath.

"What will the rest of it say?"

"I'll let you know when I find out."

Slowly, he removed his hand from her wet, sticky heat. Her face flamed when she caught a glimpse of just how much she'd fallen over the edge. The scent of her soaked sex drifted up and swirled around them, weaving a potent spell of arousal.

Keeping his gaze on hers, he circled her parted lips with the wetness on his fingers. She tasted herself, the essence sweet and musky and heady in a way she'd never have anticipated. Over and over he coated her mouth, his movements slow and erotic.

Then, pulling his hand away, he leaned in close until his mouth brushed hers, until his own lips glistened with her juices.

"I'll make you another promise, sweetheart. For the next seven days, I promise to fuck you so hard, so completely and thoroughly, that every bad thing in your existence will become a distant blur. You will have no room to think of them, much less let them attempt to interfere. You're a magnificent, incredible creature, Leia Michaels. Somewhere along the line, someone's attempted to make you forget that. With every fuck, with every orgasm, I intend to remind you of your sheer glory."

His mouth crashed onto hers, ramming the words home so forcefully, they were branded on her skin... on her psyche. He forced them down her throat with his tongue, imbedded them into her body with his hard hands and didn't relent until she gasped for breath.

Tears spiked the back of her eyes, brimmed underneath her lids when he reluctantly released her, picked her up and strode into her bedroom.

With gentle hands, he laid her on the bed, pulled her pants off and tucked the heavy sheet around her. He turned to walk away and she stared at his retreating figure, unable to fathom the swirl of emotions whizzing through her. "Why?"

He stopped at the door and slowly turned around.

"I told you, you deserve nothing less."

12

"Ready?"

Leia checked her skis one last time. The wind whipped up her hair, the air frigid and bracing, reminding her she was alive.

As far as she could see, snowcapped mountains glinted under the cloudless blue sky the exact shade of the eyes of the man next to her. The helicopter had dropped them off on top of the Swiss peak ten minutes ago.

But the rush of the impending race wasn't the reason her blood all but sang through her veins. And it wasn't the reason he was asking the seemingly simple question.

She looked at him. "Yes."

His eyes shone with approval and she beamed, unable to stop herself from basking in the hunger that vibrated off him.

How very quickly she was coming to know him. While Leia didn't fool herself into thinking she knew nearly enough about him to form a solid judgment, in the past six hours he'd been relentless in seeing to her every need, starting from his firm knock on her door the moment they'd landed.

He'd whisked her away to breakfast at an exquisite little café near the Jet d'eau in Geneva, leaving the crew to deliver her bag to the private lodge they'd be spending the night in before their flight to Vienna in the morning. They'd been picked up after breakfast and delivered to the heliport. From there, the private helicopter had flown them straight to where their ski guides waited in Zermatt. In the few hours since they'd landed, she'd learned enough about Noah to know what pleased him.

He was possessive. That would only become a problem if he found out about Warren. And she didn't intend to let that aspect of her life intrude on this moment in time.

He loved to touch her. She didn't have a problem with that.

More than anything else, he preferred it when she

used her voice. No problem there either. To Noah King, the reverse of the idiom *actions speak louder than words* was true.

With another smile, he pulled down his goggles. "I'll race you."

"What do I get when I win?"

His brows shot up. "*When?* You feeling brave, sweetheart?"

"I have a few surprises up my sleeve."

He waited until the couple next to them shoved off the summit. They were fast, experienced, and traversed the trail with smooth speed and efficiency.

But she knew they would be nowhere as magnificent to watch as the man beside her. And nowhere near as fast.

Her body was in good enough condition, thanks to the three-times-a-week training sessions she'd been taking since she turned eighteen and the once-a-week sparring matches with Warren.

But Leia hadn't hit a black run for almost two years. If she were to have a hope in hell of winning, she'd need to bring her A-game.

She calculated how quickly she could traverse the terrain and turned to find his eyes trained on her. The look in the blue depths terrified and excited her at the same time. Predatory and determined, his eyes also held a gentleness that unsettled her a little.

"If you win, I'll let you come as hard and fast as you want to the first time."

Her heart slammed against her ribs and her body grew hot, despite the sub-zero temperature. "And if you win?"

Blue eyes darkened to midnight and a muscle twitched at the corner of his mouth. "I get to dictate how long I keep you on the edge."

Recalling how excruciating the pleasure/pain had been the last time, she bit her lip. She couldn't fathom how she would remain sane if he kept her on the very edge of her endurance as he'd promised last night.

She eyed the steep run, which until recently had been a black run but had been re-classified to a yellow.

"I tell you what, I'll give you a one-minute head start," Noah drawled.

The fine hairs on her nape bristled at his superior tone. "What makes you think I need one?"

He shrugged. "Take the minute or don't. I'm just trying to get us off this mountain before my balls turn into ice cubes."

Her gaze trailed over his black and red ski suit. Her mouth watered at the sight of his broad shoulders and lean hips, then immediately dried at the latent power of his thighs as he flexed his legs on his skis. The thought of all that power unleashed on her should've made her take a step back.

Instead, she closed the gap between them and raised her face to his. "I'll tell *you* what." She deliberately kept her voice low so he'd have to bend to hear her. Her mouth brushed his ear. His throat bobbed in a swallow. "I'll be waiting at the bottom to warm your frozen balls for you. And if you're very, very lucky, I might even use my tongue. *How's that*, sweetheart?"

Before he could respond, she planted an open-mouthed kiss on his startled lips, turned and launched herself off the mountain.

The skin-flaying course whipped past her eardrums as she dug her ski poles into the soft powder and hurtled down the steep white slope.

The two couples who'd left minutes before had taken the safest path to the base.

Leia chose a more challenging route, which she'd tracked when the helicopter turned to land. It held a steep drop about halfway down, one that most skiers would think twice about before using. She didn't dare look behind her even though she could hear the faint swish of Noah's skis as he came after her.

She veered to the right at the last minute, tucked

her knees beneath her, held her breath and careened off the edge.

Noah's "Shit!" ripped through the clear frigid air.

She laughed, knowing he'd left it too late to follow her shortcut. She landed hard, her teeth jarring as she absorbed the shock and fought to stay on her feet. Luckily, almost twenty years of experience came to her aid. Memories of skiing with her father flashed across her mind.

Logan Michaels had loved skiing. Aspen had been his favorite winter playground, followed by Val D'isere. He'd taken her along each year. By the time she'd turned ten, she'd transitioned to yellow runs.

Unfortunately, his vow to have her on a black run by the time she was thirteen never materialized.

She blinked hard at the tears that prickled her eyes and shoved the accompanying pain back beneath the heavy blanket she'd thrown over her memories. She'd mourned her father—as much as it was possible to do when her life had been turned upside down after his death.

Besides, now wasn't the time to revisit the past.

The growing sound of skis prompted her to speed up, pushing even harder against the power of the man behind her.

She flew over a small outcropping of rocks and

felt momentarily free as she soared mid-air. Her landing was smoother this time, and she slammed her skis harder into the snow. A small copse of alpine trees stood between her and the finish line.

She hated skiing through trees. Despite her skill and agility, she was very aware that one wrong move and it would be over. She forced herself to reduce her speed despite the fire of the challenge burning in her veins.

The other worrying thing was the reckless promise she'd thrown at him on top of the mountain. She'd never warmed a man's balls before, never mind with her tongue. But no way was she about to confess to Noah King that she'd only had two sexual experiences in her life. The first had been clumsy and embarrassing.

The second had been life changing...

She had to win.

But if she lost... being kept on the knife-edge of orgasm for hours on end couldn't be so bad... could it? *Yes, it could.* She'd foretasted that insanity on the plane and that had lasted barely twenty minutes.

God, she would lose her mind if he kept her in a heightened state for even one hour.

The shush of skis drew closer. Digging deep, she ignored the burn in her thighs and raced through the trees. Bursting into blinding sunshine, she spied the billowing flags that signaled the end of the run.

The group made up of guests and crew stood to one side. One or two turned to watch them, and Leia saw their excited gestures.

Too chicken to check how close Noah was, she pushed herself harder.

The whole group had turned to look and most were shouting encouragement.

"Come on!"

"He's right behind you!"

"Give it up, baby. I'm going to win."

That he had to raise his voice told her he wasn't as close as she'd thought. She ventured a quick look over her shoulder and saw he was at least ten meters away.

"No chance in hell, King," she shouted.

His teeth bared in pure intimidation before she whisked around and gave it everything she had.

Her skis skidded across the finish line just as the tips of his swept into her eye line. Leia punched the air to applause and turned to see Noah shaking his head, his eyes narrowed on her face.

"So, you like winning."

"I like teaching cocky guys a lesson or two every now and then, yes."

The corners of his mouth lifted in a smile so sexy,

fire flared through her belly. "Touché. Congrats on winning."

For some reason, she was sure he meant it, although he continued to smile in a way that made her jumpy.

His next words confirmed why he was so damned pleased with himself. "Although the view coming down wasn't that bad either. In fact, watching you move gave me a fair idea of how well you can hold certain positions."

"Excuse me?"

He leaned close and whispered in her ear, "No, baby, you're not excused. Not when watching that little ass move has made me as hard as that fucking mountain. You won't be excused until I am well and truly satisfied."

Bjorn chose that moment to approach and relieve her of the ski poles. Another valet bearing hot drinks followed him closely.

She watched, half-amused at Noah's narrow-eyed look in Bjorn's direction before she picked up the mug of cognac-laced cocoa to warm her fingers. He eyed her as he drank his coffee.

The look in his eyes told her he intended to claim her on his terms in the very, very near future. As she watched, he knocked back the rest of his drink and strolled to her.

"Are you done with your drink?" Impatience throbbed in his voice.

She relinquished it with a glare. "Am I ever going to finish a drink with you around?"

"Not when there's the urgent matter on the line of your diamond-studded tongue, a private lodge and my frozen balls that needing serious and immediate attention."

13

Noah was pretty damn sure this hard-on was going to kill him. His vision blurred every time he so much as breathed. Or the jeep bounced over the snow. Or Leia slid him one of those surreptitious glances she thought he couldn't see.

She coupled each look with a tiny mangle of her lower lip. She was nervous. Understandable. Hell, he was too. But she didn't know that each time he caught a glimpse of those small, sharp teeth, he grew harder, his cock throbbing a dire warning that he was going to die if he didn't do something about his erection soon.

Their driver turned into a single-track lane and the chain-covered tires squealed as they went up a steep incline for almost a minute before leveling off into a circular driveway.

One look at the private lodge and Noah was immediately glad he'd chosen it instead of returning to the five-star Indigo Geneva Hotel where the rest of the guests were staying.

After watching her ski, seeing how sleekly and sexily she handled herself on the slopes, he'd almost lost it by the time he'd crossed the finish line. Waiting for an hour to get on the chopper back to Geneva had been out of the question in his state.

Hell, he'd have fucked her in a yurt in the middle of a snowstorm or up against a tree and risked cock frostbite if it came to it. But this would do fine.

"Wow, this place is perfect!"

He hid a smile and unzipped his jacket, drinking in her pleasure as she took in their surroundings. Tall alpine trees, heavy with snow, embraced the thick wood and stone lodge and provided a backdrop of refreshing green and white. The three-story house was secluded with the next house almost half a mile away.

"I'm glad you like it. Wanna explore the inside too?" Noah knew he didn't quite succeed in keeping his wild anticipation out of his voice. The only exploration he intended to do was with her. Fully and thoroughly.

She turned from admiring the trees and snows-cape around them and looked at him. She slicked a hand through her hair, flicking it to the side in a gesture he'd come to learn as a nervous tick. Hell, nervousness vibrated from her.

He'd need to take it slow.

Fuck. That might be a problem.

Deliberately turning away from her, he dismissed their driver and walked up the steps into the house.

The living room soared two stories high, with a giant granite fireplace that crackled with a log fire. On the polished wood floor, a large furry rug had been laid, complete with half a dozen pillows. On the slab of rock that passed as a coffee table, a sterling silver bucket chilled a bottle of champagne, and two long flutes stood next to it.

The scene was set with one thing in mind, and he was having a hard time not grabbing her and getting started. He shrugged off his jacket, threw it on the nearest chair and headed to what he hoped was the kitchen.

He needed to occupy himself with something before he gave in to the hot images flooding his mind.

"Are you hungry?" he threw over his shoulder.

"Umm... yes. I could eat."

He groaned under his breath and entered the large kitchen. He was sure shiny, expensive gadgets must have lined the countertops and every conceivable luxury had been provided. But Noah couldn't see a thing beyond his lust haze as he blindly pulled open the fridge and eyed the neatly arranged silverware and plates of food. More than enough to sustain them for the next eighteen hours.

He picked up the nearest tray containing handmade finger food and set it on the countertop.

"Oh. Smoked salmon and cream cheese mini bagels. Love those."

He breathed a sigh of relief. "Great. Would you mind grabbing—"

He gripped the edge of the counter so hard his bones screamed in agony.

While his back had been turned, she'd shed her puffer jacket and the bottom half of her ski pants. The long sleeve thermal shirt molded her small breasts so perfectly that saliva flooded his mouth. His gaze dropped to the black leggings clinging to her taut, shapely thighs and legs, and he groaned again under his breath.

She stopped in the process of grabbing the plates

from where they'd been stacked on the counter. "Noah, are you okay?"

He speared a hand through his hair. Thought about cracking a joke to avoid the stark truth. Then decided against it. She needed to know who she was dealing with.

"Hell, no. I can't look at a surface in this place without imagining you spread across or over it and me fucking you into oblivion on it. So no, I'm not okay. But I'm trying to take it slow for you."

Her eyes widened. "For me? Why?"

He laughed. "You're nervous. I thought doing something mundane like eating a meal and talking might set you a little at ease."

"At ease. Before you devour me?" Her breath hitched at the end, like she was having a hard time breathing.

He laughed. The sound came out rough and alien. "Shit, am I being that obvious?"

"A little. Okay... a lot."

"Fuck." He grimaced and shut his eyes.

"But... that's not why I'm nervous."

He raised his head. "What is it?"

She traced a finger absently over the hard countertop. He wanted that finger tracing his skin so badly he locked his knees to stop from launching himself over the aisle and grabbing her.

"That thing I promised on top of the mountain?"

"Yes," he croaked, his gaze dropping to the lips she'd worried until they were now plump and pink. "I remember."

"I don't think I can do it…"

Crap. He barely stopped himself from cursing as a healthy percentage of his fantasies evaporated into thin air. "You don't have to do it if it's not your thing."

"No, I didn't mean that. I meant I've never actually… done it before." The odd inflection in her tone made him pause.

Noah understood nuance. Hell, he'd had to learn very quickly when he set up his business and realized dealing with billions of dollars meant catering to egos that could test even the saintliest temperament. And after ten years at the top of his game, he could spot the trickiest opponents who thought they could test how far to push his resolve a mile away.

But he couldn't grasp the nuance slapping him in the face.

He'd played his fingers thoroughly between her thighs last night, explored her sweet pussy so expertly he could close his eyes and recall exactly how she felt.

Except he'd pulled back before enjoying her as fully as he'd wanted to. "Jesus, sweetheart, please don't tell me you're a *virgin*?" Another soul-destroying dose of erotic images vanished. He clutched the counter harder, the pain of knowing he'd have to walk away almost debilitating.

"No, I'm not."

His breath rushed out in thankful relief as elation flooded his system. He swallowed down his roar of joy. "Are you sure?"

Her face tightened. "Is that a serious question?"

"No, I meant are you sure you can't do it?" *Please God, let her be willing to try.* He needed to feel the back of her throat like he needed to breathe.

"I don't want to mess it up."

His bark of laughter slammed around the room, a harsh noise that made her flinch. He rounded the counter and grasped her arms. "Sweetheart, I've seen you move your body like a siren while I pleasured you. I've seen you ski with an innate rhythm that's almost a part of your DNA. I'm willing to bet you'd be a natural."

"And if I'm not?"

"Then I'll teach you." He kissed her plump mouth and moved away before he gave in to the urge to start the lesson straightaway. "Before I'm done with you, you'll know how to suck my dick like a champ. Let's eat."

How he managed to calmly dish out the food, sit across from her on the center aisle and actually chew and swallow would forever remain a mystery to him.

Watching her long black nails rip her bagel in chunks before popping them piece by piece into her mouth was pure fucking torture.

He cleared his throat loudly. "Right. Small talk. You joined the IL trip in Miami, so am I right to assume you live there?"

She nodded. "I've lived in Florida all my life. But we... I've moved around a bit."

"So where's home now?"

"Palm Beach."

She named the exclusive area and he nodded, not even a little surprised. Old Money.

He'd toyed with buying a place there when he'd relocated from New York. In the end, he'd resisted Gabriel's strong-arm tactics to buy the mansion next to his and bought a condo instead. Noah loved the view of ocean from his penthouse apartment... when he bothered to leave his office long enough to appreciate it.

"You?"

"Condo. West Palm Beach."

Her wide eyes drifted down his torso. "Fitting."

"You trying to peg me, sweetheart?"

"I suppose you *could* fit the billionaire surfer profile. If you grew your hair out a little and invested in a bead necklace."

His mouth twitched. "Sorry, I've never surfed in my life. Where did you learn to ski so well?"

Her eyes darkened a touch, and he sensed he'd hit a painful subject. "My dad taught me. He took me skiing from when I was three until he... he died." Her mouth quivered for a second, then she pressed her lips together and forced a smile. "You?"

"My cousin and I bought a resort in Aspen eight years ago. He runs it. I go whenever I can during the season."

"You own a resort?"

He nodded. "So you didn't stop skiing after your dad died?"

"I did for a year. It was too painful. But I got my mom to take me the next year."

Something in her voice tweaked his radar. "Your mom didn't like skiing?"

The faintest hint of a smile whispered across her

lips before her eyes shadowed. "There was a reason we lived in Florida. She hated the cold. It was a choice between Florida and California. My dad was born in New Jersey. Florida was as far as he wanted to stray from his roots."

Again, he noted the affection in her voice when she spoke about her father and the distinct lack when she touched on her mother.

"What happened to him?"

Pain shrouded her eyes, and he kicked himself for letting curiosity get the better of him. She swallowed a mouthful of bagel then answered. "He drowned while he was diving off the Florida Keys. He got entangled in fishing gear and ran out of oxygen."

"Hell."

"It's okay. I don't mind talking about him. I had twelve unforgettable years with him."

"Sounds like he was a great dad."

She nodded. "The best. He made living with my mom bearable. I miss him every day."

Noah popped a square cold cut into his mouth and chewed. "What's it like living with your mom now?"

She dropped the last bite of her bagel and brushed her fingers in a no-nonsense way. But he wasn't fooled. The very air vibrated with white-hot anguish.

When she looked up, the shadows and ghosts she'd promised wouldn't come between them loomed large in her eyes. "My mom's dead too. She shot my stepfather when I was seventeen. Then she shot herself."

14

His slack-jawed shock unequivocally rammed home to her that she'd said the words. Invited the ghosts to lunch. A shiver slammed through her, followed closely by several more.

She pushed away from the counter and strode quickly from the kitchen.

What the hell was wrong with her? She'd had the makings of what promised to be a weeklong relief from remembering everything that was fucked up in her life. Instead, she'd dragged her past kicking and screaming into the present.

Seeing the crackling fire, the rug and the champagne just waiting to launch the scenes she'd been dreaming of since she met Noah King, she froze in the middle of the room.

"Leia." His voice was steady, strong, betraying none of the horror he must surely feel. "Sweetheart, I'm sorry."

Enough time had passed and the world had long since moved on from the gruesome events, which had occurred the summer of her seventeenth birthday, but she still recalled the whispers and the looks of horror on people's faces like the images were branded on her brain.

"I'm guessing you want to call the driver?"

Firm hands gripped her arm and turned her around. His gorgeous, heart-stopping face held irritated surprise. "Why the hell would I want to do that?"

"I promised you I wouldn't let in the ghosts. I'm sorry, I don't... I've never voluntarily told anyone about this." She shook her head. "I don't know what came over me. I'll understand if you want to end this before it gets too—"

"So your past isn't a goddamn fairy tale. Trust me, sweetheart, mine isn't a bundle of laughs either. But I'm damned if I'll let you walk away because you assume I can't handle what you just said."

"This wasn't what you signed up for. I didn't plan on spilling my guts."

"I got that impression when you ran from the room. Why did you run?"

The sound that left her throat couldn't have been deemed as laughter. "Are you serious?"

His mouth twisted. "Sure, I guess as small talk goes that was a hell of a doozy, but need I remind you again that I don't do light?"

She looked up into his face and realized he meant it. "So *this* is what you wanted to know about me?"

"I want to know as much of you as you're willing to share, sweetheart. Nothing you say to me will make me walk away."

"Don't to be too sure about that."

His intense gaze probed until her skin tingled. The hands on her arms moved up, cupping her shoulders before they caressed higher to her neck. Both hands circled her neck in a bold and possessive hold that fractured her breathing. One thumb tilted her chin up, and he stepped closer until his nose almost touched hers.

"*Nothing*," he breathed. "Do you hear me?"

This close, the blue of his eyes was so mesmerizing, she couldn't look away. And she didn't want to, despite the real fear that Noah King could unravel her with minimum effort. "Yes."

"Good." He didn't move away or release her. "So, now we've dealt with the small talk and thrown in a dash of heavy. Tell me what you want to do."

The heat from his body was warming hers, burning away the cold that had invaded when she'd blurted out words she needed to keep locked away.

"I don't want to talk anymore."

He stilled, then his fingers tightened a touch. "No, baby. We can change the subject but you *will* talk. I'll need to hear everything you're feeling, everything you're thinking. That's the only way this works. Understand?"

Could she do it? She'd spilled enough in the less than twenty-four hours she'd known this man than to anyone else, besides Warren. The police who'd investigated the incident at the time didn't count. Even the psychiatrist, who Warren initially hired, hadn't been able to coax more than monosyllables from her in the three months she'd seen him. After Dr. Hatfield, Warren had agreed with her that therapy was a waste of time.

They'd found their own way to heal.

The ease with which she vocalized her every thought to Noah frightened her.

"Leia?" His voice was a sharp blade cutting through her jumbled words. But the arms, which came around her and pulled her back into his body, were surprisingly gentle.

"Will you return the favor?" she asked before she lost her confidence.

A slow smile spread across his face. "Are you sure you're ready to hear everything I think of you and your incredible body?"

She raised one eyebrow. "*Quid pro quo.*"

He laughed, and she could've sworn her heart stopped. "Don't say I didn't warn you, sweetheart."

Closing the tiny gap between them, he kissed her. It was hard and unapologetically demanding in a way that promised there would be no going easy. She reveled in it, desperately in need of anything that would wipe away the memories that washed through her mind as fresh as if they'd happened moments ago.

"Hey, I'm losing you." He bit her lower lip, pulled it into his mouth.

"I'm here," she groaned. "Do that again," she pleaded.

He bit her again. Harder. The shudder of pleasure rocked her to her toes. She leaned into him, eager to feel more of his hot body against hers. Hands gripping a taut bicep, she raised up on her toes and threw herself into the kiss.

His hand tightened around her throat, restricting her breathing in a way that made her treasure each breath. Stunned, she realized her senses were heightened, her pulse hammering in her head as her world grew hazy with need and desire.

Her fingers tunneled into his hair, holding on to him as pleasure screeched across her senses.

One arm circled her waist, and he lifted her high. "Put your legs around me."

Complying brought her hot center flush with his rigid cock. Unable to resist, she rubbed herself against him. He stumbled after a single step and dragged his mouth from hers. "I'm pretty sure there are condoms somewhere down here, but I don't have time to search. But, sweetheart, we won't make it upstairs if you keep rubbing that sweet cunt on me like that. So be a good girl and hang on a few minutes, okay?"

"What if I don't want to be a good girl?" She flexed her hips once more, the blaze in his eyes and his urgent pants empowering her in a way she hadn't felt empowered in a long time.

He took another step toward the stairs. "Then you'll find yourself ass up, face down in front of the fire getting the slowest, rawest roasting of your life."

Her breath hitched and her fingers clenched in his hair at the raw, potent image his words evoked. He stopped and one brow slowly lifted. "Is that what you want?"

Leia wanted him so badly that she almost said yes. But she also had a feeling going slow the first time would drive her insane. "I'll behave. For now."

He laughed and carried on walking, swiftly scaling the stairs and turning into a wide hallway with two doors. He entered the right doorway and over his shoulder, Leia saw the stunning glass room opposite.

She gasped but barely managed to say a word before she was sailing through the air. Her back hit the bed, and she bounced once before Noah stayed her with a splayed hand on her belly.

"We'll explore the rest of the place later. Right now, I need to fuck you more than I need to breathe." He started to lift her top, then paused. "Are you ready?"

She read the concern in his eyes.

Her inadvertent confession about her past still lingered in the air. "I'm fine, Noah. I promise."

He continued to stare down at her, his nails slowly grooving the skin above her navel, sending goose-bumps racing over her body. "Once you're naked, once I put my hands and my mouth on you, I won't let you go."

She grabbed the bottom of her top and slid it over her head, baring herself from the waist upwards.

His fierce growl echoed around the room. "Fuck, baby, you won the race fair and square. But please don't drive me over the edge before I get the chance to pleasure you a little."

In answer, she hooked her thumbs into her leggings, ready to tug them off. He stopped her with a hard grip.

"Leia!"

"Yes?"

"Slow the fuck down."

Her gaze dropped to the hard, thick bulge between his legs, and she squirmed on the bed. "But I want you now."

Bending forward, he kissed her. Slowly, teasing his mouth over hers, then catching her lower lip between his teeth, making her squirm harder.

"When we fuck, I will pull your hair and grab your throat. I'll dig my fingers into you and use my teeth. And that will be for starters. What comes after that will depend on how close you are to screaming. Because I won't stop until I make you scream. And even then, Leia, I may not stop. I may be so fucking lost in your hypnotic beauty that I may go too far. If you think you can't handle that, or you're not ready for that, then tell me now. Don't give me hope. Don't take me to the edge and leave me there. I've had that happen before. It fucking tore me apart. So think very, very carefully before any more clothes come off."

"I want that, too. I want everything."

His throat bobbed and he nodded. His thumbs replaced hers, and he started to slide her leggings off. When he paused mid-thigh, she groaned.

"You need to learn a little patience, sweetheart. Trust that I'll give you what you need." He planted a hard kiss on her mouth and sat back on his heels. When she started to rise, he stopped her with a look.

"Stay."

Swallowing, Leia relaxed against the pillows and watched him lift her feet to plant them on his chest. She flexed her toes, dug them into his pecs. A hard smile twisted his lips.

"Looks like I'm going to have a tough time taming you, my little rebel."

"You can do whatever you want to me. I just need this... first time to be quick. Please."

He froze. "Why?"

She shook her head, supremely conscious that she'd let yet another important piece of her brokenness through. What was it about Noah King that made her lose her senses to the point of spilling her guts?

"Answer me, Leia. Or this ends now."

She took a deep breath and scrambled to find the appropriate words that wouldn't make him recoil from her. "The last time I did this, it wasn't very... satisfying. I need new memories. Please."

15

She waited, her heart in her throat, praying he wouldn't probe deeper. Needing to distract him, she slid her feet down his chest to the rock-hard plate of his abdomen.

To her relief, he nodded and resumed his task of removing her clothing. "I'm all for making new memories, sweetheart. Trust me, I know a little bit about unsatisfactory sex."

Her incredulous laugh earned her a bite just above her ankle, once he'd freed her of the restrictive leggings.

"You don't believe me?"

"You're gorgeous. And miles past adequate in the

endowment area. I find it hard to believe you have bad sex."

His fingers drifted down her inner calf, messing with her breathing some more. "Like most areas in life, all it takes for bad sex to happen is a lack of proper communication. Which is why I need to hear you, loud and clear, at all times." He planted a kiss in the crease behind her knee, but his eyes were locked on hers. "I will control your pleasure, but if I do something you don't like, *Stop* is all you need to say. Try it now."

She shook her head. "I don't need to—"

"Say it, Leia."

"Stop."

His fingers dug into her upper thighs and he sucked in a breath. "Louder."

"Stop!"

It was only as he exhaled that she realized how tense he'd grown. A thread of concern slithered down her spine, erasing a layer of excitement. Bitter experience had taught her that monsters came in different shapes and sizes. It was why she'd learned to rely on her instinct first and foremost. They were still calm where Noah was concerned but it didn't make the anxiety disappear.

"Why do you need to hear it, Noah?" she asked,

her pulse accelerating again when his grip eased and he began trailing his fingers down her inner thigh.

Eyes so unbelievably blue they seemed unreal darkened before his eyelids swept down. "Because I have monsters too. Monsters that scream very loud at times like these. I want to make sure I hear you above their noise."

"You will."

He nodded. "Good. Between your ghosts and my monsters, we might struggle to hear ourselves above the noise. But I intend to make you scream so loud, you'll drown them out."

This time when she tried to get up, he didn't protest. Raising herself on her elbow, she cupped his cheek, gloried in the roughness of his stubble as he turned his head to kiss her palm.

"Fuck me, Noah. Is that clear enough?"

He groaned. "Shit. I thought it was cute and sexy when you blushed before you said fuck. Hearing you say it like that makes me so fucking hard."

He reefed the thermal top over his head, ruffling his thick black hair in the process so it flopped over his forehead. The combination of his heart-stopping face and deep, mouth-watering chest was too much. She gasped in a euphoric breath at all that incredible maleness.

He stopped and stared at her. "What?"

"You're magnificent."

A faint flush spread across his cheekbones. "I think you win the gorgeous stakes hands down, sweetheart." He pushed her back down, his gaze drifting over her legs, which were still propped on his naked chest, and across her flat belly to her breasts. His stare lingered long enough to cause a sizzle between her legs.

"Your nipples are so pretty. I want to lick them for hours."

Her back arched in direct reaction to his words, offering them up to him in a silent plea. He refused, choosing to kiss her feet again, her ankles, her calves until he reached her thighs.

Finally, he parted her and saw her underwear for the first time. Sliding his forefingers underneath the edges, he rubbed his thumb over the material. "Interesting lingerie."

"It's... it's what I do. Design them, I mean." His raised eyebrows made her shake her head. "Later, please. I'll tell you later."

He smiled. "Just get on with it?"

"Please," she gasped.

"You will learn patience, Leia Michaels."

"Yes, Noah," she responded in her most agreeable

voice. Anything to make him hurry and put his hands and his mouth on her.

"Fuck. You're determined to cut me to shreds, aren't you?"

She frowned. "What? Why?"

"Never mind. We'll explore that later, too." He kissed the sensitive skin of her inner left thigh, his eyes fixed square on hers, absorbing her every reaction. Her mouth dropped open on a wordless gasp as he used his teeth, then his stubble on her quivering flesh.

"Do you like that?"

She nodded jerkily.

"Vocalize. Remember, I don't hear, you don't get."

"Yes, I like that. I want more."

He started to turn his head, then paused with his mouth inches above her mound. He breathed her in, swallowed hard as his eyes connected with hers.

"You smell incredible, baby. I can't wait to taste you."

She curbed the urge to scream for him to do it now. She was learning very quickly that fast and hard didn't mean the same thing to him as it did to normal people. She would be lucky if he allowed her to come this side of sunset.

She moaned, half in frustration as he dropped

lazy kisses down her right thigh. Her fingers dug into the sheets, her back arching off the bed when he grazed his chin over her clit.

"God!"

Moving her hips, she tried to connect with him, desperate for the friction; hell, anything to ease the pressure building inside her. She almost cried in relief when he grabbed her panties and pulled them off.

But when she parted her thighs again, to eagerly accommodate him, he pressed her legs together.

"No!"

"Not yet, sweetheart. The way you're feeling right now, if I use my mouth on you, you'll come."

She slammed her head against the pillow in frustration. "Isn't that the whole point?"

His mocking laugh made her teeth grind. "Just a little longer, baby."

"You really need to look up the definitions for fast and hard. What you're doing right now is most definitely *not* it."

Strong hands kept her legs together as he raised them high. Her heart hammered and a tinge of embarrassment bled into her at the knowledge that with her exposed this way, he couldn't miss how wet or hot she was.

"Beautiful. So fucking beautiful."

The breath she hadn't noticed was locked in her lungs burst free. He blew a cool breath over her and she jerked. A finger slid up her entire pussy, light, barely grazing her heated flesh but she felt it in every atom of her being. He repeated the action, grazed past her clit. It wasn't enough to send her over the edge but it was enough to make stars burst behind her closed lids.

"I can't wait to fuck you, Leia."

"But you are! You're taking forever. I won the race so you owe me fast and hard. I'm going out of my mind. Please, Noah. Fuck me."

He didn't respond. Just continued to slide his finger up and down, dragging her shameful stickiness all over her pussy while crooning beautiful words to her in that deep, low voice that added another pleasure dimension to her already-heightened state.

He finally let her legs fall apart and reared between them. Keeping his eyes on her, he tasted the finger slick with her wetness then slowly inserted one finger inside her. "I like hearing you beg, but I won't be hurried. You think you don't, but you need time. You need care. I don't want this to be a quick blitz across your memory. You're special. Your body needs to remember how special it is." He slowly withdrew his finger and pushed it back in. Her internal muscles closed greedily around him. He groaned and his Adam's apple moved in a hard swallow. "Will you give it a little more time? Is it worth it to you?"

"God... yes."

"Good girl."

He pulled out and pushed back in, this time with another finger. A shudder raced down her body. She rocked her hips, felt him stretch her, and cried out.

"Dammit!"

She raised a heavy head and stared at him. The rigid look on his face made her heart stutter with apprehension. "What? Did I do something wrong?"

"You want me to fuck the shit out of you. But you're so fucking tight I seriously doubt I can get my cock more than a couple of inches inside of you."

She whimpered. "Don't stop. Please. It'll be fine."

He relaxed a fraction, and a half smile twitched his mouth. "You sound so certain. Have you been experimenting, sweetheart? Stretching this sweet little cunt with your naughty toys to see how much you can take? Or did you touch yourself? When the hunger got too much, did you finger-fuck that tight paradise, desperate for relief?"

She shuddered at the dark pleasure in his tone. "Yes. I needed... something."

"Did it help?" He pushed his fingers in, and her focus hazed.

A blush burned her face, and she bit her lip and shook her head. "It wasn't enough. I needed more."

"I want so very badly for you to show me, but for the sake of both our sanities, I think we'll leave that for another time."

16

Using the broad width of his tongue, he licked her from puckered hole to clit, careful not to flick against her throbbing nub. It was more than enough to drive her precariously close to the edge.

Sensing how close she was, he pumped his fingers fast, once, twice, then withdrew.

Convinced she was about to die from the sheer torture, she concentrated on restoring oxygen to her severely deprived lungs and watched him reach for the box of condoms on the bedside table. He ripped it open and tipped the contents onto the bed.

"That should do for starters."

Shocked laughter fractured up through her throat. "There must be over a dozen there."

"We have more than half a day before we fly to Vienna. I intend to spend all of it buried balls-deep inside you."

He passed her one condom and reached for his belt. Undoing it, he slowly lowered the zipper, his face creased in a taut grimace. In one fluid move, he tugged off his trousers and boxer briefs.

His cock was smooth. And straight. And thick. Two veins ran from the base and stopped beneath his broad, golden-brown head. There were no white marks around his neatly groomed crotch or hips, which meant he was no stranger to sunbathing nude.

Her eyes were drawn back to his thick, heart-stopping length, and her breath stuttered out. He was magnificent. Before the trip was over, she promised herself she would lick every single inch of that beautiful organ.

"Unless you want nine inches of hard cock rammed down your throat, you want to stop looking at me like that right now."

A fresh blush burned up her face. "Crap!"

Chuckling, he plucked the condom from her fingers, tore it open and stroked it on, his face contorting in a tortured grimace that unbelievably heightened her arousal.

Piercing blue eyes raked her from chest to crotch,

and she barely breathed as he prowled, large and glorious, over her. He trailed his hand up her torso to her throat and slid his fingers into her hair. Holding himself above her with his other hand beside her head, he looked deep into her eyes.

"You want to know what I like, Leia?" he asked in a low, deep growl.

"Yes," she responded, secretly grateful for the guidance.

"Your nails, I want to feel them. And that stud. Use it."

"Okay."

She slid her hands up his sleekly muscled arms. He stayed where he was, his gaze unwavering as she explored the smooth hot skin beneath her fingertips.

She reached his shoulders, felt the weight of his expectancy and dug her nails into his flesh.

He gave the tiniest of jerks but didn't move. "Harder." The harsh order made her wetter, her breath coming out in pants. She dug her nails in deeper and his eyes darkened. Leaning down, he smashed his mouth on hers, devouring her with ruthless need. His arm lay heavy between her breasts, anchoring her down to receive his full possession.

When she'd dared to imagine herself in this position, if not completely free of her ghosts then at least at a far enough distance, she'd never imagined she would be okay with being restrained like this.

Noah's strength and virility was undeniable. Fully unleashed, he would overwhelm and devastate. And yet...

She squirmed, anticipation at fever pitch when he finally nudged her entrance with the broad head of his cock.

Wrenching his mouth from hers, he watched her face as he eased inside her slick heat. Tight muscles stretched, took an inch of him, then two.

Then the burn began. She tensed, gasping as tears pricked her eyes.

"Shit, I'm too much for you." Jaw tight, he started to withdraw.

"No!" Leia clamped her legs around his waist.

"Easy, baby. Look at me." He angled her face up to his. His eyes compelled her, branding his words into her fevered senses. "I'm going nowhere, I just need to take this slower. When things get rough between us—and they will—it'll be because we both want it, not because I'm careless. Okay?"

Breath rushing out, she gasped, "Okay."

He pulled out, slicked the length of his cock through her wetness and slowly pushed back in. Stars danced across her vision as he filled her. Her nails clawed him and he groaned.

Knowing she'd pleased him made her relax. He pushed deeper, and her thoughts fractured. Leia melted into the bed as he rocked in and out at a steady pace. Delirium washed over her, the walls of her sex welcoming each thrust as if he meant to imprint his body inside her. She began to shake, the long held-out orgasm encroaching much too soon.

"Holy hell, Leia. You feel unbelievable. So fucking tight and lush."

Her back arched off the bed as sensation ripped through her. His mouth slid down her jaw to her neck, nipping at her throat in erotic bites that exploded along each nerve ending. He pushed deeper. The burn stroked the edge of pain.

"Noah."

He tensed and whispered in her ear, "Use the word if you need to, sweetheart."

She shook her head. The pain had dissolved, leaving behind incredible pleasure. "I don't. More. Please."

Wanting to feel more of him, she slid her hands down his torso, remembering to use her nails as he'd instructed. A full body shudder raked through him.

"Fuck. I could get addicted to you." He bit her earlobe, then raised his head and took her mouth in another potent kiss. He didn't stop until her lips burned and her lungs were starved of air. "Are you ready to come for me?"

Her fingers gripped his waist and dug in. "Yes!"

"How hard, baby? How bad is it?"

She twisted her hips, her skin ready to burst with the force of the pressure building inside her. "Bad! Oh God, I can't... *Noah!*" she screamed when he stopped moving.

He trapped her arms between his own and pressed down on her with his body. "Shhh. No, don't move."

"Why?" she cried plaintively.

He tasted her mouth and raised his head. "You're so fucking hot. I want to make this worth it for you."

"Dammit, I just want to come! Please."

"Stay still then. Now take a deep breath and hold it."

"No..."

"Yes." His tone brooked no argument.

Swallowing the protests that built, she obeyed, pulling precious air into her lungs.

"Good girl. Now feel each stroke of my cock inside you. In a few seconds you'll want to exhale. Don't. Let me fuck you a little while longer." One hand slid beneath her and cupped her ass, tilting her pelvis to receive his next plunge.

Pressure and pleasure trebled, her every nerve zeroing in on this wild sensation building between her legs. He watched her, absorbed in whatever expression had taken over her face. "I can feel your heartbeat in your pussy. You're so fucking close, aren't you?"

Yes, she mouthed. His eyes showed his approval.

"Sweetheart," he murmured. "Almost there."

Her lungs burned and her fingernails dug into his waist. He slid almost all the way out, leaving only his cockhead inside her. Then lowering his mouth to hers, he breathed, "Come, Leia. Now."

His hard thrust sent her over the brink, the edges of her consciousness blurring with the painful ecstasy thundering through her.

"Fuck!" he roared. She clamped around him, then milked him in hard spasms. Leia had no comparison to the sensations rolling through her, but she had a solid glimpse of what it felt like to die with bliss.

Noah rode the wave with her, his groans harsh and beautiful as he continued to thrust hard and fast.

After endless minutes, she started to drift to earth, her shudders still strong enough to rock the bed. But he wasn't done.

He continued to fuck her, the sounds decadent, wet and dirty, his hands rough, unsteady caresses as his breath grew harsher.

In a bold move, she raised her head and slicked her tongue over his collarbone, her stud abrading his flesh. When he groaned deeper, she repeated her action harder, using the rough edge of the diamond on his throat. Then she bit his chest. Hard.

It set him off. "*Shit!* I'm coming." The words were a deep, guttural rumble. His sweat-sheened body bucked hard, and he gripped her tighter. He pulsed long and hot, his cock thickening as he spent himself inside her. After several minutes, he turned his head and kissed her jaw, his breathing still harsh and ragged.

Angling her head, she looked at him. A lock of hair was plastered to his forehead, his face still caught in the after-burn of passion. But his eyes were wide open, fixed square on hers with an intensity that robbed her of breath.

"Noah..."

His eyes darkened, and when he spoke it was in a low, fevered whisper. "I think I'm in serious danger of becoming addicted to you, baby."

17

The moment the words left his mouth, he knew he shouldn't have said them. Especially not seconds after experiencing the most mind-blowing orgasm he'd felt in a long time. From his knowledge, words like those could go either way.

She would either take them as leave to burrow deeper into his life. Or she would see them as a way to lead him around by his cock, the way Ashley had started to do the moment he'd admitted he was into her.

Bitterness encroached and he slammed the lid on his memories. He'd been deaf, dumb, and blind to her wiles for a stupidly long time. He refused to live in that place a moment longer.

"It's a good thing you'll be gone in six days, huh?"

A shadow crossed her face, and he thought for a moment he'd upset her. "Yeah," she replied lightly, her delicate eyelashes sweeping down to stare at his mouth. "Short, hot and fantastic. No room for addictions." Her gaze rose, and he saw nothing but carnal anticipation in the endless, mesmerizing grey.

Perversely, a different sort of irritation lanced through him.

Hell, he was losing his mind. He should be glad she wasn't angling for more than he could give.

She'd just proven she had the potential to be what he wanted. She could be the near-perfect tool to blunt the edge of his clamoring need. In twenty-four hours, she'd given him the high he'd craved for years.

A high he knew couldn't exist in his everyday life. He needed to take what she was offering. And walk away when they were done. Not get annoyed because she agreed with him.

"I'm a little rusty on after-sex etiquette. Should I be content with this silence?" she asked.

He refocused on her face—on her words—and was once again struck with the jagged innocence that blasted from her in intermittent waves. He remembered how tight she was... her confession of not having had a good sexual experience.

Fuck. Her age—another thing he'd forgotten. Just how many sexual partners had she had? And what did her last one do to her that she was desperate to forget?

The irritation grew, turned darker. He tried to shake it off but it lingered.

Jesus... What the fuck was wrong with him?

He jerked back into reality when she moved away, disengaging his still-hard cock and drawing a shudder in the process. The sense of immediate loss had him reaching for her. She released herself from his hold with a strength and dexterity that spoke of specialist, possibly martial training.

He frowned. "Where are you going?"

She shrugged, rose from the bed, grabbed her panties and headed for the door. "I'm giving you space."

It took another minute to find his voice again, having been rendered speechless by the sight of her incredible body. She was lean and curvy in all the places that mattered, her hair falling down her back in reddish-gold waves. He itched to bury his hands and face in that silky mass, but he stopped himself from lunging for her. "I don't recall asking for space."

"Take it anyway," she threw over her shoulder. Her

voice had grown cooler. She was withdrawing from him.

Like hell...

Springing from the bed, he caught her just as she reached the bathroom door. "What the hell is going on?"

She shook her head, and her curls tumbled over her shoulders. "It's... nothing, really."

He gritted his teeth. "That's even worse than remaining silent." He caught her chin and propelled her gaze to his. "Spill."

"I... Right after we... you got this look on your face."

Tension seized his shoulders. "What look?"

"I don't know... a cross between anger and regret? It was obvious you were caught up in something. I just thought you needed a minute to sort through it."

"If I need a minute, I'll tell you. Or you can ask me. Don't assume. And don't walk away."

Wide grey eyes met his, triggering that drowning sensation. "Do you need a minute, Noah?"

He glanced down at her stunning body, at the small round tits he was yet to taste to his satisfaction. At her sleek torso inked with words he had yet to decipher fully—her smooth, lush hips, the neatly trimmed triangle of hair that gatewayed her incredible pussy. His cock pulsed to full and eager life. "What I need is to fuck you again, feel your tight little cunt clench around my cock as we both lose our minds." He looked over her head to the room beyond. "But I'm guessing you're sore and need something else more?" He nodded to the room behind them.

She followed his gaze to the bath and nodded.

Curbing the hunger that roiled through him, he turned her and pointed her to the room she'd been heading for, restraining the need to bend her forward right there in the doorway and experience that bliss all over again.

She took a step into the room and gave a small sound of delight.

Floor-to-ceiling windows gave a three-sixty view of the snow-laden pines surrounding the house. Snow had started to fall in slow, lazy flakes.

"I love snow."

It was less of a bath and more of an indoor hot tub, heated to a perfect temperature. Disposing of his condom, he managed to draw his gaze from her naked body silhouetted against the glass long enough to toss a few bath salts and scented beads into the water.

"Come here."

Something hard tugged in his chest when she turned and obeyed.

Hell, she wasn't good for his blood pressure.

He took the panties dangling from her fingertips and helped her into the tub. The water came up to mid-thigh, bubbling around her legs. She gave a little shiver of delight, and he forced himself to remain where he was. "Kneel."

Instead of using the sides of the tub to steady herself, she grabbed his arms. She watched him as avidly as he watched her and slowly lowered herself into the water. She gasped as the water lapped her pussy, and Noah swallowed a groan.

Jesus, he was truly losing it if every single thing about her drove him to the edge.

Dropping her panties on the side, Noah watched her widen her stance in the water.

"Is that comfortable?"

"Hmm."

"Vocalize, Leia."

"Yes. It's *heavenly*." She smiled.

"Good. Let it soothe you." Unable to help himself, he let his fingers drift down her sides. "How do you feel?"

"Aroused. Incredible. Boneless." Her gaze dropped to his erect cock, and her smile turned saucy. "Quite unlike you. The boneless part, I mean."

Laughing, he got in behind her and relaxed against the huge slab, complete with waterproof pillow, and pulled her back against his chest, his thighs bracketing her. His cock was getting heavier, more than eager for another round, but he'd felt how tight she was, knew he had to give her time. Not enough time to fully recover though. He wanted to take her again when she felt bruised from his last possession... When she would still feel the burn...

His senses flooding with anticipation, he watched her pull her hair up and twist it in a bun and contented himself in washing her neck, watching the water slide over her creamy skin. Unable to resist, he cupped her shoulders and bent forward to inhale her intoxicating scent.

Her soft sigh was music to his ears.

"Tell me about the lingerie."

"When my dad died, I inherited 51 percent of his company. La Carezza specializes in lingerie for a certain type of woman."

"I can tell," he teased. She flicked a handful of water in his direction. "Not that sort, thank you very much. Yes, most of my designs are aimed for the sensualist, but they're not kinky or lewd—well, not all of them. They're designed to remind a woman that she's wearing something special against her skin."

He shifted a little and plucked her underwear from the side of the tub. Rubbing it between his fingers, he nodded. "This isn't silk, but it feels like it. It feels more like the smoothest, lightest leather. It's nothing like I've picked up in Victoria's Secret, that's for sure."

Shit... Nice one, Noah. He watched her closely and breathed a sigh of relief when she didn't react to his tactless comment.

* * *

Leia congratulated herself on keeping a straight face at the thought of Noah buying underwear for another woman, but it was damned hard not to react to the twinge in her chest.

Clearing her throat, she stayed on subject, aware that those blue eyes were fixed on her face. "It's a fabric I had specially developed. It warms the skin, especially when the woman is aroused."

His eyes widened. "How the hell can you tell that?"

"Nanotech and pheromones. This is one of the prototypes we're testing. I'm working with engineers to iron out a few kinks before we go into full production."

A wide grin slashed his lips. "You realize you've just divulged a trade secret? What's going to stop me from taking your little panties here and selling them to the highest bidder?"

"Because I—" She stopped herself just in time. *I trust you* wasn't something she'd intended to blurt out to a man she'd just met. Although to an extent she did.

He was the first man she'd trusted her body with in five years. Even though on some level he spelled danger for her, she'd taken the risk and reached out with what was broken and damaged inside her. But wherever that tiny bud of faith had sprung from and regardless of him saying he didn't do light, she didn't think a man like Noah King was ready to hear the silly utterings of a wounded soul. "Because you'll never get it out in time. It's new technology."

"So when you're turned on it gets even silkier?" he asked.

"How do you know?"

"When I took it off you, it felt like silk. Now it feels more like warm leather."

"Yes. That's the way it works."

He brought it to his nose and sniffed.

"Noah!" She tried to grab it from him.

Laughing, he held it out of reach. "Sorry, sweetheart, I'm keeping this one. How many more of these have you got?"

His avid interest made her blush. Placing the panties out of her reach, he brushed his knuckle down her cheek. "How many, Leia?"

"A good selection."

He replaced his knuckle with his mouth, and she shivered, fresh waves of need rolling through her body.

"I'm so fucking glad you're spending the week with me," he breathed into her ear.

"Why?"

"Because the thought that you could be showing someone else your amazing body drives me nuts."

"You would never have known what I looked like underneath."

His chuckle was dark and decadent. "That's what you think. I've seen you move without your underwear. It's different from when you're wearing them. Both are sexier than is legally recommended for any man's blood pressure, but I can tell the difference now. And I look forward to seeing you giving me a first-class hands-on demonstration of your talent." He pulled her down, kissed her for a good long while before he released her. Tucking her against him, he trailed his fingers over the shaved area of her scalp. She trembled, getting as much pleasure from his touch as he seemed to derive from touching her there.

They stayed silent for several minutes, absorbing the sensations that came with exploring one another.

"So you're a CEO of a successful company at twenty-three?"

She shook her head. "I elected not to take the CEO spot until I was twenty-five, so I'm not in charge of the day-to-day running of La Carezza. I have a board of directors who run things. I vote on major decisions when I'm needed." She thought of the papers Warren had sent over yesterday that needed her signature. Then she thought of Warren and what he'd think of what was happening here. She imagined his dark hazel eyes flickering with the barest hint of disappointment at giving her trust to someone she'd only just met—

"I think it's my turn to get pissed that you've drifted off."

She laughed, but it sounded forced even to her own ears. "I wasn't pissed earlier."

"Oh, really? Your cute nose was pointed in the air in a way that would make the British royal family proud, and your fists were clenched. If I'd been closer, I think you would've sucker-punched me."

"Okay. Fine. I was a little... unsettled at the thought that you were thinking of someone else right after giving me—" She stopped and stared down into the swirling water.

"Giving you what?" he murmured in her ear.

"Right after giving me the best orgasm of my life," she whispered.

18

Noah gripped her nape, turning her head firmly so her gaze met his. Satisfaction blazed blue and true. Against the small of her back, his cock jerked as if responding to her revelation. "Sweetheart, I'm going to give you so many of those orgasms, you'll beg me to stop. But I won't. You know why?"

"Because you like it when I beg."

He smiled. "No. *You* like it when you beg. As to what I was thinking before... I was thinking about my ex."

Her spine snapped as if she'd been shot. For a moment, Leia wondered morbidly if that was how it felt like. His hand tightened in her hair, staying her in place when her senses screamed for space to handle the confounding emotions.

"I know we agreed to leave our ghosts locked tight, but I don't want you wondering about why I drifted off."

She swallowed. Thought about not asking the question and decided the not knowing was way worse than the knowing. Which was crazy considering how long she'd known Noah King.

"What was her name, and why were you thinking of her?"

"Her name was... is Ashley. I was thinking of her because I was hoping you weren't like her."

"Why, what was she like?" she blurted before she could convince herself she was better off not knowing.

He frowned. "She knew she had a power over me. And she used it." A wave of mingled disgust and bitterness washed over his face, making Leia's senses scream. The hard bite to his voice was clear evidence that his ex wasn't a specter in the past.

"I don't have that sort of power over you, Noah," she murmured.

He refocused on her and slowly, his expression cleared. His gaze dropped to her mouth, then traced over her chest, lingering at her breasts. "You don't think so?"

She shook her head.

His free hand drifted down her shoulder and under her arm, his fingers brushing the curve of her right breast before his large thumb grazed her nipple. She caught her lower lip between her teeth and bit down hard to stop from moaning out loud. The corner of his mouth flicked as he noted the action.

"Yes, you do," he rasped. "Every time I touch you like this and you gasp, every time your body sings to my demands, you gain more power over me. Because I crave those things. More than you know. More than is wise. It doesn't matter that we're doing this for only seven days. You have the power."

"Having power and misusing it are two different things. Especially if the latter is used deliberately to hurt." She should know. Her mother was dead because of it.

"I know, but so is having power and not knowing its true and full force. That can be equally as dangerous." He slowly withdrew his finger and slid it back in.

Her ragged inhalation made his eyes darken. "I'd never use it deliberately against you. Is that what she did?"

A small smile twisted his lips. "Let's just say she loved to play with her power."

She licked her lips, and his eyes dropped to her mouth. "If she's your ex, then..."

He dropped his head to the crook of her shoulder, rubbing his stubble hard into her skin. "She played her hand one too many times. The results were... ugly."

Again, she heard the odd note in his voice, the one that flared across her instincts, warning that he could be a merciless opponent, even if she somehow gained the dubious upper hand.

She tried to think a bit more about what he'd said, but her mind was fraying in the heat of what he was doing to her.

Against her back, his cock pressed insistently, its demand reminding her how much power *he* had over her.

Gripping his thighs in the water, she scoured her long nails over the taut muscles. That earned her another finger inside her wet sheath. When she dug her nails in, he groaned.

"Are you sure you can handle another fuck, sweetheart? I can't guarantee it'll be gentle."

"I want to try."

He released her hair, hit the button that stopped

the water's frenzied swirling. In the clear pool, she looked down and groaned at the sight of his hand firmly between her legs. "Does that turn you on?" He slowly withdrew his fingers and plunged back in.

"Uh-huh."

He cursed and his fingers stilled.

Her senses screamed. "Please don't stop."

"I don't want to, baby. But we don't have any condoms in here."

The thought of him stopping almost tipped her over the edge. "We don't have to... I mean I don't—" She stopped and shook her head, her senses fighting the battle for common sense and barely winning. Sucking in a deep, fortifying breath, she swallowed. "Okay. I'll wait."

He kissed her neck and slid his fingers out of her.

She sensed his curious gaze as he stepped out of the bath and went into the bedroom. He returned with a handful of condoms and dropped them on the side, ripping one open to slide it over his cock.

Helplessly caught in the fever of need, she watched him approach and step back into the water. But he didn't resume his previous seat. He moved to the far side of the tub where the view of the trees was at its most advantageous. "Get on your knees."

Her limbs heavy with lust, she positioned herself

at the end of the bath, her knees splayed in neat grooves in the tub.

He got in behind her, his body easily towering over hers even though his knees were two steps below hers. He loosened the knot in her hair and speared his fingers to hold her in a tight grip. Her scalp tingled, and waves of feverish anticipation blanketed her.

He pulled back her head. "What were you going to say?" he demanded in her ear.

She fought against the blazing need that continued to play havoc with her loose tongue.

"I took the mandatory blood test before I joined the trip."

His grip tightened and his cock nudged her ass. "So did I. Are you saying what I think you're saying, Leia?" His voice was low and rough.

"It's not as reckless as it sounds."

His free hand resumed its torture between her legs. "No, but is the issue of birth control up for debate? A clean bill of health is one thing. Pregnancy is another—"

"I can't get pregnant," she blurted. In that moment, she realized just how vulnerable she was when it came to Noah King. How very effortlessly he wrung her deepest, darkest secrets from her without so much as lifting a finger.

His shocked inhalation made her squeeze her eyes shut. "Damn..."

"Open your eyes, Leia."

She opened them but kept her gaze on his chest, afraid to look up, heart lurching sickeningly at the pity... or worse, indifference, she expected to find blazing in his eyes. "God, why the hell do I do that around you? I don't know why but there's something about you that makes me blurt out the most intimate details—"

He caught her chin and tilted her head upwards. "Stop. I'm going to fuck you now. But afterward, we'll talk about this if you want to."

A trace of apprehension fizzled through her. She'd exposed more than enough to make any man think twice about having anything to do with her. What if her next revelation sent him running? "Or we can forget I said it."

"We've gone past pretending we can keep this to the physical. Do you know you're the first person besides my shrink I've voluntarily spoken to about my ex?" he ground out, his tone a touch dazed.

"I am?"

He nodded as his hand drifted down over her tattoo to grip her waist, hard. "So I'm thinking maybe we just let things roll out naturally. You tell me whatever you're comfortable with telling me." He positioned himself behind her and slid the head of his cock along her pussy. "As long as it doesn't involve any other guy doing anything remotely close to what I'm about to do to you."

Her shocked laugh turned into a scream at his brutal penetration. He buried himself as far as he could go and grunted his pleasure. Her internal muscles, which had spasmed with his entrance, grappled to accommodate him.

Frenzied need burned through her as he moved within her. She gave a sharp cry as he withdrew, and his hand tightened on her waist. "Were you about to say something, sweetheart?"

Her arms shook from her death grip on the edge of the tub. Squeezing her eyes shut against the sensations bombarding her, she tried to remember what she'd been about to say. "Nothing comes close... I've never done anything like this before," she stuttered, then cried out again when he pushed back in, adding another inch, making her eyes water. "Oh God!"

"You're shaking, baby. Is this too much?"

"Yes! But I want more."

"You want me to make you even more sore? Shall I

make you burn, baby?" His voice held a compelling promise, a dark relish that pushed her closer to a hypnotic abyss.

Sublime bliss rolled over her with each relentless thrust. Noah King fucked her with an expertise that fueled her craving for him with each penetration. By the time he lifted her left leg and draped it over the side of the tub, opening her wider to his invasion, she was almost at the edge of the abyss. Gladly contemplating throwing herself into the unknown.

He pounded her hard, wrenching a scream from her with each breath. The fingers in her hair jerked her head back, exposing her throat to the vicious kiss of mouth and teeth. She didn't care that she would be marked from head to toe by the time he was finished with her.

All she wanted was to drown in the beckoning paradise, insulate herself from the horror she'd inadvertently unearthed.

He gripped the back of her neck and pushed her forward until her torso hung over the tub. With each thrust, her stomach dug into the edge, knocking the breath from her lungs. Still he came at her, unleashing power and vitality that fried her brain.

"Holy fuck. I can't get enough of you. You're like

one of those impossible dreams you never think will come true."

"I'm not a dream," she gasped.

"No, you're not. The way you're turning me inside out, you have to be real. But I'm still terrified to stop in case you disappear."

His next thrust was so hard, so deep, a tidal wave of water surged over the side, drenching her torso on the way down. Bent almost double, blood surged into her face, her windpipe cloying for breath as a flash of pain sizzled through her pleasure.

"Noah!" she screamed, the sensations almost unbearable.

"You're real. Please tell me you're real," he pleaded hoarsely.

"I'm real. I'm real!"

His fingers dug into her hips and he leaned into her, his torso blanketing her in sexy, fiery heat. She jerked when his teeth bit into her shoulder. "You better fucking be. Or there'll be hell to pay. Now come for me, baby. Give me *everything* you've got," he growled.

Whether it was the dark command that undid her or the simple fact that she was at breaking point, she was too far gone to tell. A small part of her reeled in stunned surprise as she flew apart a second after his command.

Leia came with an explosive scream, the air sucked from her lungs. Unending convulsions shuddered through her, milking his thick, heavy length over and over until he shouted his own release.

Sliding an arm around her shoulders, he raised her up and held her against his chest, his cock pulsing hard and deep inside her, his breath harsh and ragged in her ear. "You're real."

Her hands curled over his arm, gripping him tightly as she fought to catch her own breath. "Yes."

His free hand drifted up her side and whispered over her tattoo. "I don't know who did this to you or what happened to propel you here, but I'm glad you're here. With me. I may not be able to fix you, but you need to know that you're amazing, Leia. No matter what happens to you, don't let anyone or anything lead you to believe otherwise."

19

"You're drifting." Soft fingers caressed his cheek, dragging him from the questions swirling in his mind. She lay tucked against him, her head pillowed on his shoulder and her face turned up to his.

Christ, she was gorgeous.

His heart hammered as he stared into her mesmerizing eyes. He felt himself stir again and groaned inwardly.

They'd eventually left the tub when he could risk carrying her out without fearing his legs would turn to jelly. They slept for a couple of hours before the hunger that didn't show signs of abating had him reaching for her again.

He guessed they'd fucked on and off for the last

six hours before trudging downstairs just after midnight to demolish the rest of the food. She'd joined him when he opted for beer instead of champagne, her cute nose wrinkling at the taste before she soldiered on like a champ to finish the bottle.

For her brave foray into beer country, he bent her over the slab of concrete that passed for a coffee table and took her from behind, after which they'd collapsed on the rug in front of the roaring fire and fallen asleep.

Now his senses sang with an alien sense of peace, and when her fingers drifted along his jaw and down his neck, he suppressed a smile. She loved his stubble. He'd found out how much she liked it when he encouraged her to sit on his face. He was willing to bet she'd come twice as fast because of the friction of his rough beard on her inner thighs as much as from his mouth on her sweet pussy.

"That look in your eyes scares me."

He laughed, then sobered when he saw her expression. It was a mixture of wonder and puzzlement. He recognized it because it was the same sensation he'd experienced since he saw her in the Ozone Bar twenty-four hours ago. He stroked the side of her head and relished in her sigh of pleasure. "I have no answer for this level of intensity, sweetheart."

"But you don't think this... what's happening between us is crazy?"

He rolled her onto her back, and she parted her thighs and welcomed him. "Since crazy runs in my family, I can't plead innocence. My father met my mother on a Thursday. He asked her to marry him on Saturday. They've been together for thirty-five years. Theirs is a rare form of crazy. I accept that. But I guess I'm proof that crazy happens. The Indigo Lounge is geared to heighten our senses. We're bound to let other inhibitions down besides sex. You can hold back if you want to. But once you let it out, I won't let you take it back."

"But what if being with you makes me let out things I normally wouldn't?"

He kissed her parted mouth and lingered far longer than was wise. "Then I'm honored to trigger such feelings within you."

She rolled her eyes. "Could you sound any more smug?"

"What can I say, sweetheart? I have a special touch."

She snorted. "God help me."

He laughed and kissed her again. "The car service will be here in a few hours. Do you want to try and get some sleep?"

She shook her head. "I'm not sleepy." Her foot rubbed on the back of his thigh and he shuddered.

"Sweetheart, I know I said I'm greedy, but if we keep going like this, you'll be out of commission soon."

"I told you, I'm stronger than I look. But I'll let you recuperate if you're feeling worn out?" she said cheekily.

He snorted and adjusted his hips so the blatant evidence of his readiness was in no doubt. "I won't rise to the challenge. Much as I want to. I want the pleasure-pain in perfect balance when we fuck."

She made a pouty face but wrapped her arms around his neck. "What shall we do then?"

He slid his hands beneath her shoulders and cradled the base of her neck, awed by the fragile bones of her scalp. She was strong in some ways, yet so easily breakable in others. Someone had taken advantage of that fragility.

Broken her...

Red-hot fury rolled through him. It took several beats before he could speak. When he did, his voice emerged strained. "You said you couldn't get pregnant. You want to tell me why?"

He would've been blind to miss the wave of harrowing pain that darkened her eyes before she took control of it. When a small shiver wracked her frame, he leaned down and kissed her. Her eyes were less haunted when he lifted his head.

"I spent time in the hospital when I was seventeen... I was hurt. The doctors couldn't fix me completely. The specialist I saw afterward confirmed it would take a miracle to get me pregnant."

Noah sensed there was a lot she was leaving out, but he decided not to push. The past twenty-four hours had been intense in ways he never saw coming. Hell, *he'd* cracked open a can of worms he never dreamed he would touch without full body armor.

"Hell, I'm sorry, sweetheart."

Her eyes shimmered bright for a few seconds before she shrugged. Swallowing, she speared her fingers into his hair in a rough caress that tore at his heart.

"I haven't given up hope completely. In my darkest moments, I choose to believe miracles still can happen."

He didn't answer because he had no evidence to prove her theory. There had been a time long ago when he foolishly believed he could replicate what his parents had. He'd believed he'd found his soulmate. Having that belief turned to ash had hammered home the rarity of his parents' relationship.

"My turn."

He refocused on her. "Shoot."

"*Vocalize*. Why?"

He pressed his lips together and told himself he only needed to tell her what he was comfortable with, as per their agreement. "I need to know what you're thinking. That's all."

"No. That's not all," she countered.

He didn't realize how tightly his jaw was clenched until her fingers touched his face. He forced himself to relax. "My ex—"

Her fingers clenched in his hair. "Use her name, Noah."

Surprise arrowed through him. "Why?"

"I don't know why, but every time you say *ex*, I get a little dart of jealousy that makes me want to claw at something."

The unexpectedly blunt admission stunned a laugh out of him. "What?"

"Oh, come on! You've never had a woman express visceral, possessive jealousy before?"

"No one that mattered enough for it to count."

Another admission that shut them both up for a full minute. He cleared his throat and she swallowed, her eyes square on his as she sucked in a deep breath.

"Okay, well... since I have a claim of ownership over you for the next six days, you'll do as I say."

He speared his hands into her hair and gripped it tight. "As long as the ownership goes both ways, I don't have a problem with that."

She raised her head and he gave in to what they both wanted. When the kiss threatened to get out of hand, he raised his head.

"So, you were saying?" she asked, her voice so huskily sexy he wondered why he was continuing to fight the inevitable. Why he wasn't tugging on another condom and fucking them both senseless.

"Ashley thrived on innuendo and assumptions. I made the mistake of thinking I knew her inside out. Especially what she was thinking. When it suited her, she made me think my assumptions were right. It took me a while to realize she got off on fucking with my mind. She was the original gaslighting queen."

Leia frowned. "But you did realize and you don't strike me as a guy who would leave something like that unresolved."

His smile at the veiled question felt tight and uncomfortable. "I told you she had a certain... power over me. We connected on a level I thought I'd never connect with anyone." Ashley hadn't initially recoiled from the fact that he preferred an edgier, pain-rimmed side of sex, that his need for total control was strong enough to make most women run a mile. Even after he'd suspected her acquiescence was a careful act, she'd denied it, kept him dangling on her hook with lies and half-truths. "She made it so I didn't see anything but what she wanted me to see." And when he'd snapped, when he'd finally uncovered her true colors, he'd nearly done the unthinkable.

The memory threatened to turn his stomach.

Leia cupped his face. His breath shuddered out at the keen, perceptive look in her eyes. She didn't have to vocalize her feelings for him to know she knew exactly what he was talking about.

"Sad but true fact that those closest to us have the greatest power to hurt us."

His laughter scraped out, scalding and bitter. "Unless you cut them off."

He watched the shadows flit through her eyes. "It's not always that easy. Especially when they leave scars behind." Before he could ask her to elaborate, she continued. "You don't need to worry that I will be anything but unequivocal with you."

His blood began to thrum in his veins. "Yeah?"

"Yes."

"Vocalize. Tell me what you want." He leaned down and brushed his lips over hers.

"I want you to f... fuck me," she whispered.

He shook his head, slipping his hand down her silky, firm body. "Sorry, sweetheart. I can't hear you. Speak up."

"Fuck me."

"Fuck me, what?" He slid his hand between her legs, felt her wet, slick heat and unleashed the need pounding through him.

"Fuck me, please, Noah. Please."

"There it is. You're drenching me. But I want more. I want you to flood me."

"Please." Her nails scoured groves in his back as he readied himself and positioned his aching cock at her entrance. "*Please, please, please.*"

"God, Leia, you make insanity look like pure heaven."

20

Noah wrapped a towel around his waist and entered his bedroom suite aboard the plane.

He jerked to a stop at the sight of the empty bed. Leia had been fast asleep when he went to shower five minutes ago. Frowning, he started towards the living room, only to stop at the sound of his cellphone ringing.

Since only a handful of people had this number, he didn't waste time with pleasantries when he grabbed it. "What the hell do you want, Damon?"

He received an unapologetic grunt. "Give me a break, man, I drew the short straw for this phone call. Biting my head off doesn't help either of us."

"Speak for yourself. I feel like tearing chunks out

of it right about now." He flicked on the bedside lamp and turned back toward the bed. Its emptiness unsettled him. "And what the fuck are you drawing straws about? I'm beginning to worry that you three have nothing better to do."

He headed for the sitting room, a part of him thankful that they were on a plane and thus finding her would be easy. A greater part of him was even more thankful he'd had her moved into his suite before they took off from Geneva. He wanted her close.

At Damon's silence, he paused, apprehension gripping him. "Has something happened?"

"Nah. We called your office. Maddie said you hadn't been in for a couple of days, so we're guessing you made the trip after all?"

He resumed walking. "You called me at three in the morning to ask me that?"

His friend sighed. "Don't jerk my chain, I knew you'd be up. Or are you saying you've found a cure for your chronic insomnia?" he asked, sounding hopeful.

Noah strolled into the living room and drew to a halt. On the oversized sofa, Leia sat with a large pad balanced on her knee, tapping a pencil against her cheek as she frowned at the page. She was wearing a forest-green slip. From what he could see of her upper half, the design was seriously sexy, cut daringly in places that made his mouth water and his hands itch to explore.

"If you want a blow by blow of what I'm doing right now, you're out of luck."

Leia glanced up and her eyes connected with his. Whatever expression he wore—and he had a feeling it was one of bone-deep hunger—made her eyes widen and her lips part.

Christ, just looking at her intoxicated him.

Keeping his gaze pinned on hers, he answered Damon's question. "If you must know, the experience is proving to be worth it. Why don't you go and report that to your knitting committee?"

Damon's laugh held a touch of uneasiness and his nape tightened. "Yeah, sure... I'll do that."

The easy agreement and the fact that he wasn't griping about Noah's jibe made alarm bells ring harder. He reached the sofa, crouched in front of Leia and slid his hand over her knee. Her smile tugged at his heart.

"Damon, what the hell is going on?"

"Fuck, forget I called. It's nothing that can't wait until you get back."

Noah watched her lips part wider, her need for air growing as he explored the silky flesh of her thighs. This close, he could see her slip was made of the same material as the panties she'd worn in Switzerland. And that the bits covering her breasts were made of decadent lace triangles.

He forced himself to concentrate on the call. Something wasn't right, and as much as he loved his childhood friend, Damon had never been good with getting to the point fast. Taking into account the time difference, the day of the week and the music in the background, he said, "It's Tuesday so you're at The Sphere. Let me to talk to Gabe."

"He... uh, he's not here."

"Where is he?" he snapped. The pencil dangled from Leia's fingers. Reaching out, he took it and slowly traced the blunt end over her collarbone. She shuddered and her nipples pearled against the lace.

"Bora Bora, I think."

"What the hell's he doing there?"

Damon cleared his throat. "Angela broke things off with him. Or she's trying to, anyway. But you know how stubborn they both are. She's pissed that he's refusing to let her dump him and she's gone into hiding at Savage's place. Gabriel hopped on his plane and hightailed it down there first thing this morning. I'll have him call you with an update when he gets back... Hold on a sec," he interrupted himself. Noah heard heated murmurs, then Damon said in a rush, "I gotta go. So everything's going great, right?"

Noah's eyes trailed the stunning vision staring back at him with a hunger that almost equaled his own, and he swallowed before he could speak. "Yes. It is. And Damon?" He leaned down and drifted his mouth over the soft curve of her shoulder.

"Yeah?"

"Thanks." No matter the reason behind the call, Noah was thankful his friends were looking out for him, albeit in ways that irritated the hell out of him.

"No problem, buddy."

He hung up, tossed the phone away.

Leia looked from the phone to his face. "What was that about?"

"Hell if I know. Come here, baby."

As she melted into his arms, he growled his satisfaction. Bending his head forward, he caught one lace-covered pink nipple in his teeth and bit down hard.

* * *

A couple of thousand miles away, Mike stared at his friend for several seconds then he shook his head. "I can't believe you fucking chickened out."

Damon shrugged, the back of his neck heating up at the embarrassing truth. Feigning bravado, he quipped, "So shoot me if I don't see the point in upsetting the balance of things just yet."

"Things have been unbalanced for a long time. And trust me, he *will* shoot you when he gets back and realizes we knew and didn't tell him."

Damon grimaced. "Then I'll happily celebrate my stay of execution while the celebrating is good." He made eye contact with the waitress and held up two fingers.

She brought their drinks a few minutes later and frowned at their somber looks. "What's up, fellas? Somebody die?"

Mike glanced over at him and smirked. "Not yet but this time next week, I'm sure one of us will."

Rolling her eyes, she slid their drinks on the table and left.

Damon took a healthy gulp of his neat vodka before he glanced up. "You think I should call him back?" he asked halfheartedly.

Mike eyed him, tapping his finger against his glass. "How did he sound?"

"Good. Great, even. Not his old self but then are any of us our old selves?"

The tapping increased in tempo, reflecting his

friend's agitation. The sick feeling churning through Damon's stomach grew.

"I think we should leave it, let Gabe get back, then draw straws again," Mike said.

"Crap, are you sure that's a good idea?"

"Hell no, but like you, I'm not in a hurry to tell my best friend the reason he left New York two years ago has turned up on his doorstep."

* * *

"Who's the knitting committee?" Leia gasped out the question, stunned she could speak coherently considering every inch of her body was on fire.

Noah's head reared up from where his tongue was sliding down her inner thigh. "What?"

"Your call. You said something about a knitting committee?"

His mouth curved, and her stomach flipped over at the sheer beauty of his smile. "Yeah. My pain in the ass friends. They're nosier than a gaggle of high school girls and they're not ashamed to own it." He rubbed his stubble over her skin and she shuddered.

"They called to check up on you?" She slid her fingers through his silky hair, making sure her nails grazed his scalp the way he liked it.

He groaned and blew a hot breath over her wet, hungry pussy. "Yeah, at three in the morning. Like I said, they're a menace to my sanity."

She thought of her own life, of the absence of friends or any meaningful relationship in her life besides Warren. Her social life had come crashing to a halt the moment her mother put the gun in her mouth and blew a hole in the back of her head. By the time Leia surfaced from her own fog of horror, Warren had taken control.

He'd been in control ever since—

She jerked at the merciless clamp of teeth on her flesh. Gasping, she stared into sexy... *suspicious* blue eyes.

"Did we not agree that I own your attention completely when we're together?" he rasped.

"I... Yes."

"You were drifting just now. Where were you?" he demanded.

"Nowhere important."

His eyes narrowed.

"Honest," she insisted.

His nostrils flared. Bending his head, he opened his mouth and dropped a hot, wet kiss at the top of her pussy, right above her clit. Then, keeping his eyes on her, he parted her with his fingers and rotated his chin over her throbbing nub.

She gripped a handful of hair and angled her hips, her heart racing, her whole being centered on achieving maximum friction for that pebble of need.

In one smooth move, he lifted himself off her. Her senses screeching in disbelief, she tried to lunge for him.

He caught her hands and imprisoned them above her head.

Intense blue eyes blazed down at her. "Where were you, Leia?"

"I was thinking about my mom. About her killing herself. She left me alone at a time when I needed her most. I hate that she chose to end her life that way. I've tried to forgive her but I don't think I ever will. Does that make me a horrible person?" she whispered.

His eyes gentled. "It makes you human that you've tried. It makes you human that you feel bad about not succeeding. But it doesn't excuse you from evading my question the first time I asked it. Total honesty at all times, Leia."

She swallowed and tension raced over her skin. "Are you going to punish me?"

"Do you think you deserve punishment? Or are

you just saying that because you think you'll enjoy the punishment I'll give you?"

"I'll do whatever you want, Noah."

His eyes darkened. "You mean you'll do whatever it takes for an orgasm."

She started to deny it, and he leaned down and sucked her lower lip into his mouth. When he released her, his displeasure hadn't abated. "Were you about to lie to me again, Leia?"

She closed her eyes and shuddered. "Please... I need you."

"I know. But you'll have to wait even longer for your orgasm. That's your punishment."

He released her and sat back at the end of the sofa. Gloriously naked and carefree despite the huge, proud erection, he leaned back in the seat and picked up her pad.

He thumbed through a few pages. His eyes flicked to her and back to the designs she'd been working on. A different kind of tension seized her. Besides Warren and a select few on her trusted design and development team, no one had ever seen her designs. Certainly no one like Noah King, a powerful, shrewd businessman who also knew the female body inside out.

"These are incredible." Relief burst through her

only to short-circuit when he gripped his cock and began stroking it. "Are they all yours?" he asked, his voice low and deep in a way that told her he was extremely aroused.

"Y-yes." She couldn't take her eyes off what he was doing, what she yearned to do. His movements were slow, hypnotic. "Noah..." she started, knowing very well she would beg if that was what it took for him to see to her needs.

He ignored her, thumbed through her pad then closed it. He glanced at her and nodded at her slip. "Is that another one of your special designs?" he asked, his hand still moving up and down.

She nodded.

"Vocalize."

"Yes. It's one of my favorites."

"How many do you have with you?" he rasped.

"I brought about a dozen," she said.

"Get up."

The weight of her want felt like a physical force pressing down on her, but she managed to stand. He opened his legs wider, inviting her to stand between them. The sight of his balls hanging full and heavy had her swallowing. She licked her lower lip and his nostrils flared. A part of her was secretly thrilled she did that to him.

"Will you model them for me?"

"Will you make me come if I do?" she whispered.

"I'll always make you come, sweetheart. Just not at your command. Go." This time it was less of a request and more of a demand.

She tried to move but couldn't take her eyes off his lazy strokes, or the bead of pre-cum at the crown of his magnificent cock. Slackening her jaw, she opened her mouth and deliberately curled her tongue so he'd see the diamond stud.

His hand jerked and he swallowed hard. "Are you fucking with me, baby? Because if you are you might want to think about this—for every minute you delay in doing what I ask, you get to wait another half hour to feel my cock pounding that tight little cunt."

"What? That not fair!" she yelled.

"Then move your ass," he sizzled back, his voice deeper. She noticed he'd pinched the base of his cock hard and his jaw was clenched, holding back the power of his arousal.

She wanted to shout some more, demand he put them both out of their misery. But she was terrified of the payback.

21

Forcing herself to move, Leia rushed into the bedroom and yanked open the closet where she'd moved her things on returning to the plane.

It would take at least a half hour to present all ten pieces—if she was quick. Thirty minutes to keep the ever-expanding pressure between her legs from exploding and turning her into a gibbering wreck. Oh, who was she kidding?

She was one self-pleasuring touch away from coming on the bedroom floor. Only the knowledge of how much more powerful and intense Noah could make the experience stopped her from fingering herself back to sanity right there in the closet.

Fingers shaking, she plucked the first item from the hanger. The powder-blue silk teddy brushed her skin as she slipped it over her head. From the outside it looked like an ordinary teddy, but the special lining running down the insides of the garment immediately reacted to her skin's temperature.

She walked into the living room and her eyes zeroed in on Noah. He was in the exact position she'd left him minutes ago except for the glass of whiskey balanced on his thigh.

He twirled a finger. "Turn."

She dragged her eyes from his cock and pirouetted, loving the sexy feel of the material on her body.

"I can't see the tech on this one."

"It's... inside."

His gaze slid over her, lingering at her breasts then down to her feet and back up to stop at her stiff, peaked nipples. "You're covered in goosebumps. Are you cold?"

"Yes."

"Why?"

"The technology on this garment is slightly different from the other one."

His eyebrows rose. "How?"

"When the bra cups come into contact with my skin, they caress my breasts in hot and cold waves."

"You mean right now you're getting stimulated each time you move?"

The amazement in his voice made her smile, despite the growing ball of need between her legs. "Yes, I thought just because I'm not adequately endowed in some places doesn't mean I can't have fun with what I wear."

"Anyone who sees you and doesn't think you're a knockout better not say it to my face because they'll eat my fist. Now, come here."

Smiling, she walked forward till she stood between his legs again. Setting his glass on the arm of the sofa, he reached up and cupped her breast, testing the fabric. "Fuck. This is incredible." He squeezed her nipple hard. When she shuddered, he released her. "You're a sexy and clever little thing, aren't you?"

Her smile stretched, her insides melting at his praise.

He released her, sat back and slid his fingers down to cup his balls. "Next one."

Leia hurried away, the fear that she was at breaking point hammering through her. She'd never come without physical stimulus before. But she was pretty damn sure that watching Noah stroke himself like that for much longer would set her off.

Tugging the teddy over her head, she flung it into

the closet and grabbed the next item—a cream thonged unitard that could be worn as an undergarment or with a skirt or pants. She'd barely pulled it on before her clit swelled to almost twice its size. Heat creeping into her face, she went back out.

Noah noticed immediately. "You're walking differently."

"It's the thong. It sends tiny electrical pulses to my clit." A tremble rolled over her body and she moaned.

"Jesus!" he croaked. "You design these for women to wear out in public?"

She shrugged. "Women go out in public every day wearing discreet sexual gadgets. This is just another tool for pleasure. It's not strong enough to induce an orgasm unless you're already super turned on."

"The only tool I want pleasuring you is my cock."

"When?" she asked plaintively, her voice breaking.

His gaze lingered at her crotch and he swallowed. A tiny hint of stress marred his face but he smiled. "When I say so. Next one."

Her fingers tingled. "I don't think I'll last much longer, Noah."

"If you come without me inside you, sweetheart, I'll make you scream so hard for your next orgasm, they'll hear you in China."

"God! You're a fucking maniac!" Whirling, she ran back to the sound of his strained chuckle, tearing the unitard off before she reached the closet.

The next was a bustier and pant set in red and black that delivered the same caressing stimulus when she moved. By the time she fastened the hooks and pulled the sides of the panties over her hips, she genuinely feared she wouldn't last.

The light flush across Noah's cheekbones attested to his own battle with the consuming fire of desire. She turned, displaying the garment in all its glory before she faced him again.

"Describe."

"There's a tiny button here." She indicated the sides of the panties. "When I touch it, the red lines on the panties deliver a shock that simulates spanking."

He let go of his cock and jerked to his feet. Striding to where she stood, he lifted her chin with a finger. "I don't know whether I'll enjoy fucking you for your brains or for the naughty little minx who resides inside your stunning body," he rasped.

"Both. Fuck me for both," she whispered fervently, her body raw with the need to feel the satisfaction he held back from her, the powerful friction of his cock inside her.

"Yes," he said simply. "Stay here."

Her breath shuddered out as he walked into the bedroom.

God! Finally...

Heart accelerating, Leia wondered whether to start undressing, then thought better of it. Noah loved doing that. She was learning very quickly that when it came to the bedroom, he loved calling all the shots. If he'd wanted her undressed he'd have told h—

"Why are you dressed?"

Black designer jeans hugged his hips and he'd thrown on a light grey T-shirt that clung lovingly to his shoulders and torso. As much as she wanted to appreciate him, right now he was fucking with her head in a way that sent a fireball of anger smashing through her arousal. "Noah, this isn't funny anymore."

He eyed her, as if testing to see how far gone she was. "I'm not laughing, Leia. Put these on."

He raised the items in his hand, and she frowned. His shirt. Her shoes.

"Why?"

"Because we're going out and I sure as hell don't want anyone seeing you in that getup."

Confused, angry and so aroused she feared she'd fly apart if she so much as breathed the wrong way, she took his shirt and shrugged it on. The tails of his black shirt reached her knees and the sleeves swallowed her arms.

He folded back the sleeves and buttoned her from neck to knee and stepped back with a satisfied nod. "Shoes."

She stepped into her Valentino pumps and he slid his fingers through hers. "Not long now, baby."

Too wound up to ask where they were going, she followed when he tugged her to the door, each step an excruciating reminder of the escalating pressure and extreme wetness between her legs.

She was so busy putting one foot in front of the other she didn't notice their destination until they reached the door marked *VICE*.

"Time to tick high number three off your list."

Lifting two of the weird-looking black and indigo goggles off the hook, he pushed the door open. They entered a small squared-off area. When the door shut behind them, he carefully slid one pair over her head then adjusted it in place. "How's the fit?" he asked.

"A little tighter."

He made a rough sound in his throat, like a growl. Leia registered that his fingers weren't quite steady as he tightened the band above her ears. The further evidence that he teetered on the same brink as she did calmed her down a touch.

"Okay now?"

"Yes."

Having kept her eyes closed as he adjusted the goggles, she opened them now and gasped. The room pulsed with music and color. Blues, greens and reds swirled high above her head and spiraled to the floor. The decorations, moving in slow psychedelic shapes, made her smile. Reaching out, she touched the nearest green swirl and watched it curl over her finger before it drifted away.

Noah's hand slid against her palm, the heat from his fingers pulsing yellow as they grasped hers.

He led her deeper into the room and body shapes flowed into view. She counted seven figures, one behind the bar and two sipping drinks tinged blue by their cold temperature. Two couples were engaged in heavy fondling against a wall and the other couple was much further down the line, with the guy on his knees with his head buried between his partner's legs. The woman sat on a stool, her head thrown back and her mouth wide open as she gasped out hot breaths that coated the air with orange puffs.

The act drew Leia's attention to her own precariously aroused state, heightened further as the woman moaned loud and deep.

She searched out Noah's profile. "Are we... Will everyone see us?" she blurted.

"Hell no," he growled in her ear. "We're heading in here."

"Here" was a large booth with green and blue lines running along the outside. Inside, the usual custom-built chaise longue took up one side and on the other side was a purple stool a few feet from the wall.

Noah shut the door, led her to the stool and helped her onto it. He reefed his T-shirt over his head and dropped it. The outline of his body glowed reddish-yellow, the colors deepening under his arms and his groin as he lowered his zipper and tugged off his jeans.

Stepping close, he unbuttoned her shirt and slid it off her. Then his hands spanned her waist and trailed upward.

He hooked his finger into the top line of the fabric and used it to pull her close. "Your scent drives me insane. I can barely think straight around you."

He trailed his tongue over her heaving breasts and they both watched the hot glow slowly fade to a warm yellow. He yanked down the bodice of her bustier and groaned at the sight of her nipples ringing a faint orange. Wrapping his hands around her breasts, he squeezed hard, capturing her nipples painfully between his thumb and forefinger until they glowed red-hot.

"Lord, you're so gorgeous."

"More. Please."

He squeezed again, harder this time, making her cry out. He tensed for a moment, then repeated the action. Freeing one nipple, he bent and sucked it into his mouth. Then without warning, he slapped her other breast. Hard.

"*Ah!*"

He tilted his head and she knew he was watching, searching for signs of her displeasure. She couldn't have been further from displeased. Sizzling arrows of pleasure and pain chased through her belly, the visual evidence of her arousal heightening her senses like nothing ever had before. He waited a few seconds, then slapped her flesh again. Her moan was loud and guttural.

"You like that?" There was an unmistakable hesitancy in his voice that triggered an immediate response.

"Yes. Very much."

He shuddered and she saw his throat move in a convulsive swallow. "You haven't forgotten what you need to say if you don't like anything I do, have you? I may forget to ask later."

"No, I haven't."

"Good. Raise yourself up for me."

Grasping the side of the stool, she obeyed. He yanked her panties down and threw them over his shoulder. Sinking onto his haunches, he hooked her heels into the lower rung of the stool. She heard the rattle of metal on metal, then cold braces snapped around her ankles.

Leia jerked, the unexpected restraint firing a bullet of unease through her. Again, his head angled up, waiting for her to object. Heart hammering, she waited for the unease to grow, for the panic that resided beneath all the therapy and soft conversation with Warren to rear its ugly head. But as the metal warmed against her skin, the panic subsided. Reaching out with shaking hands, she traced Noah's jaw. Her silent acquiescence spurred him into action.

With barely leashed restraint, he yanked her legs apart, baring her center to his gaze.

"God, baby, I can literally see how hot you are for me."

Her gaze dropped to his groin where the glow of his erection burned a fierce, bright orange. "Ditto."

"Hang tight, sweetheart. Things are about to get a

whole lot hotter." Grasping her ass in both hands, he pulled her forward in the seat, her stance baring more of her sex to him. "Hold on to the back of the chair, Leia. Don't let go until I'm done."

She whimpered and did as he asked, biting her lip when he began trailing hot kisses along her inner thigh. He stopped when he reached the outer lip of her pussy and started along her opposite thigh.

Her groaned protest earned her a wider parting of her legs and a merciless bite she was sure would leave a mark. She swallowed any further protests and watched his mouth, tinged a darker orange, move closer to her core. His lips parted and she cried out as his tongue lapped her from anus to clit, stopping to swirl over her nub once, twice.

Pressure tightened harder in her pelvis, desperate for an outlet. But Noah wasn't ready to free her. He savored her, taking his time to work his mouth over her as he squeezed her breasts and tortured her nipples.

Leia watched, fascinated as her temperature soared, her body glowing a bright orange, with her nipples and pussy turning redder with each caress.

Desperate for relief, she angled her hips, her butt almost off the chair as she sought the friction she needed to get her off.

He released her clit and slapped her pussy hard with the flat of his hand.

"*Ah... God!*"

"You try and shortcut this, you get punished." He slapped her again. She shuddered and pulled back an inch, her senses frying with the overload of sensations. "Will you behave?" he rasped.

She groaned. "Yes."

Another slap but this time, softer. All pleasure, no pain. Absurdly, she missed the sting. "Harder."

He froze, then a shudder transmitted up her thighs. "Shit, baby. Are you sure you know what you're asking? Because I *will* mark you, brand myself all over you until you can't take a step without thinking of me."

"Yes, I want that, Noah. Do it."

Another slap, the wet sound merging with the vibration of the throbbing lounge music and turning her on even harder. His next slap was harder, wetter. The burn brought tears to her eyes. Leia blinked them away, biting back a sob of pleasure in case it made him stop.

Her thighs tensed along with the muscles in her back as her orgasm gathered. He repeated the slaps, keeping to rhythmic intervals, alternated with flicks of his tongue against her pussy.

Leia lost sense of time and space, her whole world centered on what Noah was doing to her. She may have lasted one minute or ten, she had no idea. All she knew was that she was poised for his command.

"Now, baby. Explode for me. Show me just how beautiful you are."

Her orgasm slammed through her, jerking her off the stool and into his waiting hands. He buried his mouth in her throbbing core, his hands gripping her ass as he sucked hard and rhythmically on her clit, stretching out her climax.

When she collapsed, boneless, onto the seat, he rose and clamped an arm around her waist. His kiss was hot and demanding, frenzied and heady with the taste of her pussy. He released her to kiss along her jaw, his stubble creating a different burn as he bit her earlobe.

"Now you're going to get the fucking you deserve," he whispered in her ear.

A sob burst through her throat, her vocal cords incapable of speech.

"Leia?"

"Y-yes," she croaked.

"Let go of the chair and put your hands on me. I need you to touch me."

A light coating of sweat on his skin made sliding

her hands over his hard muscles feel like heaven. Going with her instincts, she scoured her nails hard down his torso. Through the goggles, the trails flared bright red.

"Jesus. Again."

She repeated the act, and his cock jerked against her pussy, his breathing choppy. "Do you like hurting me, Leia? Drawing blood?"

"I like what you like."

Both hands grabbed hold of her waist and jerked her forward, his movements rough and merciless. "You know what hearing that makes me feel?"

"How?"

"Powerful. Insane. You drive me to the edge with just a moan. Seeing you, spread before me like this, ready to take my cock... God, I can't think straight."

He slid his hands under her knees and spread her thighs even wider. Her center was still red hot, still on fire for him.

"Watch what you do to me."

She watched nine inches of hot, thick cock slide inside her inch by delicious inch, and reality splintered into useless shards. Shaking uncontrollably, she grabbed his waist, her fingers digging in hard, breaking through his skin. "Oh my God!"

He slid out slowly and slammed back in, shuddering when he was buried in deep. "Oh, baby, you've turned me into a fucking mess."

He rolled his hips once more, then stopped.

Need built with a swiftness that stole her breath. She tried to move but his hands held her still. "God, Noah please. I need you... Oh *please, please, please.*" Her words blurred together in a desperate litany.

22

Every plea fell on Noah's ears like an anointment of power.

He lost another hold on reality. He released her knees and grabbed her ass, lifting her off the stool to slam her onto his cock. Her sharp yelp drove him closer to the edge. The knowledge that she liked the pain, that she wasn't running screaming from him or ridiculing his 'weakness', sent a shaft of pure pleasure through him. He'd told her he was in fear of becoming addicted to her.

He was beginning to dread that it was already too late.

He gripped her ass harder, the insane need to brand her as his and his alone overcoming him again.

Widening his stance, he pumped his hips, felt her flinch even as she met his thrust with a juicy roll of her hips.

Christ... this was insane... but he wanted to keep her. To make her his in ways that would in all probability scare her. The urge to see her tied up, open fully and helplessly to him, unable to move as he fucked every orifice, rushed through his mind, saturating his pleasure even deeper. The image was so powerful he bared his teeth and growled long and deep.

She shuddered at the sound, her nails sliding round to dig into his ass. Her raw hunger and the scent of her arousal blew his mind. He leaned in close and sank his teeth into her shoulder. Supple and salty with her exertions, she tasted like fucking heaven. He bit harder and earned himself another shudder.

He was on a downward slope to seriously unsafe territory with this woman. This woman who still held questions he'd come nowhere close to answering. Questions he'd kept putting off because he'd been too terrified of asking.

Like who had hurt her so badly she'd had to brand her skin with those heartbreaking words? Because he feared once he knew he'd have only one option.

An unthinkable option that might revisit New York on him all over again.

"Noah." The sweet whisper of his name brought him back to the searing pleasure ramming through him. Pleasure that sent him spiraling over the cliff when she scraped the rough diamond edge of her stud over his nipple in short hard flicks, then sank her teeth into him.

"Holy shit, Leia!"

So tight, so deliciously tight was his Leia that her juices spilled out, coating the base of her ass and his fingers as he pummeled her.

Sliding a finger up her ass, he teased her second hole, then pressed down hard, popping through. Her mouth dropped open on a shocked groan.

Then she was coming hard, her cunt a closed silky fist that milked his cock so fiercely he could barely move inside her.

Noah had thought feeling her come was incredible enough. But watching through the goggles as waves of orange-red washed up her body, suffusing her in pleasure—he'd never experienced anything so soul shaking.

He buried himself to the hilt and came in a thick, helpless rush, his climax so powerful, he roared himself hoarse.

God knows how he managed to stay on his feet, how he found the strength to take off her leg restraints before he carried her to the lounger.

They collapsed in a tangle of arms and legs, their breaths nowhere near normal. He gathered her close and felt his heart lurch all over again when she tucked herself into his side. Like she belonged there.

"Are you okay?" he asked gruffly several minutes later when neither of them had broken the silence.

"I'm not sure. Ask me again in a month's time," she slurred.

Something kicked in his chest. "If that's an invitation to call you when we get back to Miami, I accept." He tried for light, but it felt short by a mile.

She tensed. "I didn't mean to... I wasn't trying to..."

"Whether you were or not is irrelevant. I want to see you when we get back to Miami."

He watched her worry her lower lip, the color flowing orange and red depending on the pressure she put on her flesh. He wanted to take over the biting. Hell, he wanted to do so many things with her, his mind reeled with just what he was contemplating. Considering he'd only known her for forty-eight hours, for fuck's sake.

"We're only on day two. You may not want to know I exist come Friday."

He slid his fingers into her hair and tightened his grip. Her hand immediately splayed on his stomach, their need to connect with each other almost visceral. "The only reason I won't want to know you exist is if you stop responding to me the way you just did. Or if you play mind games with me. Are you about to do either?"

She shook her head. "The way I feel when you touch me... I can't turn it off," she whispered.

"Neither can I. So going on the basis that we haven't fucked each other to death by Friday, this thing between us isn't over."

He may have been arrogant enough to think he'd have her immediate agreement. When she kept silent, cold dread flared up his spine. "Leia?"

"Can we talk about it later, Noah?"

He kicked himself when he heard the weariness in her voice. He'd been relentless since he chased her down the mountain yesterday. In less than an hour, they'd be in Vienna and she'd barely slept more than a few hours.

He kissed her, then got up and located their clothes. He tucked her panties in his pocket and buttoned her back into his shirt. Handing over her shoes, he swept her up into his arms and headed out of the booth, fighting the urge to demand an answer then and there.

"Sure, sweetheart. As long as you get that I'm not taking no for an answer."

* * *

They ended up staying on the plane and sleeping for six hours straight after they landed in Vienna. They woke with barely enough time to check into their hotel before it was time to get ready for the jazz concert.

Noah walked into the bedroom as she was stepping into another pair of sky-high heels. He stopped in the middle of the room, a fireball landing itself in his belly before shooting down to his groin.

"Is everything in your wardrobe made of leather?" he rasped.

She jerked around, shrugged and drifted her hand over her short, flared leather skirt. "When I can get away with it. Which is most of the time." She smiled.

His heart kicked, then went into overdrive. Christ, did she have any idea how breathtaking she looked when she smiled? He found himself moving toward her before his brain kicked back into gear. "You're determined to explore my every weakness, sweetheart, aren't you?" His voice hadn't quite returned to normal, and he doubted it would when her smile widened.

"What other weaknesses do you have?"

He stopped in front of her, looked down at her top. It was short sleeved, made of sheer purple lace with two silk pockets over each breast and a broad black zipper that went from neck to waist. Taking her by the waist, he turned her around, several million brain cells frying when he confirmed his suspicion. She wasn't wearing a bra.

He pulled her back, rubbed his throbbing erection against her ass. "You want to know my other weakness?"

"Yes," she whispered.

"Small, bite-size tits that bounce when I fuck you."

She wriggled against him and gave a little pleased sigh. "I'm glad you like mine. Most men are obsessed with big boobs."

He shifted her hair to one side and gripped her nape. "I'm not most men, baby. Get that through your head now."

Her head fell forward, her first vertebrae nudging against his palm. "Yes, Noah."

A tremor ran through him. "Those two words can

pretty much guarantee you get whatever you want when it comes to me."

She glanced over her shoulder, her eyelids fluttering when their eyes met. "Yes, Noah."

Something shifted in the air between them. A knowing. A demand. An acceptance. A connection much more intense than sex. Noah wanted to grab it, bottle that moment, and never let it go.

She blinked and the moment was gone. He let go of her nape and slid his hand down her back to her ass. "I'm not sure how I feel about the length of this skirt though, especially knowing you're wearing another of your lingerie sets under it."

"If I have to change then you do too."

His brows rose. "You object to what I'm wearing?"

She stared him up and down, and her tongue swirled over her upper lip in an unconscious gesture of want that spiked fire through his blood.

"Yes, I do. The way your jeans hug your ass isn't legal. And that blue T-shirt brings out your eyes way too sexily for me to even want to think about you leaving this room dressed like that." The deadpan delivery drew a stunned laugh from him.

"Are you telling me you like what you see, baby?"

Her eyes met his and that rawness exploded between them again. "You know I do," she said in a hushed voice. She stepped closer and her hand slid up his chest to curve around his nape. It felt like the most natural thing in the world to lean down and kiss her.

His hands skimmed her back, curved over her ass and squeezed.

Her flinch made him freeze and pull back. "How badly does it hurt?" After the insane frenzy of their fucking last night, he'd known she would bruise but even he hadn't realized how far things had gone until he'd seen her ass and breasts. The marks on her shoulder and neck were covered by her top and loose hair.

Grey eyes met his and a wave of heat swept into her cheeks. "It's not that bad."

"Leia?"

"I mean it. The pleasure I got from what you did made the pain worth it. In the bathroom just now, I touched them just to remind myself how good I felt."

The rush that broke free threatened to cap him at the knees.

He cupped his hand around her throat and brought her face up to his. "Tell me again. Slowly."

"I like it, Noah. The pain, the pleasure. All of it."

He smashed his mouth down on hers, kissing until they both couldn't breathe. When he raised his head, the beauty of her face sent him under once again.

"This jazz thing. How wedded are you to the idea of attending?"

"Fused Realms have hit the billboard charts consistently for over fifteen years," she whispered against his lips. "This is an opportunity of a lifetime."

Growling, he grabbed her hand and splayed it over his aching groin. "I have an unending opportunity of a lifetime right here, baby. We don't even need to leave the room."

She laughed despite the dangerous currents flying through the air. Caressing his cock, she answered, "Let's go rock out, baby. Then you can bring me back here and rock my world again."

He held her against him, let her stroke him for another minute before he reluctantly stepped away. "I'll agree on condition you don't bend over at any point during the evening. If I catch even a hint of your ass on show, we're coming back here and I'm making your ass sing again."

She tilted her head and stared up at him. "Yes, Noah."

A clock chimed somewhere in the room. Had he been able to look away from her stunning face to look at his watch, he would've known the exact moment he relinquished part of his soul to Leia Michaels forever.

23

"Should I be jealous that your heart is racing and you have a blissful smile on your face that has nothing to do with me?" Noah growled close to her ear to be heard above the sound of band rehearsals.

Leia laughed and turned in the circle of the arms caging her in on either side. Behind them, the huge stage in the Vienna Stadthalle, where the bands would perform in an hour, gleamed under powerful colored lights. Sliding her arms around his neck, she stood on tiptoe and kissed his jaw.

"Sorry, for the next few hours, you have to share me with a serious addiction to jazz funk."

He grunted but allowed her to tease him with

light kisses before their inevitable hunger for each other threatened to fire out of control.

When he raised his head, his blue eyes were dark and his breathing a little ragged. Leia was beginning to think she would never get over how staggering their hunger for each other was, or how this breathtaking man seemed to be as caught up in the turbulent emotions swirling around them as she was.

"Don't worry, baby, I'll be right next to you to remind you of your other addictions." He cupped her ass and squeezed. Her gasp at the fused spike of pleasure and pain darkened his eyes further.

"So you've changed your mind about singing backup with me?" she teased.

One corner of his mouth twitched in a purely masculine, insanely sexy smile. "Fine, maybe not right next to you but close enough to make sure you stay on the right side of groupie lust."

She laughed again, and it suddenly struck her how easy it was to laugh with Noah. How very little of it she'd done for a long time. How different her life would be a week from now once she was back home. Back with Warren.

He cupped her chin. "Hey."

She glanced back at him, fighting to stay in place. "Sorry."

"What was it?"

"A whisper of ghosts. Nothing more." She visibly shook herself out of thinking about the future. "I'm awesome groupie material. The right ingredient to being a good groupie is to project enough crazy awe without coming over all stalkerish."

He stared down at her, head tilted thoughtfully. "So if I were in a band, you wouldn't chain yourself to my trailer or drape yourself naked over my drums?" he asked with a salacious wink.

She laughed. "No, but I'd wear your headband and let you sign your name on my boobs. Possibly consider holding your joint when the muse suddenly struck and you didn't have an ashtray nearby."

His laugh was a deep and sexy rumble that wove its way through her body to her toes before whooshing back up to curl around her heart.

"If I had you, I wouldn't need a muse or weed. You already go straight to my head," Noah whispered against her lips.

God, he was gorgeous. And hers for only a few more days...

Unless she contemplated the impossible and let herself see him once they were back in the real world.

The temptation was strong. It tantalized, drawing her in deeper, even as she pushed it away.

Dr. Hatfield had tried to steer her into thinking that what happened five years ago wasn't her fault. But deep down, Leia knew she wasn't guiltless. In the dark of night when the ghosts gleefully woke, she couldn't shut them off because they were right. She might hate her mother for not being strong enough to withstand the horror that had befallen their cursed family, but she couldn't hide from the fact that part of that horror had been of her own making.

A series of rapid African drumbeats rumbled through the auditorium, effectively distracting her from the dark sojourn into the past.

She tightened her arms around Noah's neck, closed her eyes and swayed to the throbbing beat.

Noah's hands clenched on her waist. "Fuck. Open your eyes, Leia. Now. Before I find somewhere dark and disturbing to remind you that you're mine."

"Kiss me first," she challenged, her heartbeat still echoing with wisps of what she'd done. How she'd made it so she carried an incomplete tattoo on her ribcage, too scared to complete it.

He didn't. Her breath caught because she knew what he wanted. Knew what she had to say to get what she needed. "Kiss me. Please, Noah."

One hand dragged her closer. Held completely immobilized, he sealed his mouth over hers in punishment and lust. She opened for him, drank him in, infused her senses with the breathtaking man who could make everything fall away. The drumbeats increased in tempo as Osibisa, the band her father had loved and whose music she'd known since childhood, built up to a wild and frenzied crescendo.

Noah pressed her against the balcony railing, her bottom digging in to the metal frame, sparking a riot of pain that mingled with the pleasure of his kiss.

Her clit throbbed to life, her pussy clenching with desperate hunger.

"Miss Michaels? Mr. King?" a hesitant voice said above the music.

Noah broke the kiss, his chest rising and falling rapidly as he pressed his forehead to hers. "Shit. I'm going to make you pay for the next four hours of blue balls I'm going to suffer," he muttered.

"I'll be a good little groupie and let you use me however you want," she whispered back.

Noah was still cursing when she craned her neck to see a woman about her age with a clipboard, earpiece and slightly panicked look in her eyes that spelled "harried usher" standing in the doorway of the exclusive box the Indigo Lounge had hired for tonight.

"Hi, I'm Greta. The band is getting ready to go on

stage. If you'd both like to come with me?" she asked with a smile that flashed on and off, her fingers drumming impatiently against her leg.

Noah took Leia's hand and tugged her behind him, making no effort to hide what must have been a very evident arousal.

Leia held her breath, but the girl was too busy getting the shock of her life once she caught a glimpse of Noah's handsome face to lower her gaze.

When he smiled at her, her mouth dropped open along with the clipboard, which landed on the floor with a clatter. Still smiling, Noah bent and retrieved it for her.

She didn't move.

"After you," he said pointedly.

"I... Thank you. Umm... yes. Please, follow me." She walked backward, gawping some more at Noah until the outside wall stopped her progress. Stumbling, she finally pried her eyes away and cleared her throat. Then she took off down the long circular hallway.

"Did you enjoy that?" Leia had meant to keep her voice even, her tone modulated in a way Warren would've been proud of. Instead, it emerged rough and edgy.

"Enjoy what?" He raised innocent eyebrows at her.

"Reducing her to a puddle of stupid?" she snapped.

His smile disappeared. "I'm not responsible for the way I look or feel when you have your hands on me. That's what she was reacting to."

"Sure, keep believing that." A part of her was drowning in mortification. The rest couldn't step out of the quagmire of jealousy swallowing her up.

"Hey." He pulled her to a stop, drew their clasped hands behind her back and used it to propel her forward. His free fingers drifted up her cheek to caress the swathe above her ear, a gesture that immediately soothed her. "If I can lose my shit over the way your valet looked at you, then you're allowed to lose your shit every now and then, too. Within reason. And hell, you're going up on stage in a place that will have over ten thousand people watching you in that getup. Have you stopped to think how I feel about that?"

She frowned. "When you put it like that..."

He lowered his hand to trace her lips with his thumb. "Knowing you're a little possessive over me helps a bit. But you don't need to be jealous. Okay?"

"That's easy for you to say."

"It's not, but I'm hoping you'll make me a better person."

A tiny frown marred his brow after he said that, his face contemplative.

They turned the corner to see the usher waiting by a back elevator. Her eyes grew huge when her gaze landed on Noah, and Leia fought the urge to snap again.

In the lift, Noah tucked Leia in front of him and clamped his arms around her waist. Ignoring the girl, he proceeded to kiss his way down her neck.

Despite knowing he was proving a point, by the time they exited the lift, Leia felt bad for the girl, especially when she caught a look of mingled embarrassment and envy in her eyes.

She delivered them to a large green room and left them there, hurrying away when a loud voice called her name.

"Hopefully, she'll be too busy to find somewhere dark to rub herself off with an image of you in her mind. Otherwise I'd have to hunt her down and make her feel my claws." Thankfully her tone was light enough to make the joke passable.

Noah laughed, raised her fingers to his lips, and trailed his mouth over her long nails. "That would be such a waste. The only skin these claws are allowed to mutilate is mine."

A loud cough broke them apart for the second time in less than ten minutes.

They turned. The lead singer of Fused Realms, Kendal Spikes, stood behind them in full leathers and long spiky hair.

"Which one of you is Michaels?" He looked between them, one carefully plucked eyebrow quirked.

Leia raised her hand, a different excitement scything through her. "That would be me." She stepped forward, and his gaze drifted down her body, widening a touch as it went. "Please call me Leia... and thank you for the opportunity. I've been a huge fan of yours since my dad bought me your first record. I won a high school talent contest when I sang 'Blue Noise'."

He gave a lopsided smile. "Ouch. Thanks for making me feel every minute of my forty-five years, darling," he drawled in a distinct British accent.

Leia gasped and furiously backpedalled. "Oh no, I didn't mean—"

"It's okay. We adore all our fans, especially if they come as gorgeous as y—"

"Noah King." Noah stepped forward and held out his hand.

They shook hands and locked eyes for a long moment. Kendal nodded as if he'd received a subliminal message. Or a warning.

"Come and meet the rest of the band." He turned and walked out of the room.

She glanced at Noah, noted the gathering storm in his eyes. "Losing your shit is allowed. Within reason," she said, paraphrasing his words back to him.

His eyes met hers and he nodded. "Okay, I'll behave. Maybe."

She laughed.

Two flights of stairs later, they went up a rigged staircase and onto the stage. Introductions were made to the six-man band and two backup singers. The band members drifted away to their instruments, leaving them with Gary, a thickset black man, and Fliss, a young blonde with tattoos down her left arm.

Kendal strolled toward them, carrying a mic and a song sheet. He handed her the song sheet. "Guys, Leia will be joining you in backup for the last three songs. You mind working on the chorus of the songs with her?"

Leia looked at the titles of the songs and shook her head. "There's no need. I know all your song lyrics."

Kendal smiled and held out the mic. "Give us a taste of your pipes then."

Noah's hand tightened on hers. She didn't dare look at him.

"The chorus to 'Blue Noise'?"

Kendal nodded. "That'll do."

She took the mic and tried to free herself from Noah. He delayed that freedom until she looked at him. His eyes gleamed with myriad emotions: possession, lust, anger, and a touch of vulnerability, each stamping its way into her heart.

Her fingers curled around the cold mic, her breath snagged somewhere in her chest as Noah took two steps back, folded his arms and sat on the stool someone had brought for him.

"When you're ready." Kendal's voice bounced on her consciousness like rain on gravel. She didn't want to look away from Noah; she wanted to explore those emotions sizzling like lightning between them.

But she had the leader of a world-famous band standing in front of her, waiting to make her dream come true.

She cleared her throat, resisting the urge to tap her finger on the mic like she'd seen so many amateurs do. She looked at Kendal and he nodded.

A bass guitar struck a chord somewhere behind

her, strumming the tune of the first chorus line. She waited till the guitarist was done with the practice run. Then she joined in:

> You turn your back, and I am grey
>   noise
> When you're away, my life is black
>   noise
> When we make love, my world is gold
>   noise
> Love in your eyes, my heart is blue
>   noise
> Sweet baby mine, I'd give my last dime,
> My heart and soul, my every dol-
>   lar sign
> To have your love, to have your blue
>   noise
> My heart and soul, to hear that blue
>   noise

24

Everything tightened in Noah's body and he struggled to stay upright as the incredible sound of her voice boomed through the auditorium. Her sultry come-pour-yourself-all-over-me voice was sinfully sexy, evoking images he had no doubt every man on stage was thinking.

His stomach clenched and he forced himself to sit still. She'd taken her place beside the other two backup singers after wowing everyone with her initial test.

Now he watched her sing another track, one about a fast and loose heart in New Orleans. He tried to look away, take a beat. And failed.

What this woman was doing to him. How fast she was consuming him. Three days. Just three fucking days, and he couldn't imagine his nights without her. Couldn't imagine fucking anyone else but her. And he still knew only less than a handful of facts about her. Granted, a couple were facts he was sure she'd told no one else but...

Things were escalating too fast, spiraling out of control.

She wrapped both hands around the mic, meshed her long fingers and slid them up and down. Gold and blue spotlights danced over her face and upper body, bathing her beauty in soft lights. She tilted her head and that swathe of shaved scalp made his breath catch. Made him yearn to know what had triggered that and her tattoo.

The song ended. Fliss said something to her. A smile split her face, and she blushed and responded, happiness radiating off her.

He swallowed as she came toward him, his heart banging harder against his rips. He wanted to haul her off the stage, find the nearest private room and pound all the feelings he didn't want to name into her. The moment she was within touching distance, he curled his arm around her tiny waist.

Mine, he barely stopped himself from growling.

"Hey, King, you play an instrument?" Spikes shouted from the center of the stage.

Noah shrugged. "I dabbled a little with bass guitars years ago."

"No shit. Hey, Steve, we have a spare guitar lying about?" he shouted at the drummer.

Steve nodded and murmured to the stagehand. The requested instrument materialized within a minute.

Kendal waved him over. "Join us for a quick turn. Don't let your little lady here have all the fun. We'll go for a pure fusion—you know Hancock's 'Chameleon'?"

"Sure."

"Great."

Noah wasn't sure whether the offer was genuine or a ploy to keep them there for longer so the asshole could keep ogling Leia. He started to shake his head and paused when a huge smile split her face.

"Omigod, I'd love to see you play!"

That stomach-hollowing feeling rushed back, overpowering every other emotion. Her beauty flattened him, her smile a ray of pure sunshine on his desolate soul.

Add that to what she did to him in the bedroom

and he knew he would have a very, very hard time walking away from Leia Michaels.

"Please, Noah?" she whispered in that voice that sparked every primitive atom in his body.

Jesus.

He took his hand off her waist and nodded. "Sure, let's do it." He shrugged off his leather jacket and draped it over her shoulders. He placed her on the stool and took a hard, fast kiss. "Remember you're *my* groupie. Keep your panties on, your knees together and your eyes on me."

"Yes, Noah."

Two words. Two fucking words that tore his insides to shreds, caused the world to tilt beneath his feet.

When he'd told her to vocalize her responses, he'd done it because he didn't want any misunderstanding between them. He hadn't anticipated this, hadn't imagined that each time she said those two words, he'd feel like a king even as he fell to his knees to worship her.

Yes, Noah.

Those two words could be his undoing.

Grabbing the five-string bass, he pulled the strap over his head. He plucked the strings, adjusted the back pick-up a touch and stepped onto the stage.

The drums followed the piano intro. He blended in at the same time as the electric guitar and couldn't stop his grin as the melody flowed through his fingers.

Halfway through the track, he glanced over at Leia. She was doing exactly as he'd told her, staring straight at him with the fixation of the perfect groupie. He rocked back and forth on his feet, his fingers sliding up and down the strings as an old love rekindled inside.

He'd sacrificed so much to Ashley's toxic mind games. Some things he'd never bothered to reclaim once he left New York, mostly because he'd been furious with himself for losing sight of them in the first place. Furious with himself for turning his life inside out to hold on to something that hadn't been there in the first place.

Thank God that was all behind him...

"Take it away, King!" Spikes nodded at him to take the penultimate solo. Noah's fingers flew over the strings.

Leia cupped her hands around her mouth and whooped. He winked at her and smiled when she blushed.

Hell. *Perfect* was slowly creeping into his mind. There was no other word to describe her. Everything else seemed *lame*. Yes, she was broken. But then so was he.

Whatever had broken her had made her ideal for him. Ideal... *Perfect*.

The session ended in a crescendo of drums, piano and guitar strains. Leia broke into applause, and a smile split his face.

Even when Spikes glanced her way with another of those furtive lusty-heavy looks, he didn't feel as homicidal.

Leia was his. Only his. And he aimed to keep it that way.

He handed the guitar to the stagehand and walked over to her. Grabbing the lapels of his leather jacket, he pulled her close and kissed her, reveling in her touch when her hands curled around his waist.

"Was I a good groupie? Will you let me into your trailer or do I still have to chain myself to it?" she murmured for his ears alone when he raised his head.

"Sweetheart, if I had a trailer I'd fuck you on every surface inside it, then I'd fuck you on top of it, under the stars so your beauty can touch the very heavens."

Her pulse fluttered wildly and she grinned. "You say the hottest things, Noah King."

"Enjoy the concert, you two." Spikes walked over. "Leia, I'll see you back here in ninety minutes."

Noah shook his hand and hustled her back to their private balcony before his mood turned sour at the thought of letting her anywhere near Spikes.

The next ninety minutes passed in an excruciating medley of enjoyment and frustration. He basked in Leia's delight at the talent on show but each time she leaned over the balcony and wriggled her ass against him, his knees threatened to buckle.

Many times he bit his tongue against ordering them to leave. She'd never forgive him if he thwarted her dream. But hell, he had to fuck her soon or he'd go blind.

She wriggled again. He grabbed her waist. "Stop it." His voice was rough, lacking the force he wanted to project.

She glanced over her shoulder at him. Then wriggled again.

On the balcony, the other three Indigo Lounge couples who'd joined them were absorbed in the band and crowds below.

Blocking their view with his body, he spanked her ass hard and heard her yelp.

"Stop. Wriggling. You've been torturing me for the last hour, determined to drive me over the fucking edge." He soothed the burn, then spanked her four more times in quick succession. She bit her lip and her nipples hardened to rigid nubs beneath the silk.

He petted her ass as Fused Realms ended a third song to roaring applause and launched into the fourth. "After this one you're on. You'll be down there, making your dream come true with my handprint on your ass. Does that turn you on?" He kissed his way down her jaw and licked at her skipping pulse.

She gave a delicate shudder. "Yes."

"Good. Have fun and be prepared to leave straight after."

He took her hand and led her the way they'd gone earlier. Backstage was a frenzy of excited post-gig high, flowing booze and roadies trying to haul equipment amid the chaos.

Noah scrubbed his intention to return upstairs and stayed put at the curtained-off entrance of the stage. Fliss spotted them and indicated a small darkened section near the back of the stage without breaking the rhythm of the high note she was singing.

He nodded and led Leia there. From where they stood, they could see the fifteen rows of the auditorium and the two giant big screens strung high on the walls.

A smile broke over her face, another wriggle

working its way through her body. She stopped halfway and glanced at him.

"You know I could pull you back against me, lift your skirt, and fuck you right here and no one would notice?"

She turned her head and rubbed her cheek against his stubble. "But you won't."

"No. Because I'm addicted to seeing you reach a new high each time we fuck. Those highs only come with time and patience. And I'm finding that I'm getting invested in your pleasure, Leia Michaels."

She opened her mouth to answer just as the song ended. Gary looked their way and nodded. This time Noah let her excited wriggle go and basked in her sheer excitement as she hopped up onto the stage and took her place.

The first song—"Toxic Yin and Yang"—dealt with the edgy underbelly of jealousy, an emotion Ashley had excelled in evoking from him—

Hell, why the hell couldn't he stop thinking about her? And why now when before last week in his office he hadn't given her a thought in months and only during therapy?

He leaned against the stage wall and let his gaze wander over Leia. She was hot, incredibly responsive and a borderline submissive, not that he was into that whole Dom/sub scene. But hell, he could see the attraction in that, could feel the power in that push/pull control. He craved control in bed, but he loved pain more. Pain reminded him he was alive. It did the same for Leia. He could tell.

They'd barely scratched the surface of their possibilities.

So what the fuck was he doing dwelling on his ex-fiancé, the woman he'd cut out of his life like a cancer two years ago?

Closure.

He shook his head. Fuck, he was screwed if he was hearing his shrink's voice in his head in the middle of a jazz funk concert in Vienna.

The song ended. The crowd roared. Leia glanced back at him, her face flushed with happiness. He smiled back, and she gave him a little wave.

Fuck Ashley.

Fuck his shrink.

He was living in the now, with the sexiest, most intelligent, most fuckable woman he'd ever met. A woman who had the serious potential to be everything he'd ever wanted, who didn't flinch from his dark side.

The next song started, an up-tempo one Leia began dancing to. He pulled his phone from his pocket, intending to capture her enthralling movements on his video camera.

He activated his phone and froze. Premonition slid an icy hand around his nape.

You have 4 missed calls and 6 text messages.

The calls were from Gabe.

The texts all said the same thing:

Call Me. Ashley.

25

How do you tell a man you didn't know three days ago that you are addicted to the slap of his hand against your ass?

Especially when said man hadn't spoken more than two words to you since he hauled you off the stage before the last note died?

The shocking realization wouldn't go away. Nor would the growing inkling that something was wrong.

"I really wanted to thank the band for letting me perform with them," she said.

"You already did. Many times. Hell, you even blew them kisses as we left. I hope I score for not being a dick about that."

Although he smiled, his jaw remained tight. She

frowned. "Is there something bothering you? Something you want to talk about?"

He reefed stiff fingers through his hair. The corner of his mouth lifted in a mirthless smile. "What I'd like is for the driver to go a little over half a fucking mile an hour." He started to lower the partition to the limo taking them back to the hotel.

Without pausing to think about the wisdom of her action, she slid onto her knees on the seat and pulled off her panties.

He hit the *up* button again. "Jesus. What he fuck are you doing?"

Dropping her panties, she straddled him and slid her arms around his neck. "Something's wrong. You can either talk about it or you can allow me to distract you. But I don't want it keeping you from me. I'm still buzzing from high number four. I don't want anything to bring me down."

"I'm not fucking you in the back of a limo, Leia."

She squashed the touch of disappointment. "I know. So... talk..." She kissed his firm, delicious mouth. "Or distraction."

He groaned and dragged her close, pushing her down so her hot center dragged over his rigid erection. "I've never been this hard for this long, sweetheart. You're lethal to my mental and physical wellbeing." His hands squeezed her thighs, then he slipped one hand between her legs. His groan morphed into a hiss of disbelief, and his forehead dropped to her chest. "And you're so fucking wet."

"Put your fingers inside me."

"Put your fingers inside me, what?"

Her fingers gripped his hair. "Please, Noah."

"Did you forget your manners so quickly, or did you do it deliberately so I'd spank your tight, sore little ass?"

Her blush drew his first genuine smile since the one he'd given her on stage before her performance.

"Are you trying to make me feel better?"

"Yes. Tell me what's wrong, Noah. Did I do something?" Between the start and end of her backup routine, something had happened. As much as she wanted to brush over it with sex, she couldn't ignore the layer of unease.

His chin snapped up, a dark frown between his eyes. "Of course not. Why would you think that?"

She shrugged. "If you're going to punish me for something I've done, I'll take the punishment but I want to know now. I don't like surprises."

He didn't answer straightaway. But he twisted the hand between her legs, rubbed his knuckle hard against her clit. She gasped, her fingers digging into his scalp as she held on tight. He rubbed her roughly for a full minute, then buried two fingers between her legs.

A long kiss later, he raised his head.

His eyes had gone dark and turbulent. "You haven't done anything wrong. I got a few missed calls. I've been trying to reach Gabe. He's not answering. I'm not sure what the time is in Bora Bora right now—"

"Minus twelve hours from right now. It's the middle of the night there."

He pulled his fingers out slowly and plunged them back in. "You're a sexy genius. Did I tell you that?"

Her breath hitched. "Maybe. Please don't stop."

He repeated the action. "I'm pissed off that he called me four times then doesn't answer when I call. And he didn't leave a message."

"But that's not all."

"I got texts from Ashley."

Leia froze, suspended somewhere between acute arousal and disconcerting anxiety. "I'm not sure how I feel about you mentioning her name while you have your fingers inside me."

"You asked me what was wrong. I'm telling you

because I don't want you to think you're the reason I'm in a bad mood."

Irrationally, she wanted to tell him he could've chosen distraction over talking about his ex. She wanted to ask why his ex had his number. But considering her own messed up life, who was she to question his?

"What does she want?"

"Fuck if I know. She wants me to call her." The disgust in his voice was unmistakable.

"You think Gabe knows?"

"I'm guessing he does. Otherwise, it's a hell of a coincidence since they called within minutes of each other." He flexed his fingers and arousal kicked anxiety's butt, but didn't knock it out totally.

"Are you going to call her back?"

His jaw tightened but the visceral edge of lust in his eyes didn't fade, much to her satisfaction. "We haven't spoken in two and a half years. The last time I saw her I made it very clear I never wanted to see or speak to her again." His voice was a blade of raw anger. "That position hasn't changed on my part."

But something clearly had changed on Ashley's.

He pressed a hand into the small of her back, urged her to rock her hips against him. The action forced his fingers deeper inside her while she rubbed herself on his erection. Leaning down, she kissed him, slowly running her tongue over his mouth before sliding it in.

She continued twirling her hips. The tension gradually oozed from his shoulders. Several minutes later, he drew back and leaned on the headrest. His eyes were dark and intense as he watched her. "Lift your skirt. I want to see you."

She let go of his nape and lifted the front of her skirt. His gaze dropped to where his fingers were lodged inside her. He circled his thumb over her wet clit. Reality took on a definite hazy edge.

"Why don't you like surprises?" he asked, his eyes intent on what he was doing to her.

"Wh-what?"

"You said that earlier."

"Oh. My mom was the queen of spontaneity, and not always the good kind. My dad used to say she had a chronic impulsive disorder. Her solution to every problem was throwing a surprise luncheon. I got into a fight with a school bully once. Mom thought it would be helpful to throw an anti-bullying party and make the girl and her parents guests of honor, only she didn't tell them until they got there. The week before my sweet sixteen party, I came home from school to find that she'd invited all the boys from my class and paid them each a thousand dollars to make themselves available to escort me to the party."

His eyes met hers. "Christ."

"And those were the lamer ones. Imagine walking into your bedroom to find a full-grown Amur leopard on a leash for you to play with because you'd lost a softball game. It got to a point where I'd call Sonia, our housekeeper, to find out whether it was safe to come home."

He smirked. "She had exotic animals on tap?" His free hand went to her shirt and unbuttoned her halfway. Exposing her breasts, he caught a nipple between his fingers and squeezed. Her breath hitched.

"She had crazy good connections. If she liked you enough she could get you five minutes with the president with a single phone call."

"But you just wanted a normal life."

She nodded. "It got worse the older I got. It took me a while to realize why she was going off the rails." Leia's words slurred with the pleasure gathering through her body.

He paused in his ministrations. "Why?"

"She married my stepfather barely six months after Dad died. The marriage got very turbulent very quickly. I think that was the only impulsive decision she ever regretted."

"You think if she hadn't, she'd still be here?"

Guilt and sorrow threatened to overtake pleasure. "I *know* she would be." Unwilling to stray into much more painful and disturbing territory, she placed her hand over his on her breast and silently begged him to continue. He pinched her nipple hard. Pleasure rolled through her. She threw her head back and pumped her hips.

"Don't come."

She gasped. "Oh God! *Please.*"

"Baby, we're almost at the hotel. You're not walking through reception with a just-climaxed glow on your face for every guy out there to see." Pure possessiveness throbbed through his voice.

She bit her lip and tried to bring herself down a notch. It was one of the hardest things she'd done in a long time. "Are you like this with every woman you date?"

"I don't date. Ashley was the last woman I dated."

Once again, his ex loomed large between them and she tried not to think of how much power the faceless woman still had over Noah. "What do you do with your women, then?"

"Catch." His thumb circled. "Fuck." Again. "Release."

Her eyebrows rose. "Are you serious?"

"You're the only woman I've seen for longer than a five-hour stretch in a very long time."

"Why?"

Blue eyes filled with shadows met hers. "No expectations. No mind games. No attachments."

"Did that satisfy you?"

He kneaded her breasts. "Up to a point and barely in the last few months. But you... you satisfy me so much more. I'm addicted to you. I want everything you have to give and more. I want to give you untold pleasure, push you way out of your comfort zone and make you die with bliss. I want to make you mine, Leia. And I haven't wanted that in a long time."

Her heart lurched and her sex clenched around his fingers, reacting to the intense words. "Noah..."

He shook his head and that contemplative look she'd seen on his face earlier returned. "It's a little insane, I know. We'll work it out when we get back to Miami."

Either he was too busy lowering his head to her nipple to feel her tense or the unsettling conversation had thrown off his radar.

But even as she lost herself in the pleasure he drew so effortlessly from her, Leia was scrambling for emotional safety. Noah King was slowly drawing her into his orbit. An orbit she was sure she wouldn't be able to inhabit no matter how much she wished to.

The car pulled to a stop, and he slowly raised his head, pulling his fingers out of her. "Don't think I haven't noticed that you've avoided answering me about Miami for the second time." He traced her wetness over her lips, then licked his fingers. "It's happening, Leia. *We're* happening. I'm willing to give you another day or two to get used to the idea. Then I expect to hear that *Yes, Noah* you've become so perfect at saying."

He kissed her hard, lapping at her mouth with broad hungry strokes before easing back to button her up. By the time they alighted she was once again respectable, albeit minus her panties, which he'd stuffed into his jeans pocket.

A party going on in one of the hotel event rooms had spilled out into reception. He kept her tucked firmly to his side and hurried them to the elevator. They were stepping in when his phone rang.

He looked at the screen and his jaw tightened. "About fucking time, Gabe. What the hell's going on?"

26

With each floor they climbed, Noah's fury grew. "Wait a second. Are you saying Ashley's in *Miami*?" He detested the vibrations in his voice but couldn't stop them.

Gabe grunted. "Yeah. Has been for the three days. You must have missed each other by a few hours."

Which was just as well. Noah wasn't sure what he'd have done if she turned up unannounced at his front door. "What the hell does she want?" he rasped.

Beside him, Leia tensed. He looked down at her, but her eyes were averted. He tucked her closer and breathed easier when she slipped her arms around his waist.

"She won't tell me. I tried to see her before I headed down here. She'll only talk to you."

"Fuck that. If she has anything to say, our lawyers can deal with it." They exited the elevator, and he reluctantly let go of Leia to open the door. As they entered their suite, she started to move away. Catching her to him, he pressed his lips against her temple. She mouthed *Shower* and he nodded.

"Yeah, I tried that route. She hinted that it wouldn't be something you wanted on the record."

Ice cracked down his spine. "What the hell does that mean?"

"Jesus, man, I don't know." Gabriel sounded weary. "Hell, I thought this thing was behind you. Don't think I don't kick myself every fucking day for ever introducing you two."

Noah wanted to be generous and reassuring and forgiving, but the fury bubbling in his bloodstream made that impossible. "Whatever the hell she's after, she's going to have to cool her heels until I get back. Then she'll have to deal with my lawyer anyway."

Gabe paused. "You think that's wise? Whatever she wants made her leave New York to seek you out. Maybe a face-to-face will—"

"Like hell that's going to happen," he snarled. "I

stopped jumping through her fucking hoops a long time ago, Gabe."

"I know. I'm just saying, we both know the shit she's capable of. Antagonizing her may not be the best solution."

"I'll take that under advisement."

"Which in your pig-headed way means *fuck no*." Gabe sighed again. "I don't blame you, buddy. If she was my ex I'd probably start mixing Molotov cocktails at the sound of her name, too."

Noah breathed deep and tried to calm his irate nerves. "How are things going down there with you?" he asked, seeking a distraction to his anger. He glanced toward the bedroom where *his* perfect distraction was waiting for him.

"Fucking impeccable. My girlfriend is determined to leave me unless I spend time with her. Now I'm here, she won't talk to me because I'm not 'committed enough' to our relationship. Fucking women!"

Noah smiled despite his mood. "I'm sure you'll rise to the occasion. For some odd reason, Angie's nuts about you." The two had fallen over each other like a ton of bricks the moment they'd laid eyes on one another. He'd been too cynical to trust that it would last. He still was, but he wasn't about to tell his best friend that.

Everyone was entitled to crash and burn their own way. And if by some miracle they didn't, then kudos to them.

"I'm hoping she remembers that pretty fucking soon. There's only so much powder-blue sky and sun-kissed sand I can take before I hurl something."

"You live in Miami. Blue skies and beaches aren't alien concepts to you. Besides, according to Damon, you've been there less than a day."

"According... I can't believe that asshole managed to give you the lowdown on my sex life and neglected to mention Ashley, the main reason for his call. He's picking up the tab for poker night drinks for the rest of the year."

The reminder of his ex's name made his stomach roil all over again. He heard the faint sound of a shower, and his fingers tightened on the phone. "Call me if she contacts you again. Or better still, don't. Deal with your shit. I'll handle her when I get back."

He hung up, deleted the texts and blocked Ashley's number. He threw the phone onto the bar on his way into the bedroom, unable to shake the fury and underlying edginess clawing through him.

Toeing off his shoes, he undressed and entered the bathroom.

She stood between the powerful shower jets, her body coated in fluffy suds and scented steam.

The knot she'd secured her hair into started to slip. She leaned back to fix it. He slid his hands under her arms and cupped her breasts.

Lust-heavy grey eyes met his, and her lips parted. "Hi," she murmured.

Holy hell, she was stunning. "Hi."

"Everything okay?"

"No. Most definitely not." He couldn't stop the acid bite of his response.

She leaned back further, laid her head on his shoulder and trailed her mouth over his jaw. "Distraction?"

"God, yes." He plucked at her nipples until they peaked under his touch. When she curved her arms around his neck, granting him unfettered access to her body, his mood improved greatly. He squeezed and teased, pinched and bit, drowning in her whimpers and shuddering exhales. He wanted to absorb everything she was, lose himself in her and forget the bullshit waiting for his return.

"You're incredible, Leia. Your generosity slays me."

"I want to give you more." She jerked and flexed her hips when his fingers slid between her legs.

He increased the pressure. "Why?"

Her breath caught. "Because... you've shown me that sex can be ugly and beautiful at the same time," she whispered. "That I don't have to be ashamed to give in to the hunger. I want to satisfy yours which- ever way I can."

He kissed her neck and used his teeth on her shoulder. Raising his head, he watched her skin turn red. Satisfaction spiked through him, pushed him fur- ther. He caught her clit between his fingers and squeezed. She cried out and her knees buckled.

"I'm greedy and I'm insatiable. I'll take everything you have to give, and I'll demand more. What will you do then?"

She twisted and faced him. Then slowly sank down to kneel before him.

"Leia?" he croaked.

Wide grey eyes stared up at him, then dropped to his stiff cock. The flash of innocence and determina- tion fired up his blood. He angled the showerheads toward her lower body so he could see her face prop- erly and caught her chin in his hand.

She looked up again and slowly circled her lips with her tongue. "I'll learn ways to give you more. Teach me, Noah."

God.

"Put your hands on my thighs."

She obeyed immediately, her nails lightly grazing his skin. He shuddered and eyed the bench a few feet away. If this went the way he intended it to go, he'd lose his mind and possibly the power of his legs before this was over. But right then, shifting even an inch from where he stood felt impossible. So he planted his feet more firmly. "Open your mouth. Wider. Eyes on me."

He slid in slowly, giving her time to get used to his thickness. Her mouth started to close over his head, the warm suction tugging at him. "No, don't suck. Not yet. I want to feel that stud."

She opened again. He pushed in further, scraping against her teeth and sliding over her tongue. Her jaw lowered as she struggled to accommodate him. He pulled out just before he hit the back of her throat, savoring the moment, torturing himself. He fucked her mouth, groaning each time his cock emerged glistening with her saliva. After a few strokes, she began to curve her tongue around him, applying subtle pressure to the underside of his shaft.

Fast learner.

"Do you want to suck me off, sweetheart?"

"Hmm," she mumbled, her eyes affirming her answer.

"You have my permission," he said.

Her mouth closed over him in a greedy gulp, pulling him as deep as she could take. She barely reached halfway. "You need to flatten your tongue, baby. I need to be deeper inside you." He pushed in another inch, scraped his cock over her diamond stud, and stars exploded across his vision.

Fuck.

It wasn't enough. He slid his fingers into her hair and tightened his grip. "Suck harder. Make my cock hurt."

She hollowed her cheeks. He slammed into her mouth, hit the back of her throat. "God, yes!"

A smug look entered her eyes and she quickly established a rhythm, sucking him deep and hard. Sensation exploded all over his body. He began to shake. His balls tightened, and he gripped her harder.

Her nails dug in deeper, and he knew he was about to lose it. Not yet. Fuck no, not yet. "Hands behind your back and open your legs," he barked. That she managed to obey without losing her rhythm blew his mind.

He retreated a half step, forcing her to lean forward, arch her back. He looked down at her ass, at the clear spank marks marring her skin, and his cock swelled thicker. She gagged and he cursed.

Quickly locating the button he needed, he pressed

it. The powerful jet hit her pussy in a hot spray. She jerked wildly, and his cock slipped out of her mouth. Making a sound of distress, she twisted her head and caught him back with a sloppy, greedy pull, then doubled the pressure of her suction.

His free hand slammed against the wall. "*Jesus*. I'm so fucking grateful you've never done this to any other guy. Otherwise I'd have to hunt him down and destroy him."

She sucked him relentlessly, eagerly, until he lost the ability to think straight. With a thick, guttural shout, he jerked into her mouth. Hot, thick and endless, he came like a damned freight train. And she took it all. Dear God, she swallowed every drop of semen like a champ. All without once taking her eyes off him.

He released her hair, noticed his hands—hell, his whole body—were shaking. He caressed her cheek, her neck, anywhere he could touch without moving too far and losing the balance in his kitten-weak legs.

"Leia. Jesus, you're so damned near perfect." He couldn't speak above a croak.

She started to answer, then moaned, her hips moving in a series of helpless rolls. Watching her with her hands behind her back, legs wide open to the powerful spray of water, struggling not to come, re-energized him. Cracked the door to his fantasies wider.

He grabbed her arms and hauled her up. She was so close her whole body trembled. He contemplated just fucking her right there against the wall. But he wanted to make it good for her. And yes, he also wanted to test her boundaries a little bit more. Make her crazy with need the way she drove him over the edge with desire.

He carried her over to the smooth wooden bench and placed her in front of it. "Bend over. Lay your cheek against the seat. Hands behind your back."

Another wild tremble, followed by compliance. He trailed his hand down her back to her ass, then lower to her crease. She was soaking wet, slick, silky and hot. He smacked her pussy and she cried out.

"Does that hurt?" he demanded.

"Y... yes."

"Do you want me to stop?"

"No."

"What do you want?"

"More. I want more, please." He gave her more until her cries smashed into one another, her legs shaking as she struggled to stay upright.

Then he sank down and kissed her raging-hot sex, soothing her with his tongue. He pushed his tongue inside her, and she clenched hard around him.

"Don't come."

"I can't... hold it."

"Yes, you can."

He crouched next to her and looked into her flushed, beautiful face. Her mouth was open, gasping in desperate breaths. He trailed his fingers down her cheek. "Do you trust me? Not with everything outside this time and place, but right here, right now. Do you trust me to take care of you?"

"Yes."

His chest tightened, and his jaw clenched against an emotion he hadn't been aware of as it trawled through him. Doubt. He'd been afraid he would fail, that she would reject him if he took things too far.

"Noah?"

He blinked. "Yeah."

"I need you. Don't let her get in your head."

He surged to his feet and stumbled back a step. For a second he wondered whether it was wise to feel this visceral connection with another human being.

Opening up to Ashley about his needs had nearly brought him undone. She'd twisted him inside out and nearly ruined his life in the process. He'd had to seek therapy; *therapy*, for God's sake. He'd allowed someone else in his head, someone who'd reassured him he wasn't crazy, even while she eye-fucked him and then spread her legs for a taste of what he was capable of.

He looked down at Leia, perfectly laid out for him, waiting, trusting. She was getting under his skin. Fuck, who the hell was he kidding? She was already there, wedged deep.

She could be everything he needed.

Yeah, but for how long?

He pushed the voice away. "Don't move. I'll be right back."

27

She waited, her ass in the air, her heart hammering. Waited for him to come back and do goodness knows what to her. It would involve fucking... that much was guaranteed.

But the rest was all mystery. Anticipatory. Predatory. But still a mystery, tinged with danger that snapped like an electric current along her nerves. But no fear.

She trusted him.

She needed time to process that. Time to ponder why handing over the most damaged part of herself to a man she'd only just met could be so... freeing... so mind-blowing.

He returned, and her thoughts fractured.

Her lowered stance meant she saw his muscular thighs first, followed by his stiff, thick cock. She'd tasted that beautiful organ, still had the sticky, salty taste of him in her mouth. Another heady experience she'd never anticipated she'd relish so much. She wanted to do it all over again...

Her gaze shifted higher, and her breath snagged in her lungs. He was holding a black leather belt and two silk bathrobe ties.

Her heart rate kicked up several notches. Her hands started to slip from her back. "Noah..." Her voice quivered.

He stopped beside her. Ran his hand over her cheek, her neck, down her arm to rub his fingers over the tattoo covering her ribcage. "Remember what I said to you when we first met? About you deserving only the best?"

"Yes."

"I meant every word. I will never break your beautiful spirit, never cause you to feel fear or regret. You're brave and amazing. You intoxicate me with just one look. I want to make you soar, sweetheart. Higher than you've ever soared before. Where no other person besides me will ever be able to take you. Will you let me?"

She could get up, walk out, any time she chose. He

wouldn't hurt her. Wouldn't take anything she didn't want to give.

That gut-deep certainty made her nod.

He increased the pressure on her tattoo. "Vocalize, baby."

"Yes."

His breath shuddered out, and she realized he'd been holding it. Power surged through her along with a sharp burning in her chest. She'd felt that burning before. A softer, deeper, less jagged version. The enormity of those similarities made her gasp.

Time...

She needed time to sort out her crazy emotions.

He laid a hand on her lower back, just above where her wrists met, and pushed her down to kneeling. Her mind ceased to track. She willingly gave up on chasing her thoughts, ceded control to the power of his touch and the excitement chasing beneath her pulse.

"Spread your legs." She widened her stance. He looked down at her. "Wider," he said in a firm voice.

She moved her left knee, then her right, teetering a little off balance with her hands behind her back.

He dropped what he held next to her head on the seat and picked up one tie. "I'm going to secure your knees to the bench."

Her heart stuttered. "Okay."

His movements were precise, efficient, his touch unbelievably gentle. Then he knelt next to her, cradled her head in his hands and kissed her. Deeply erotic and intensely passionate, it transported her to a whole different realm. But he stopped before she was anywhere near satisfied. "Now your arms."

Stepping away, he picked up the belt and looped it under her bent arms. He yanked it tight, pulled her shoulders back until her muscles burned. The pain transmitted straight to her stinging core, mingled with the pleasure as his hand slipped between her legs and caressed her from asshole to clit. Moisture dripped from her, her body a balloon of pure desire that just kept expanding with each caress.

Over the sound of the pounding shower, she heard him secure the belt into its loop and then his hand was back in her hair, tightening, caressing.

"You're so beautiful, sweetheart. I can't tell you what your trust does to me."

His middle finger explored her asshole, light then firm, but he didn't go beyond that. When she found herself pushing toward his finger, whimpering for the unknown, he chuckled and leaned over her.

"Fucking you in the ass is a gift I'll take from you when you're not tied up. For that, you need to be in control of your own pleasure. Besides, I haven't nearly had enough of your exquisite cunt."

The images that raced through her brain had a full-body flush racing over her skin.

"Do I take it from that blush that you've never been ass-fucked?" Anticipation slurred his question, tightened his fist in her hair.

"N... no."

He groaned. "We're going to be so good together. So fucking incredible."

He let go of her hair and gently massaged her neck, her shoulders, and all the way down her back. The gentle petting motion soothed even as it raised her temperature. Her insides clenched and un-clenched as merciless hunger clawed at her insides. He caressed her whole body, down to her feet and back up again. The position of her arms brought pain each time she moved. Her knees were digging into the marble floor, but she would've died before she begged to be released. Because she knew what was coming would be an experience never to be equaled. She just wished he would hurry up.

"I need you, Noah."

"You'll have me." He brought his hand down sharply on her ass, the sound hard and wet in the bathroom. "All of me. Right now."

He rose off his knees, slid on a condom and crouched above her. Then he slid slowly into her with a heavy grunt, his cock filling her so fully she squealed. And still he kept going, burying all nine inches inside her until the head of his cock brushed the edge of her womb. He held himself there, balancing her on the knife-edge of pleasure and pain. One hand slid up her back and curled around her throat, his grip firm enough to make her heartbeat echo in her ears. She clenched harder around him and shuddered from the exquisite flood of sensations.

They stayed like that for a full minute.

Against her splayed hands, his stomach muscles quivered as he fought for control. "Sweet holy heaven."

She wanted to turn her head, watch his face, but his grip and the ties held her completely immobile. She wanted to plead with him to move inside her, but he was in total control.

"Beg me to fuck you, Leia. Beg me to come."

"Please, Noah," she sobbed. "It hurts so bad."

He gave another rough grunt, then moved. Slow, long strokes at first, each soft slap of his balls against her clit wringing more pleasure from her. Gradually, he increased the tempo, ramming deep and hard.

Harder. Then all bets were off. Bliss drowned her as he fucked her with little mercy and expert strokes.

The man knew how to move, the flex and thrust of his hips so skillfully timed it felt like poetry in motion.

Tears filled her eyes, rushed down her cheeks at the sheer inexplicable beauty of what she was feeling. The pressure grew, filling her to brimming.

"Come, baby. Fly for me." He thrust hard, buried himself deep.

The first orgasmic wave was so strong it shook her off her knees. "Oh God, Noah!"

He gripped her waist, pushed her back down to receive the hailstorm of fire that rained on her, drowning her even as she burst out of her skin, soared high and wild, spasming in brutal clenches that had him shouting his agonized pleasure.

"Shit!" He pulled out and thrust back through her resisting flesh, shuddering against her as his cock thickened inside her. "God, Leia, you're destroying me," he panted. "Christ, I'm coming."

The raw agonized pleasure in his voice as he emptied himself inside her sent her soaring again. She'd always believed multiple orgasms were a myth. No more.

Noah collapsed on top of her, releasing her throat

to slide his arm around her shoulders and bury his face in her hair. Their harsh breaths steamed the air and his heartbeat drummed against her back.

Her heart was racing so loudly in her ears, it took her several seconds to understand the words he spoke against her ear. "I'm going to untie you now, okay?" he said gruffly.

She got away with a nod, probably because they were both struggling to breathe.

Gently, he released her. She remained where she was, too weak to move. Her shoulders and knees stung as blood flowed and muscles returned to their normal positions. He left her for a moment and returned with an uncapped bottle in his hand. Pouring a measure, he rubbed the lotion into her sore shoulders, elbows and knees. The scent of eucalyptus and lavender washed over her, and she sighed softly as lethargy blanketed her.

Then he scooped her up and sat on the bench, adjusted the spray of the shower so it rained a light mist over them and cradled her in his lap.

"Are you okay?" he murmured between kisses on her face and neck.

Her hand stole around his neck and emotion moved in her throat. "Yes. You made me feel... God, I can't describe it."

"You don't need to." He brushed her hair from her cheeks and tilted her face to his. "You're mine now, Leia. I'm never letting you go. Whatever ghosts or demons I need to slay in order to keep you I will slay. If you need to slay them on your own, I'll be right beside you. But know that from this moment on, you own me. And I fucking own you."

Warren Snyder watched the YouTube clip with his fingers steepled beneath his chin. Anyone who walked into his Palm Beach corner office would've been fooled into believing he was calm. On some level he was. From a very early age he'd trained himself to suppress his emotions unless he absolutely needed to show them. Most of the time he allowed enough to bleed through his voice to make a point.

But he was not calm. The overriding description he could conjure up was a sense of furious disquiet.

For five years he'd watched over her. Pieced her back together. Kept her from going over the edge.

Nurtured her.

Readied her.

His patience had been beyond exemplary, a fact for which he was quite proud. He liked to think Logan Michaels would've been proud, too, had he been alive.

But now...

Noah King.

The clip wound down to the last two minutes. Although the lead singer of the band commanded presence on the stage, it was the man who stood next to the electric guitarist that held Warren's attention. The man whose gaze was fixed squarely on the woman on the stool as he strummed the guitar, his intent as blatant as the floodlights bathing the stage in harsh light.

Warren switched his gaze to her, and his fingers pressed harder into each other. She glowed with health and vitality, and her grey eyes held very little of the shadows that had plagued her for so long.

He was responsible for that.

Everything she'd become she owed to him. She'd accepted that a long time ago. Had also accepted that the next step hovered just beyond the horizon.

He'd allowed her this one brush stroke on the canvas he'd carefully created. After all, he wasn't a complete tyrant. The victory wouldn't be sweet unless she came to him fully and of her own accord.

What he hadn't calculated for was how broad a stroke she intended to wield. He watched the last thirty seconds of the rehearsal, watched her lose herself in the embrace that was taken in full view of the world.

He inhaled and opened his senses to allow his emotions to flood in. Just enough so he could acknowledge their presence, then free himself of it and get down to the business of strategizing the best way forward.

Anger. Ten seconds.

Disappointment. Twelve.

Jealousy. Seven seconds.

Arousal. Thirty... no, forty seconds.

He processed them all and lit the match to his emotional torch paper. He breathed through the fumes, hit the *replay* button and watched the clip to the end with complete detachment.

Noah King was not his enemy. But he seemed intent on taking his prize; taking what belonged to him. It was unfortunate that he didn't know that hell would burn itself out before Warren ever relinquished Leia Michaels to another man.

Calmly, he shut off the computer and picked up the phone.

29

"Wake up, sweetheart. Lunch is here."

Leia scrambled through clouds of sleep and warm sheets. "Don't you mean breakfast?" She sat up and brushed back her hair. Lean, gentle hands replaced hers and took over the task.

She almost didn't want to open her eyes because that breathlessness that knocked her sideways each time she looked at him was getting out of control.

"Open your eyes, Leia." Unlike when they fucked, this was a gentle command.

She opened her eyes, and he smiled at her. "Hey, sleepyhead."

His gorgeous face made her chest ache, especially

when he smiled at her like that. "Hey. What time
is it?"

The sun blazed through the bedroom, bathing
him in white light that accentuated broad shoulders,
wavy hair. Unable to resist, she caressed his face.

"It's nearly one o'clock."

"What?" She glanced out the French windows and
frowned. "I've been asleep for six hours?"

His smile widened. "City-hopping and insatiable
sex catches up with you eventually. You dropped like
a log almost mid-orgasmic scream this morning."

Her face flamed. They'd barely checked into their
hotel in Cannes last night before he dragged her into
the bedroom where he surprised her by letting her go
on top and giving her free rein over her orgasm. The
power of her position had gone to her head. She'd
ridden him with every last ounce of energy she had,
which had been nearly depleted after the bathroom
episode in Vienna and the dash two hours later to the
airport to board the jet.

"Come on, the food's getting cold." He drew back
the sheets and held out his hand.

She got up, semi-conscious of her disheveled state
next to the sharply pressed black slacks and open-
necked white shirt he wore. He caught her close,

curled his hand around her throat and kissed her deep and long. A little of her agitation evaporated.

Pulling away, he tugged her to the dressing room of their Louis XIV decorated suite and grabbed another pristine white shirt from the hanger. He waited till she pushed her arms through and buttoned it up. "That should do for now. You can get dressed after we eat."

The Indigo Lounge Cannes sat on La Croisette Boulevard and overlooked the perfect blue waters of the French Riviera. From their penthouse balcony, the view to the marina on the right was picture perfect, small sailboats and launches slipping between fuck-off yachts with practiced ease.

Noah pulled out a chair and she sat down. At the far end of the table, a laptop and papers were spread where he'd been working. He strode over, picked up the hotel phone and spoke in rapid French.

She watched him pad back to her, his body relaxed but no less smoldering.

He nodded at her plate. "I took a gamble and aimed for somewhere between frogs legs and escargots, and burger and fries."

"I've braved the former and yep, it's an experience I'd rather pass. The latter is a weakness I'm trying to stay away from." She lifted the lid on her plate, inhaled the aromas and smiled. "Almost perfect."

He relaxed in his seat and raised a brow. "What did I get wrong?"

"Stuffed peppers with chicken and the truffle scrambled eggs—yum. The roasted zucchini, not so much."

He picked up the serving spoon, lifted the zucchini off her plate and onto his, and replaced it with two of his stuffed peppers. Then he poured a glass of chilled Sancerre and passed it to her.

"Is this going to cost me?" she joked.

He winked. "Of course, baby. But nothing you won't be dying to pay."

Leia thanked her lucky stars she was seated. The power behind his smile hit her like a blow to the gut and radiated throughout her body.

She'd noticed that he'd been smiling more in the last twelve hours, and she couldn't help but think the bathroom episode had something to do with it.

His words rushed through her head, filling her with equal parts excitement and apprehension.

Could she survive Noah King in the outside world, away from this ephemeral bubble they'd created with sex?

Despite what she'd revealed so far, he didn't know

nearly enough about her to make the declarations he'd made in Vienna. But telling him any more risked bringing the ugly outside in. Not just yet...

"You're frowning. We can order something else if you want."

She shook her head. "No, this is great." She picked up the cutlery and took a bite of the stuffed peppers. With a groan of pleasure, she tucked in, not stopping until her plate was clear and the wine half finished. She sat back against the cushioned seat and basked in the sun's warmth. "How long do we have before the zero gravity experience?"

"We're not going. I cancelled it a few minutes ago."

For some reason, a spark of irritation fizzed through her at his answer. She put her wine down. "I'm sitting right here, Noah. You could have asked me what I wanted before you cancelled it."

His gaze narrowed on her face. "You have shadows under your eyes, and you've yawned three times in the last five minutes. At the very least you need to be awake for an experience like that. Otherwise it's stupid and dangerous, and I don't risk what's mine."

The possessive stamp in his voice rattled her further. "Be that as it may. I'd like a say in whatever plans you made on my behalf."

"I want to take care of you—"

"I can take care of myself!"

His gaze sharpened. "I get the feeling this isn't about a cancelled trip. What's really going on, Leia? And please do me the courtesy of not saying 'nothing.'"

"I wasn't going to."

"Great. Let's hear it."

"Last night... What you said—"

"That you're mine? You are."

She swallowed. "I don't... I'm not sure if I can be yours."

His face froze into a taut mask, his eyes boring into her like lasers. "Why the hell not? It isn't arrogance to believe that you wouldn't be here doing what you've been doing with me if you weren't free to be mine. You're not a liar and you're not into mind games. But I'll ask you anyway. Are you fucking someone else back in Miami?"

"No!"

He visibly relaxed, but his eyes didn't waver. "Do you plan to?"

She pressed her mouth together and shook her head.

"Vocalize, Leia. I need to hear the words."

"Why?" she flung at him. A part of her recognized that she was picking a fight purely based on the overwhelming need to give in to what he wanted, what she'd begun to crave... Noah King and everything he had to give her. "You can have any woman you want, Noah. Why do you want me when you barely know anything about me?"

"I want you for the same reason you want me. For the same reason you let me tie you to the bench last night. We connect beyond the here and now. Beyond the fact that we've only known each other four days. I crave your surrender. You crave my control. I promised you the stars, and I intend to give it to you. You just need to be brave enough to take it."

"My ghosts are very real, Noah."

His fist clenched. "Those are fucking excuses." His deep voice vibrated in the space between them. "I warned you when we met that I don't do light. I never have. The one-night stands were different, but they were not light. You don't get to walk away because you're scared, Leia. So if you want out of this incredible thing we've created, you need to find a better deal-breaker besides your ghosts."

She toyed with the rim of her glass, not wanting to hope, not wanting to contemplate what awaited her back in Miami. If she was daring to dream of the possibility of Noah in her future, there was a lot she'd have to tell him. "Even if I was selfish enough to ask you to accommodate all my baggage, what's to stop you hating me if I can't accommodate yours?"

His jaw flexed. "Explain."

Her pulse jumped under the searing intensity of his stare. "From what I overheard of your conversation yesterday, Ashley is waiting for you in Miami," she blurted. It was something she'd pushed to the back of her mind, not wanting it to taint the precious few days they had in their erotic bubble. Now it loomed large.

"My lawyers are taking care of it."

"She doesn't strike me as the type to let herself be handled."

"I don't give a fuck what she wants. One way or the other, she *will* be handled. She has no hold over me, Leia. Not anymore."

"But she gets to you."

His eyes swept down, then back up. "Yes, she does. It's not easy to admit that she brought out traits in me that made me despise myself. But it's over and done with. Now, do you have any other issues you want me to address, or can I take you back to bed and remind you why you won't be walking away when we get back to Miami?"

He was angry. And aroused. But she caught the underlying vulnerability in his voice when he spoke of his ex. Sure, he'd layered it with thick anger, but it was there. Whatever number she'd done on him still festered beneath all the raw masculine alpha male posturing. She'd wounded him. And he hated the reminder.

"You can take me back to bed."

He shoved his chair away, and she witnessed for herself just how aroused he was. Before he could scoop her up, she placed a hand on his chest. "Some women like angry sex, Noah. I'm not one of them."

He leaned both hands on the arms of her chair and lowered his face to hers. "One day you'll trust me to know exactly what you want. You'll trust me to know how to fuck you into a mood or out of it." He brushed his lips over hers. "And you'll know that me being angry doesn't translate to angry sex. Sex between us is sacred. It will never be an outlet that causes distress, but a joy that lifts our souls. Tell me you understand that?" he rasped against her lips.

She curled her hand over his heart, absorbed its steady beat, and her world tilted beneath her feet. "Yes, I do."

He picked her up and walked her past the billowing muslin curtains that framed the French windows, past the living room with eighteenth-century chandeliers, Carrara marble floors and gilt-frame mirrors.

In their bedroom, he laid her on the rumpled sheets of their four-poster bed and started unbuttoning her shirt. Looking into his face, Leia couldn't deny that something had shifted again between them, taken them another rung up from the bathroom incident.

Their initial white-hot chemistry was transcending into something else, something she couldn't quite describe. The raw, unfettered need in his eyes reflected the need writhing inside her.

"Noah..."

The phone beside the bed rang, startling them both. He released the last button and sat up, reefing his hand through his hair.

"This had better be important." He grabbed the handset and barked, "King."

He listened for a beat. "Who is this?" His voice was less irritated, but puzzled eyes shifted to her. "It's for you." He held out the phone to her and leaned against the bedpost.

She sat up and pulled her shirt closed. Noah saw it and his jaw tightened.

"Hello?"

"Hello, my dear. Who's your friend?" Warren

asked.

Her gaze flicked to where Noah lounged, arms folded, narrowed blue eyes firmly on her.

"His name is Noah."

"Does he know who you are?"

More than I would ever have believed possible. But she knew what Warren was asking: *Does he know how damaged you are?* Sucking in a short breath, she answered, "No. I don't think so."

"Will you be volunteering that information?" Warren pressed, his voice eerily unflappable.

"Maybe, I haven't given it much thought." *Liar.*

"Are you sure?"

"You taught me to trust my instincts, Warren. It doesn't help me if you let me start questioning them."

Noah's interest sharpened, his eyes narrowing further.

"That wasn't my intention. I was merely urging you to exercise caution. Don't do anything foolish."

Too late...

"I won't." She caught a strand of hair and twisted it between her fingers.

Noah rose from where he sat and prowled closer. Catching her chin in his hand, he raised her face and stared at her, his expression fierce. His sheer willpower bore down on her with compelling force.

She swallowed. "Do you need anything else? I have to go."

Warren's pointed hesitation was a cool rebuke for rushing him. "I sent you the documents the board needs signed days ago. Production won't start on the autumn collection until we have your signature. Your delay in returning them is unacceptable."

His tone made her feel like a recalcitrant child. "I'm sorry, it skipped my mind."

"If you could see to it, I'd like to have it back by close of play today."

Demanding hands slid along her jaw and down to her throat to curl over her nape. The hold grounded her and made her soar at the same time.

"S... sure. I'll take care of it... Bye, Warren."

"Leia?"

"Yes?"

A tiny pause. "I've missed you."

She answered with the part of her that wanted everything to stay the same. The part that fought the changes and decisions she didn't want to make. "Me too."

Noah took the phone and dropped it into its cradle. He parted her shirt and divested her of it. Then he undressed without taking his eyes from her.

Prowling onto the bed, he parted her thighs and

settled himself between her legs. God, he felt so right there.

His thick cock probed her entrance, but he didn't slide in. Instead, he speared his fingers into her hair and continued to stare down at her.

"Everything okay?"

"Yes," she answered.

"Who was that?"

"Warren Snyder."

"He's not a ghost."

"No."

"Is he an obstacle?"

"No. He's my savior," she whispered.

30

Noah waited a beat to let the rush in his ears die down a little. When he was sufficiently calm, he tried to speak. "Your savior."

"Yes." She opened her mouth, changed her mind, and bit her lip.

He rubbed his thumb over her lower lip, felt it tremble against his skin. "I'm going to find out everything about you, Leia. You can speed things along by volunteering information or I can seduce it out of you. Either way, you will tell me what I need to know."

"That's not fair, Noah."

"Fuck fair. You've just told me someone holds an important place in your life. By the sound of his voice, he's not a hundred years old with fading eyesight. And I'm guessing he's not a blood relation."

She swallowed. "No."

Another red haze washed over his eyes, and he tried to suppress the clamoring in his head. "Why was he asking about me?"

"I don't know... He was curious, I guess."

"Tell me about him, Leia. How is he your savior?"

"He was there when most of the shit in my life happened."

"Elaborate."

She grew restless beneath him, flexing her hips in that helpless way that caught him on the raw. Not reacting to the proximity of their bodies was impossible, but right. What she needed to tell him was more important than his body's demands.

"Warren was my father's best friend. They lost touch for a while after college, but they reconnected at my parents' wedding. Dad gave him a job at the company and offered him a seat on the board. Eventually, he became the second majority shareholder— he owns 49 percent of La Carezza. He was there the day my father drowned. And the day my mother..." Shadows clouded her eyes. "I was seventeen and essentially an orphan. He stepped in, and the court agreed to appoint him my guardian."

Tears filled her eyes, and Noah's chest tightened painfully. He kissed her, then tried to comfort her in the most elemental way he knew. "I'm not wearing a condom, baby. Is that okay?"

Her breath shuddered out and her pupils dilated. A part of him experienced the tiniest twinge for using the blatantly powerful tool. But then her hands slid from his ribcage to his waist and her nails scraped over his skin, holding him closer. And just like that, he was drowning in her, desperate for her.

"Yes. God, yes please."

He cradled her skull and slid slowly into her fist-tight heat. A wild shudder rolled over her and her nails clawed him. By sheer strength of will, he held himself still.

"Keep talking," he grated out.

"He... he was there when I fell apart. He saw me through half a dozen therapists and a fortnight on a psyche ward."

"Christ. I'm sorry, baby."

She gripped him tight and blinked back fresh tears. "I was a mess, Noah. I still am."

His fingers tightened in her hair. "Like hell you are. You're a genius with innovative ideas that blow my mind. You're beautiful and generous beyond words, and you sing like a fucking champ."

Her watery smile turned into a gasp when, unable to help himself, he moved inside her. Heavens above, she felt like hot silk, binding him, squeezing him, fracturing his mind. But questions lingered, ones he wasn't prepared to let go unanswered.

"Is there anything else I need to know about Snyder? Is he the reason you are reluctant to give us a chance in the real world?"

Her nostrils flared. "You're the first man I've shown an interest in since... I'm scared of taking this thing out of this bubble."

"Because you don't think it'll survive or you don't want to disappoint him?" He hated himself for probing to see how important the other man was to her. But he was man enough to admit he was too far gone to pretend he didn't care.

Leia Michaels belonged to him. Any threat to that reality needed to be identified and neutralized.

"God, Noah. You're everything I've dreamed of and more. You make me... I feel like the most beautiful woman in the world when you're with me like this," she whispered. "The one thing I'd never be is worried that anyone would find you lacking. I know how you make me feel."

His breath fractured. "But?"

"I'm scared too. I don't know how to be in a relationship, casual or otherwise. The only meaningful relationship I've had recently is with Warren."

For purely selfish reasons, he despised hearing that name on her lips. "Do me a favor, sweetheart. Don't mention his name when I'm balls-deep inside you. I don't care how important he is to you. It drives me a little nuts."

"You wanted me to talk about him."

He grimaced. "I know. I'm a fucking irrational idiot. As for the rest. You feel like a beautiful woman because you are. If I contribute even a little to elevating that feeling, then I consider it an honor. I'm glad you're scared because I'm fucking terrified. Terrified that I turned your ass black and blue and you begged me for more. No one has owned me so totally by giving themselves so completely like you have, Leia. I can't imagine tomorrow or next week without you. I will fight to the death to hang on to that. You're too precious for me to lose. So live in the moment and leave the rest to me. I've got this. I've got us."

Another full body shudder racked her and she shook her head. "God, Noah, I can't... You don't know what—"

"Yes, I do. I feel it too."

Grey eyes met his and grew dark with longing that

echoed his. "Make love to me, Noah. Make the doubts go away."

Noah wondered how he could be hard as steel inside her and yet feel like every other part, and mainly his heart, was melting all over her. He swallowed hard and slid one hand under her ass. "Ah, sweetheart," he groaned around the lump in his throat. "I would slay monsters for you, all day, every day."

31

I've got us.

Leia tried to stem the giddiness in her heart but failed completely. A full day and a half after Warren's call and her conversation with Noah and her breath still caught each time she replayed those three little words.

She adjusted the off-the-shoulder diamante strap of the cream designer Grecian gown, which she'd bought in Cannes for the masked ball, and tried to stop the stupid smile from spreading across her face. After shattering her completely with slow, sizzling lovemaking yesterday, Noah had collapsed onto the bed and pulled her close. In the bathroom in Cannes, she'd been so busy absorbing the flood of sensation that came from breaking her sexual boundaries that she hadn't taken the time to savor the pure bliss of Noah taking her skin-to-skin.

Yesterday had remedied that, had shown her the sublime beauty of feeling him within her without barrier. When he came inside her, she'd cried all over again. Noah's face too had held a stunned wonder that echoed through her. The profound feeling had silenced them for a long time, until Noah had brushed his mouth across hers and pulled the sheets over them.

"The rest of today is room service, TV, and vegging-out day."

"Are you sure? I'm feeling really energized. Maybe we should revise that sex-in-zero-gravity thing."

He grinned. "It sounds like more trouble than it's worth. I've decided I like gravity much better. It keeps me anchored between your legs whenever I want. I'm not messing with that dynamic."

Her laughter drew an answering one from him. He'd slid his fingers through her hair and called her beautiful. She'd returned the gesture and called him a charming rogue.

They'd talked for hours after that, both silently agreeing to stay away from volatile subjects like saviors and ex-fiancées.

Besides cars, guitars had been his second love. He'd learnt everything there was to know about bass guitars before he'd turned eighteen. And given both his car and guitar collections to his younger brother who lived in Chicago when he moved from New York.

His closed expression as he'd said that had prevented her asking why.

She picked up her gold and cream mask and threaded the ivory plumed feathers through her fingers. There were parts of themselves they'd have to uncover eventually. If they stood a chance of attempting anything close to a healthy relationship, she needed to tell him what happened five years ago.

Her hands shook and she sucked in a breath. The bedside phone rang. She picked it up.

"Whose bright idea was it that we dress in separate hotels?" His voice rolled over her like a decadent dessert she couldn't get enough of.

"It's a masked ball, Noah. No point in making the effort if you know what I'm wearing."

"I took you shopping yesterday. I already know what you'll be wearing."

She smiled. "Wrong. I chose three dresses, so you have a 33 percent chance of getting it right."

"Sweetheart, every curve of your perfect body is

imprinted on my brain. Picking you out of a crowd, mask or no mask, will be as easy as breathing."

She didn't doubt him. The amount of time he'd spent exploring her body in the last thirty-six hours made her face redden. "I feel a distinct sense of disparity as far as exploration is concerned."

"Don't worry, baby, I'll give you the chance to address that injustice as soon as I sate my hunger for you. What underwear do you have on?" he demanded, his voice low and deep.

Heat flared across her skin. "White leather and lace thong. No bra."

"No bra," he repeated.

"I can't wear one with my gown."

"Damn." His voice had grown lower, heavier. "Who's driving you to the ball?"

"Bjorn's picking me up in five minutes."

He cursed again. "Make sure he keeps his hands to himself. Or you'll feel mine on your ass."

"Yes, Noah."

He fell silent for several heartbeats. "You will say those two words to me every day, at least a dozen times."

"What will I get in return?"

"Me. At your feet."

She gasped. "Noah."

"Hang up now, Leia, before I storm over there and put a big fucking hole in this evening's plans."

She hung up and dropped the phone on the bed. From the moment she laid eyes on him, Noah had set her emotions on overdrive. Now they were seriously threatening to spiral out of control. He dominated her with his presence, his words, his looks, his insatiable appetite.

In five short days, she'd become addicted to him. Wanted him in her life despite the caution that they might not survive full disclosure of her past. She loved his domination of her, loved losing her control to him.

Before she'd boarded the Indigo Lounge, she'd only read about dynamics like that in books. The reality of it... Hell, she could never have imagined it. He'd branded her, imprinted himself on her skin and on her psyche.

As crazy as it was real and tangible, she was falling in love with Noah King.

* * *

The limo crawled along Husova Street towards the Clam-Gallas Palace. Beside her, Bjorn made small talk that she absently participated in, but inside, Leia's pulse was jumping with the decision she'd made on the way over.

She would tell Noah before they returned to Miami. He would be horrified and judgmental... or he would not be. Either way, she wouldn't have to nurse the fear of the unknown. Pursing her lips, which threatened to tremble, she drew in a breath as the limo stopped in front of the Baroque Palace.

Music from a string quartet drifted out onto the square cobbled courtyard.

She entered the vast entry hall and mingled with other costumed guests. Leia tried not to look too conspicuous as she sought out Noah.

She recognized the blowjob couple from the plane by the guy's ginger hair. He was dressed as Caßesar and she as Cleopatra, and their costumes worked despite their coloring. The other woman caught her staring and waved.

She lifted her hand to return the greeting and felt Noah's presence. Heart thumping, she started to turn. Rough hands closed over her shoulders.

"About damn time you got here," he rasped in her ear.

"Noah, you're ruining the whole idea of the masked ball. You're not supposed to know who I am." Her protest was half-hearted since she'd been busy seeking him out. Seeing him in front of her, broad-shouldered, the sculpted perfection of his face, that unapologetic *maleness*, her mouth went dry.

"Fuck that. I've been without you for four hours. You were supposed to be here a half hour ago. What the hell took you so long?" His hand drifted up and down her back a few times before dropping to her ass. Then he did that squeeze-pull thing that brought her flush against his hard body.

"We hit a bit of traffic."

His mouth grazed the part of her cheek the mask didn't cover before he kissed the corner of her mouth. "I've missed you. It's been a little hellish imagining that Nordic beefcake's eyes all over you."

"Bjorn was a perfect gentleman."

Electric-blue eyes raked her up and down. "Are you sure you don't want to ditch this thing? We'll make up the rest of your highs in bed."

Temptation weakened her knees. "I just got here. This is supposed to be one of the most beautiful baroque palaces in Europe. Allow me a moment of culture before you attempt to debauch me."

He smiled. "To be properly debauched we'd have to do it in a church. Actually, there's a room upstairs that we can pretend is a church. The fireplace is large enough to be an altar. I can worship your tight little cunt there."

She giggled. "'Your body is the church where Nature asks to be reverenced.'"

He took her hand, placed it on his arm and steered her away from the crowd. They found a square recessed space overlooking a side street, and he pulled her close. "You can't quote de Sade unless you're sitting on my dick. It's a prerequisite. You can recite the whole thing while I make you come."

She grinned. "I don't know all of it, just the dirty bits."

He laughed, his blue eyes twinkling down at her. His fingers traced the white ropes she'd used to twist her hair into a Grecian style and touched the gold dangling earrings. "I'll teach you the rest while you ride my dick. I'm generous like that. God, you look breathtaking, Leia."

She settled her hand on his chest, absorbing his heartbeat. "Thank you. I love your mask."

The winged black silk and onyx design covered him from forehead to nose. As he looked down at her, a lock of hair fell over his eyes. She brushed it back and he caught her fingers in his, brought them to his mouth. "I'm glad you've seen beneath it. Not a lot of people have."

Her heart stuttered then sped up. It was now or never. "Noah, before this goes any further, there's something I need to tell you."

His smile fractured around the edges. "Words that makes me wish all over again that we weren't stuck in this place. Tell me."

Violin strings from the quartet struck a high-pitched chord, and she shook her head. "It can wait till we get back. I just wanted to lay the foundations before I chickened out."

Blue eyes narrowed. "How bad is it?"

She shivered. "If I could keep it a secret forever I would."

He reached out and brushed his knuckle over her cheek. "Just say the word and we'll leave. And whatever it is, if it's shaped you into the beautiful and generous person you are today, you have nothing to be worried about."

"Even if it's shaped out of self-reproach?"

He froze. "Then you'll have to find a way to forgive yourself or live with it. Don't let it pull you down." His hand drifted down to where her tattoo branded her skin. "You're already halfway to finding closure, sweetheart. You took a bold step in coming on this trip. Don't stop now."

She shook her head. "This was one step, taken under the heading of desperation."

"I'm glad you took that step. If you let me, I'll help you figure out the next. Will you?"

"I... I can't let you offer that yet. Not until you know."

He remained thoughtful for several seconds. Then he nodded. "Okay. I'll get us a drink and let you talk baroque to me until you're ready to leave."

Champagne appeared as if by magic. Noah commandeered the head valet and requested a tour after the mouth-watering banquet was served on long wooden tables. Every time his gaze slid to hers and she saw his concern, she knew her face was betraying the anxiety eating through her stomach. He touched her at every opportunity, guided her through the stunningly decorated palace and listened with interest at the history of the place. But she couldn't dismiss the vibrating tension that belied his calm.

They swept back down the grand staircase just as a gong sounded and the guests split into four groups. In the middle of the room stood a giant stone urn containing small indigo envelopes.

"What's going on?" she asked.

"According to the brief, this is where the evening takes on swinging masked ball status."

Her eyes widened. "We're not doing that, are we?"

"Hell, no. Your name isn't in there. Neither is mine. Do you want to stay for another drink or do you want to leave?"

"Leave, please."

He squeezed her hand. "Good."

The limo whisked them through the Old Town with its quaint charm and history-rich streets. Noah whipped off his mask and dropped it onto the seat between them. He settled one hand on her thigh and caressed her.

"Are you going to take off that mask?" he asked.

She shrugged and traced the velvet pattern. "In a while. I like it."

"You can't hide behind it forever, Leia." His tone was half gentle, half warning.

She swallowed. "I know."

He caught her chin and dragged his thumb over her lower lip. "Poor baby, you're shaking. Did no one teach you not to start something you couldn't finish?"

She jerked and knocked his hand away. "No, don't!"

He inhaled sharply. "Leia, what's wrong? You're as white as a fucking sheet."

As if floodgates had been open in her mind, vile words flowed over one another. "Just..." She breathed deep, struggling for calm. "Don't say that to me."

Puzzled eyes searched hers. "Don't say what?"

She closed her eyes and shook her head. "What you just did—"

The limo drew to a halt at the entrance of their hotel. She jumped out before Noah could stop her. "Dammit, Leia. Stop."

Her heels clicked on polished stone as she rushed past reception. "Miss Michaels, I have several messages for you—"

She stumbled to a halt and turned to look at the concierge and the papers he offered. She held out her hand for them and stuffed them in her purse.

Noah reached her and took her arm. "Besides Snyder, who else knows you're here?"

"No one."

"Okay, so we'll assume the messages are from him. Whatever he wants can wait until you explain what just happened."

He pulled her into the elevator and caught her in his arms. A swift, hard kiss landed on her temple before he tucked her head beneath his chin. She couldn't stop trembling, couldn't stop the sickening reel of words and images in her head.

I'll teach you not to start something you can't finish.

They rode up in silence, her arms stiff at her sides, her heart hammering loud and relentless in her ears.

When the elevator doors opened, he swung her into his arms and entered their suite. The door slammed behind them. He strode to the large arm-chair and sank into it, his arms clamped around her.

"Take off your mask." It was a command, figurative and real.

Hands shaking, Leia drew off the mask and glanced at his face.

He cursed. "Jesus, what the hell's going on? You look like someone's just killed your puppy. What did I say?" Anguish coated his voice.

"Someone said that to me once... about teaching me a lesson for starting something I couldn't finish."

Hooded blue eyes narrowed. "When you were a kid?"

"I was sixteen when he first said that to me."

"Who?"

"My stepfather. This... this was what I was going to tell you."

He tensed beneath her and his eyes darkened, but his face remained a cool mask "Go on."

"I talked my mom into letting me move into our pool house when I turned sixteen. She resisted for a while, but she knew I couldn't stand the tension and passive-aggressive fighting between her and my step-father. Anyway, she helped me turn what had been my dad's home office into my bedroom." She plucked at the corner of her mask and swallowed. "But my mom forgot that my dad had installed cameras in his office after a break-in. At first I didn't think anything of it when my stepfather walked in at inappropriate times or in the middle of the night when I took the odd skinny dip in the pool."

Noah's hand tightened on her knees, and his jaw turned to steel. "Fucking Christ."

"I hated the way he looked at me, but I was a brat back then. The world had taken the most important person in my life and replaced it with an asshole who didn't treat my mom right and looked at me with his cock in his eyes. I acted out a lot, almost dared him to do his worst." She whispered that last part, icy fingers of guilt clenching her heart.

His arms caressed up and down her arms. "Oh God, baby."

A furtive look at Noah's face showed the braced anguish in the dark blue depths of his eyes. Her heart squeezed, and she forced herself to go on.

"A couple of months after I turned seventeen, I threw a party. It was a classic parents-out-of-town party with too much booze and rich bratty kids. My boyfriend stayed over. I woke up minus my virginity and completely underwhelmed by an experience I could barely recall."

"Leia." His voice was a rough rumble. The hand on her thigh rose to splay over her stomach, and the other gripped her nape. His chest rose and fell in a jagged exhale.

She'd become attuned enough to his reactions to know he didn't like the idea of someone else having her, even if it was past tense. But it was also coupled with a gentleness and strength that calmed her roiling emotions.

"Sexual frustration and self-destruct mode isn't a healthy mix. I was using my vibrator when my stepfather walked in on me."

Noah's growl was low and deadly. She shivered.

"He told me he'd seen the video of Brad and me. He described it in vivid detail and told me how much better he would do it."

"*Motherfucker!*"

"He called me a cock tease... A shameless whore."

You're a dirty little cock tease. You deserve my cock up your ass for your little stunts...

"Then he raped me in my bedroom."

32

From a broken acorn...

Noah wanted to ask her to repeat what she'd said. But words like those couldn't be mistaken. And even if he wanted to believe he'd overheard, the look in her eyes told him he hadn't.

Several puzzles fell into place. Seventeen. The age her life had imploded. The age her mother had taken her life.

"Leia, did your mother see what he did?" He could barely speak past the fury and the harrowing sorrow he felt on her behalf.

Her grey eyes were almost black with painful shadows and unshed tears. She nodded. "She came into the pool house with my father's gun. He kept it in his safe. That's where they found the monitors, so I'm guessing she saw what he was doing and grabbed the gun. She was so calm, Noah. So steady. She told me she was sorry for failing me. She shot him. Then turned the gun on herself. I tried to get to her. God, I tried so hard but... he was on top of me. By the time I freed myself it was too late..."

Wrenching tears ripped from her throat and poured down her face. His heart broke wide open with each sound. He tugged her to his chest and closed his eyes. "Baby, it wasn't your fault. He was the sick one. The creep spied on you and got off on it. He was the fucking adult. There's nowhere in this universe where that can be turned back on you."

She shook her head, despair in each movement. "It wasn't just that. The coroner found signs of abuse all over my mom's body." She shuddered. "I'd left her alone in the house with that monster when deep down I knew what he was capable of."

"Dammit, it wasn't your fault. Think of what else he could've done to you if you'd remained in the house—"

"When we met, I called you a tease. I know what it is to be one."

"No, you weren't. I was playing hot and cold. I

wanted you beyond reason, beyond sanity, and I was scared of what I'd do to you if you gave in to me."

"My last therapist told me I won't find closure until I accept my part in what happened."

His teeth gritted hard enough to make his jaw ache. He captured her chin and kissed her hard, branding her with his tongue, his mouth, adoring her with his touch in the hope that he could wash away a little bit of the bastard's stink off her psyche.

He closed his eyes when she finally relaxed and melted into him. He slid his hand up and down her arm.

"Fuck the shrinks. Not all of them know what the hell they're talking about. Trust me, I know."

"Warren agrees," she whispered. "He thinks owning the guilt will make me stronger."

An irrational wave of anger swept over him. "Bullshit."

Noah had looked up the other guy this afternoon while he'd been holed up in the hotel across the street, wondering if he'd lost his mind for agreeing to the whole masquerade ball and separate hotels crap.

On the surface, Snyder's success and standing were impressive enough. He had other business interests besides Leia's company that Noah had dealt with in the past. But something about the guy, who was more than twenty years older than Leia, made him uneasy.

He'd seemed too perfect, too put together to the point of being icily aloof. But there was something else in the guy's eyes that made his gut clench. He'd have been the last person he pictured his passionate and generous Leia leaning on.

"Listen to me. You have nothing to be ashamed of, and nothing to feel guilty about. You'd already lost so much. The bastard not only replaced your dad, he also took your mother away. You would've been a saint not to act out in some way. That's no excuse for him to do what he did. And I'll castrate anyone who dares to tell you otherwise. Do you hear me?"

She gave a half nod and Noah knew he'd have to work harder to convince her. She'd gone far too long with her trauma of being violated and guilt ingrained in her. He kissed her, willing her chill away. She leaned into him and his heart soared.

Rising, he walked them into the bedroom and crossed over to the bathroom. He undressed her first, then himself. Keeping one arm around her, he ran a bath. Her head remained on his shoulder the whole time, until he lifted her into the heated water and slid in behind her.

When he went to settle her against him, she

turned sideways. Her eyes were slightly red and her cheeks were flushed. The water lapped her breasts and the white ropes twined in her golden hair. He'd never seen anything more beautiful in his life.

"You're breathtaking, my darling. Inside and out. I intend to repeat that until you believe it."

She bit her lip, and he stopped himself from roaring the words until she drowned in them.

"What?" he asked instead.

"I've kept a very low profile for a long time, since it happened. Warren's house is big enough—"

"Wait, you live with Warren?" Every last atom in his body froze.

She nodded warily. "He was appointed my guardian, remember?"

"That was when you were seventeen." He tried to keep his voice even, but it vibrated with the dangerous energy lashing through him.

"I saw no reason to alter the arrangement. Like I said, his place is more than big enough for the two of us."

Noah didn't even think twice about making plans to change that. Curbing the need to stamp his possession over her one more time, he picked up a sponge and rubbed it over her shoulders. "So you kept a low profile..."

"Yes, but there were cops, and lawyers, and media when it happened. Every now and then someone tries to revive the story. I just want to warn you—"

He tilted her chin. "You're worried about me?"

"You need to know that it will most probably rear its head."

He thought of the carnage he'd left behind in New York. Something he'd have to tell her when she wasn't so traumatized from rehashing the past. "Sweetheart, I've lived through worse. You have no reason to worry about me." Leaning forward, he kissed her. "But I'm glad you are."

Her mouth opened beneath his, and he deepened the kiss. When she groaned, he dropped the sponge and cupped her breasts. Short flicks of his thumb across her hard peaks earned him a beautiful gasp.

She turned fully and straddled him. Fire lashed through his veins. He slid his hand lower between her legs and found her wet and hot.

Noah sent up a prayer of thanks that what had happened to her hadn't dimmed her sexuality one little bit. It had, understandably, warped her ability to trust, and his jaw clenched as he wished her violator were alive so he could slowly squeeze the life out of him.

She arched into his touch, fucking the fingers he inserted into her.

"God, you're so soft. So generous with your body." And the fact that she loved what he did to her... That just blew his mind.

His cock grew hard against her ass. She felt it and whimpered.

"I need you, Noah."

"How?"

She pulled back and licked her trembling lips. "Hard and fast. Ravage me. Please."

Whatever she wanted, he would give. "Brace your hand on the edge, baby."

He lifted one thigh and plunged into her tight sheath. His other hand fisted a handful of hair, and he bit her shoulder.

She screamed even as her pussy grew hotter around his cock. She angled her hips, pushed her groin into his as he slammed into her.

"Yes, Noah!"

Her hands flew to her breasts, tugging at her nipples as he invaded her slick channel. He released her shoulder so he could watch her torture her stiff nubs.

"God, baby. I love it when you do that."

She leaned in closer. "Bite me again," she groaned.

He caught her skin between his teeth and ravaged

the tender flesh. Her moans grew louder, her hips circling as she worked herself into a frenzy.

"Ah, that feels so good."

"I know. And it's about to feel even better."

He stroked into her fast and steady, his cock pushing all the way in with each thrust. Her mouth dropped open, sucking in desperate air as her eyes slid shut.

Pleasure poured over her face, and his heart stopped.

Letting go of her thigh, he drew her to him. "We came on this trip with uncomplicated sex in mind. I was such an ass to you that first hour. You could so very easily have walked away. Now I can't imagine being here with anyone but you. I want to be everything you need, fulfill your every craving, slay your every fear. Say you'll let me."

He rolled his hips, and her eyelids quivered. "Yes, Noah... I'll let you."

Light flared through his chest. His every sense shook as he grappled with what was happening to him. He was unraveling, spiraling out of control with someone with as much baggage as he had.

And he didn't care.

All he wanted to do was be with her, burn with her.

Her breath grew desperate and ragged. He knew what he wanted, but he kept her on the edge for a little while longer.

"Noah... God, please. I need you."

"You're mine, Leia."

"Yes. Let me come, Noah. I'm yours... Let me come."

"Yes," he rasped, his vocal cords barely able to form the words as she exploded around him.

"Beautiful. So fucking beautiful," he whispered.

33

It felt like they'd gone to bed mere minutes before the phone rang. Noah groaned and cursed under his breath. Leia started to move away. He clamped her closer and inhaled her intoxicating smell.

"Leave it." His mouth drifted over her collarbone.

"Can't. It'll drive me nuts."

"Do I need to show you again who's in charge here?" He nipped playfully at her shoulder.

Sexy, half-drowsy eyes met his. "Maybe. But after I answer the phone." She smiled and reached for the handset. "Hello."

She brushed her hair out of her eyes and squinted at the clock. He followed her gaze. 3.39 a.m. Foreboding slammed into him. Almost nothing good came from a call at this time of the night. He sat up and hit the light remote.

In the silence, Snyder's voice came through loud and clear. "Leia. My messages. Did you not receive them?" The man sounded like every picture Noah had seen of him—eerily, unnaturally calm.

Leia's gaze shot to his. Shit. The messages she'd stuffed in her purse earlier...

"I did... Hang on a moment," she replied.

Noah rose and padded to where she'd dropped her bag and pulled out the white and gold cards. He looked down at them but nothing in them elicited a middle of the night phone call. Frowning, he handed them to her. She read the first two, discarded them and moved on to the third. "I've got them here— *No!*"

She dropped the phone as her eyes filled with icy horror.

"What the hell?"

She looked as if she'd been electrocuted.

"What's wrong?"

Jaw locked, eyes wide, she shook her head.

Noah scooped up the phone from the floor. "What the hell did you say to her, Snyder?"

"You know who I am, so you won't be offended if I tell you this is a private matter and none of your concern."

"Leia *is* my concern so you better tell me what the hell is going on. Right now."

"Mr. King—"

"Noah, stop it." Her whole body was shaking. She held out her hand to him, and he took it.

Gritting his teeth, he said into the phone, "I'll call you back."

He hung up and pulled her to his chest. "Baby, it's okay. Whatever it is, you're safe. I'll protect you." He rocked her until her shaking abated. He stared at the five message cards scattered around her. Four were messages for Leia to call Warren. The fifth had a name with a message.

He eased her away and cupped her face, willed her to stop shaking. "Sweetheart, who's Stephen Willoughby?"

Her breath grew choppy, and a shaft of fear lanced his heart. "He's—my stepfather."

Shock slammed him. "*What?* I thought he was dead!"

She shook her head so wildly her locks covered his arms. "My mom shot him. Then herself. She died. He survived."

Christ. "So where's he been all this time?"

"Locked up. He's supposed to be serving ten to fifteen at Florida State Prison."

Supposed to be.

They stared down at the message: *Stephen Willoughby is out. Call. Warren.*

The phone rang again. She answered it, her voice growing stronger with each question she fired at Snyder. When she hung up, he took her back in his arms.

"Aren't they supposed to notify you about his release?" he asked.

"What does it matter? He's out." Another shudder raked her body. Then she pulled away.

"What are you doing?"

"I'm going home." She left the bed and headed for the dressing room.

Part of him was glad she wasn't shaking with shock and fear. The other part of him wanted her to remain in his arms. Safe and warm.

"I'm sure I can catch a flight first thing."

"You don't have to. My plane will take too long to get here, but I'll charter one to take us home." He picked up the phone and dialed his assistant's number.

She stopped. "You're coming with me?"

He frowned. "You expect me to stay here? And, what, carry on with the trip without you?"

She bit her lip. "I'm sorry. That was stupid."

He held the phone to his ear and caressed her

cheek with his other hand. "You're in shock so I'll let this one slide. But you're mine to protect now. Please don't forget that."

She gave him a weak smile and turned into his caress. When he curved his hand around her nape, her head dropped to his chest. The feeling was so sweet; he closed his eyes until the phone clicked.

"Maddie, I need a plane." He gave her the instructions and hung up to find Leia's gaze on him.

"You own a plane?"

He rubbed his nose against hers. "I own two. One for business, the other for pleasure. The business one is in KL getting a refit. The one for pleasure is flying my parents around Australia and New Zealand. It's their thirty-fifth wedding anniversary this week. Mom's crazy about *Lord Of The Rings*. Almost as much as I am. Remind me to speak Elvish to you sometime."

Noah kept his tone light, banked down the rage bubbling beneath his skin at the news that her attacker was still alive *and* breathing free air.

The shadows he'd thought were banished once and for all were back in her eyes. More than anything, he wanted to take her to bed and fuck her happy again.

Instead, he contented himself with a long, slow

kiss before nudging her toward the dressing room. "Go get dressed. I'll get someone to pack your things."

She started to leave. Then stopped. "Noah, are you sure you're okay with this? You don't have to—"

"Yes, I do." The certainty came from deep within. Somewhere he didn't bother to question.

She blinked and nodded. "Thank you."

"Thank you for trusting me with this." Heading for the living room, he placed a quick call back to Miami before calling reception.

He felt no guilt for putting the plan in place. Not when Leia's safety was at stake.

* * *

They landed in MIA just before 8 a.m. the next morning. Noah had wanted her to sleep on the flight, the cabin of the jet he'd hired more than adequate for a good night's sleep. But she'd been too agitated.

In the end, he'd pulled her down on top of the sheets and kissed her for the better part of an hour before undressing and sliding slowly inside her. The gentle poignancy of the act had brought tears to her eyes and a little calm to her fraying senses.

But the thought that her stepfather was free, and possibly in Miami, never strayed far from her mind.

Warren had called again, but she cut it short when he had nothing new to report.

Hell could wait just a little bit longer.

Now she smoothed her hand down her red Fused Realms T-shirt and leather shorts and looked at Noah as the pilot exited the cockpit and started to lower the door. He caught her fingers and brought them to his lips. "I want to take you home with me. Keep you safe until all the shit goes away."

She shook her head. "I need to see Warren."

His jaw tightened, but he nodded.

Her inhale was shaky and insubstantial. "Hell, I'm already beginning to hate reality."

He released her seatbelt and helped her up. "You came home to face the monsters. Go kick their asses and call me when you're done. I'll make you dinner, and we can crash after. Sound good?"

Her heart soared at the certainty in his voice. Maybe this reality thing wouldn't be as harrowing as she feared it could be.

Dinner plans. Crashing into bed after. They all sounded like good, wholesome, *relationship* things that she could get on board with.

"Sounds good."

He smiled, and she caught the hint of relief in his eyes. When he held out his hand for her, it felt like the most natural thing in the world to slide hers into his.

They walked down the short steps onto the tarmac and Noah stiffened. "What the hell?"

She looked from his face to the cars parked a short distance from the plane. She recognized Warren's sleek Jaguar straightaway. He stood next to the back door, his tall, thin frame impeccably dressed in his favored Savile Row threads. The other two cars—a dark red sports car and a Mercedes limo—were unfamiliar.

The back of the Mercedes opened, and she realized what Noah had reacted to.

The woman who alighted could easily have stepped off the pages of *Vogue*. Straight black hair fell in layered waves to her shoulders and her green dress, white and green Hermes scarf and high-heeled shoes matched so perfectly, it made her eyes hurt.

She swayed toward them and stopped at where Noah was frozen on the tarmac. "Noah." Her voice was soft and sultry like a dawn breeze and she had an intimate smile that curved her lips like a dark secret.

Leia hated her on sight.

"What the hell are you doing here, Ashley?" Noah bit out.

Leia had never heard that tone before. He sounded like he was chewing frozen gravel.

"I would've thought it was obvious. I'm here to give you a ride home."

"I'm more than capable of finding my own way home. And how the hell did you know what time I was landing?"

The hand clasping Leia's trembled. She wasn't sure whether it was from fury or another potentially more disturbing emotion.

"Your PA, Maddie, told me."

"I seriously doubt that."

"You really should hire PAs with more grit, Noah. She buckled under pressure within minutes."

Leia glanced at Noah and inhaled sharply. His face was a taut mask of ice, and a tic throbbed at his temple. She flexed her hand in his, desperate to get a reaction from him. But he seemed to have forgotten she existed.

She looked over to Warren and caught his cool regard. He wouldn't approach. Their way had always been for her to go to him when she needed him. Never vice versa.

He said it was so she'd never have to feel he was impinging on her boundaries. Now she wondered if it was a power thing.

She flinched as Noah's fingers tightened, and he sent her a sidelong glance of apology. When she tried to free herself, he held on tight.

"Ashley, I have nothing to say to you other than get the hell out of my way. If you have a burning need to communicate with me, contact my lawyers. Approach me like this again, and I'll sue you for harassment."

Her smile didn't falter one iota, but her gaze flicked to Leia. "Are you going to introduce me to your little pixie?"

Anger flared through Leia. Lifting her free hand, she gave Ashley a two-fingered wave. "Little Pixie, Leia Michaels here. If we ever meet again, and I sincerely hope we don't, you can call me Miss Michaels. And I'll do my very best not to call you Rude Bitch." She tacked on a false smile.

Ashley paled a little and her eyes narrowed.

Leia turned away from her. "Noah, I have to go. I'll call you later."

* * *

Noah's inner smile at Leia's response to Ashley's rudeness died as he looked over at Warren Snyder.

He'd seen the way the other guy had looked at

Leia as they approached. Every hackle in his body rejected the idea of letting Leia leave with him. Grabbing her arm, he walked her away from Ashley wishing they were back in that bubble Leia had been so afraid would burst once they came back. Christ, how right she'd been. "Come home with me. Please," he breathed. "We can deal with this from my place." He needed to halt this absurd spiral before he lost his mind.

Leia's gaze flicked to Ashley, and her lips pursed. "Looks like you have your hands full with your own monsters. Besides, I really need to talk to Warren."

He struggled not to curse. "My hands want to be full with only you. Call me as soon as you're free and I'll send a car to pick you up, okay?"

Her gaze strayed once more to Ashley and she lifted her brow. "You sure?"

He caught her chin in his hand. "No excuses, remember? Don't think about her. She's less than a minor inconvenience."

She nodded. "She better be. You may have control in the bedroom but I'm trained in Bartitsu. I'll break your arms in several places if you let any part of her touch you."

He smiled at her fierce look. "I'll consider myself adequately warned."

She gave an answering smile that blew him away.

Considering the grenade the justice system had thrown into her life a few short hours ago, she was holding up pretty well.

Whereas he was fighting the very strong urge to beg her to come with him.

He contented himself with a short, hard kiss before he walked her to the Jaguar.

Warren Snyder eyed him, then held out his hand. "Thank you for bringing Leia home safely."

Noah shook his hand and curved his arm around her shoulders. "No need to thank me. I protect what's mine."

Leia stiffened, but he didn't care that he sounded like a mega-possessive SOB. If Leia objected to it later, they would work it out.

It was his turn to stiffen when Snyder's gaze shifted to Leia. "We need to go, my dear. The lawyers are waiting."

Noah's hand cupped her nape for a long moment before he let her go. He turned to the valet holding the keys to his Maserati and saw Ashley.

34

Everything inside him tightened. "Are you still here?"

"I'm not going away just because you ignore me, Noah."

Anger and bitterness fought for supremacy in his gut. "I really wish you would get the message. I wish you'd disappear off the face of the earth. That's how very badly I *don't* want to see you." He took his keys and pressed the unlock button.

"Taylor died."

Noah stiffened, one hand braced on the hood of his car. He closed his eyes against the lance of grief that flared in his chest. "My condolences. He was a great guy. But I don't think you flew down from New

York and stuck around for five days just to tell me your twin brother died. So nice try, but whatever your angle is, the answer is still no."

"One hour, Noah. That's all I need."

He faced her. "You just can't help yourself, can you? You want something, so you try and soften me up with your brother's death. Well, here's a newsflash —I'm over your mind games and your manipulative ways, Ashley. So leave with a little bit of the dignity you denied me two years ago. Or I will bring you to your fucking knees. We both know how much you hate that position, don't we?"

"It's her, isn't it? She's got you so twisted around her little pixie finger you can't see straight."

He looked at her and tried to recall what it was about her he'd found so captivating four years ago. She was very well put together, not a hair out of place or smudged lipstick in sight. Her body was well toned —the result of a fanatic gym regime. She was beautiful in a cool and classy way that turned heads when she walked into a room. But all that was just surface gloss. He knew firsthand what lay underneath.

"My first warning was free, Ash." He used the nickname she hated. "The second one won't be."

He yanked the handle and dropped into the

bucket seat. Stabbing the key in the ignition, he barely gave the engine time to tick over before he stomped on the gas.

Noah got fleeting satisfaction from seeing her jump back from the fumes of burning rubber before his thoughts veered like a divining stick toward Leia.

It had been less than ten minutes since she'd left, and already he felt a gaping desolation. The idea of her out there, under Snyder's dubious protection, stuck in his craw.

Gritting his teeth, he hit the phone button dial on the steering wheel and scrolled through to the number he wanted. "Any luck locating Willoughby?" he asked as soon as the call was answered.

"We have a lead but nothing concrete. We should have something for you by tonight."

Noah paused. "I have another brief for you."

"Yes?"

"Get me everything you can on Warren Snyder, La Carezza, Inc."

"Okay. I'm on it."

He hung up feeling marginally better. He ditched the idea of going to his condo and drove to his office instead. Maddie was headed out to an early lunch when he walked in.

"Mr. King! I wasn't expecting you in till Monday." She seemed nervous.

"I'm not stopping for long." He paused on his way to his office. "Ashley Maitland met me at the airport. You know anything about that?"

Her eyes rounded behind her boxy glasses. "I'm so sorry. She's been calling here all week. I refused to give her any information but this morning she said it was a matter of life and death. I know it's stupid, but—"

"She guilted you into it. I'll let it slide this once. Don't let it happen again."

Relief poured over her face. "Thank you."

"Enjoy your lunch. When you get back, call Tagliani's. Have them deliver the chef's special for two to my place at seven." He intended to see Leia long before then, but he reckoned they'd need food before they went to bed.

"Yes, sir."

He ploughed through two mountains of paperwork and numerous phone calls before he let himself glance at the clock.

2 p.m.

He speared a hand through his hair and checked his phone. He missed Leia. The emptiness inside him terrified and thrilled him. A part of him rejoiced that when Ashley had him carted off in handcuffs two years ago, she hadn't succeeded in killing off every emotion that made him human.

To know he was capable of sustaining the connection he'd found with Leia made his heart race as he located her number and dialed it.

She's got you so twisted around her little finger you can't see straight.

Hell, yeah. And he wasn't ashamed to admit it—

The number you have dialed cannot be reached at the moment.

He rose from his desk and strolled to the window.

He'd stood here less than a week ago contemplating the barrenness of his life, and the depths of his cloying hunger. In a few short days, Leia had changed that desolate landscape. She filled him with hope and possibilities that made him reel.

He knew a good investment when he saw one. He intended to hang on to her with everything he had.

Six hours later, Noah was pacing in front of another window, the vice around his chest tightening with each call that went unanswered. The food had long cooled on the dining table in his condo, and his appetite was non-existent.

Where the hell was she?

He scrolled through to the number he'd dialed

earlier on in the day. He was about to dial it when the intercom buzzed.

Turning off the phone, he grabbed the handset. "Yes?"

"Sir, there's a Miss Michaels here—"

"Send her up." He stalked out the door to the elevator, wishing for the first time that he didn't live in the penthouse suite of a twenty-story building. He nearly tore open the doors with his bare hands when the car stopped.

"Where the fuck have you been?"

"Don't yell at me, Noah. It's been a rough day." She wore the same clothes from this morning and weariness bruised her beautiful eyes.

He dialed his voice down a notch. "Okay. No yelling. Why is your phone off?"

"I didn't get done until half an hour ago. And my phone was off because I was in meetings all day. The board wants me to take over as CEO now or hand over the full reins to Warren—"

He frowned. "You just stepped off a plane. You're exhausted. They couldn't wait a day to hit you with this?"

"Everything sort of snowballed into each other."

He sliced his fingers through his hair. "Leia, I've been going out of my mind worrying about you."

"I'm sorry." Exhaustion lined her voice and face, and he swallowed his frantic worry that had consumed him.

The elevator doors started to shut. He slammed it back. "Come inside. Dinner is cold, but I'm sure I can —" He stopped when she shook her head.

"I'm not coming in. My car's waiting downstairs."

"What the hell for?"

"I just think this is a bad idea. You said we could withstand the baggage. But your ex turned up the moment we landed—"

"And you left with a guy who looks at you like you're his private possession," he snapped.

She recoiled. "No, he doesn't."

He stalked in and caught her up against him. "I know you're not that blind so let's talk about something more relevant. What happened today?"

She pushed against his chest. "Nothing. Let me go, Noah."

Panic surged. He strode into his condo and kicked the door shut. "When I left you this morning you were okay. Now you're dumping me? I think I deserve some answers, don't you?"

"I need a little distance. That's all. Maybe we can pick this back up when—"

He slammed her against the wall. She moaned

and her pupils dilated. His rough treatment turned her on. Just as much as it turned him on.

For them, the rougher the better. The thought that she wanted to take this from him, *from them*, nearly sent him into orbit. When her tongue flicked against the corner of her mouth and her eyes devoured him, he forgot his own name.

"Noah, what are you doing?"

"I should be asking you that." His thumbs caressed the sides of her breasts, and her breath grew shallow and fractured. "Make me understand. You haven't stopped wanting me in the space of eight hours. I sure as hell haven't stopped craving you. So what happened?" he whispered. "I know something did. Baby, please tell me." He didn't care that he was pleading.

Her eyes stayed planted on his mouth but she didn't speak, only shook her head. She inserted one leg between his, slowly sliding her naked thigh upward. The friction, the soft heat of her, made his brain scramble. When the top of her knee scraped the seam of his jeans, he swallowed hard.

"Remember what we agreed? I like the action but I need to hear the words, baby. Vocalize."

"I don't want to talk about it, Noah."

He widened his stance and she immediately

raised her knee. He allowed himself to rock his balls against her, let a dizzying wave of pleasure drown him before he trapped her leg.

Bracing his arms around hers so she couldn't escape, he caught both nipples between his fingers and squeezed hard.

Her scream echoed down his hallway.

He removed his touch and stepped back.

"No! Please…"

"I won't seduce the information out of you, Leia. You have to tell me of your own accord."

Despair wove through the weariness in her eyes before she squeezed them shut.

He refused to let her deny him. "Open your eyes, Leia. Don't be afraid."

She tensed, and her eyes snapped open. "I'm not afraid."

"You are. You're afraid to trust me, even a little. I don't want you hiding yourself from me. Or hiding what's really going on here. I won't be dismissed from your life as easily as you think. And I sure as hell will not let you run because you're too afraid to believe in our future."

"How fucking dare you! If I intended to run I wouldn't be here!"

His smile felt tight and grim. "Good. Then fight

me. Fight with me. For this! For all the nights and days we can have together. Tell me what happened today. I can't help you fix it if you push me away."

She deflated before his eyes. "I can't," she whispered.

Fear clutched his soul. "Give us a chance, baby. Or we're sunk before we've even begun."

"Maybe we shouldn't have begun at all."

Icy fingers clamped his nape. He dropped his hands and stepped away from her. "Fine." He dragged the door open. "Then leave. Run back to your little cozy hideout."

Her eyes widened in shock, then a flash of anger lit her eyes. "Don't be an asshole, Noah."

"You're ripping my guts out, and you accuse me of being an asshole? Tell. Me. What. Happened," he yelled.

"My stepfather happened!"

The jagged pain in his chest took a backseat to his fear for her. "*What?*" He tugged her back and slammed the door shut. "Did he hurt you?"

She dropped her purse on the floor and speared her hands through her hair. It tore him apart to see them tremble. "No, I didn't see him. He called."

"He called you?"

"No, he spoke to Warren."

"What did he want?"

A nauseous grimace rolled across her face. "He wants fifty million dollars in the next seven days."

"That's ridiculous, unless... Is he blackmailing you?" he growled, but the tingle along his nape didn't bode well for hoping it was something else.

"He made a copy of secret recordings... including the one of him..." Her voice broke and her hand flew to her mouth. "Noah, I think I'm going to be sick."

He picked her up and rushed her to the bathroom. He held her head as she dry-heaved, his insides twisting with every hoarse sound. When she exhausted herself, he set her down on the vanity and grabbed a new toothbrush from the cabinet.

"Have you eaten at all today?" he asked.

Bruised, beautiful grey eyes met his in the mirror as she brushed her teeth. "Half a frozen yogurt at lunchtime."

He waited until she'd rinsed her mouth and handed her a face towel. "Think you can handle any food if I rustle something up?"

"You don't have to—"

"You need to eat." He stood behind her and traced his fingers through her hair. "Let me take care of you, baby. Stay here tonight. Please."

Their eyes locked. Held.

"Yes, Noah."

Relief rushed through him and his fingers tightened in her hair. "This isn't something we brush away as inconvenient or walk away from when the going gets tough. You're mine. Even when I threaten to kick your ass, you'll still be mine. Mine to take care of." He bit her nape lightly and traced the hurt with his tongue. "Mine to fuck. Mine to cherish." She trembled beneath his touch and gripped the sink. "Walking away shouldn't be the first option when things get tough. Okay?"

"Okay," she whispered.

"And Leia?"

"Yes?"

"I'll find Willoughby, and I'll make the bastard pay. Trust that too."

He didn't demand an answer because her eyes filled with tears. He caught her to him and just held her tight through her silent weeping.

When it trailed off to hiccups, he kissed the top of her head. "Shower?"

She nodded.

He led her upstairs to his suite and pointed to the door at the far end. "Dressing room through there when you're done. Find something to wear and come find me."

"Okay. Thanks."

He left her in the middle of the room and walked out before he could voice the words tumbling through his head. Words he wasn't sure he understood completely.

They'd survived their first day back in reality.

Noah was prepared to take that as a win.

35

She started to pull off her top and caught sight of her tattoo.

From a broken acorn...

Before yesterday, she alone knew what it meant. Now Noah King knew the pain and horror that had gone into each letter. He knew, and he still wanted her.

Fresh tears threatened as she stood under the shower. She'd almost walked away from that. From him, his strength, his indomitable will and determination to right everything that was wrong in her life.

What will the rest of it say?

He'd asked her that about her tattoo. She still didn't know. But she was hanging on to the hope that one day she would. And she sure as hell was going to hang on to him if he wanted her. Part of the reason she'd fought so hard to come here tonight to end things was because she'd been terrified of the depths of her feelings for Noah. When she'd walked away from him this morning, she'd felt as if her very existence was ripping in two.

She'd carried his last touch on her nape through the day, touching herself there when her world had threatened to cave it on itself.

Then she'd compounded the torture by imagining him with Ashley.

Jealousy and dread tore through her stomach. She pushed it away and finished washing.

After drying herself, she walked naked into Noah's dressing room and peeked through his clothes. On one side, sharp designer suits hung neatly next to four trays of ties and cufflinks. On the other, casual clothes, shoes, and men's accessories had been laid out. She picked up a Vassar College T-shirt and pulled it over her head. She was about to turn away when she noticed the closet at the end of the room.

Intrigued, she opened it and froze.

She'd never shied from using sex toys for self-satisfaction when her needs had grown too explosive to handle. But compared to her paltry collection, Noah's was the super-deluxe version.

She bypassed floggers, ball gags, and cock rings and stopped in front of the heavy-duty stuff. A five-rung silver rack with black straps hung on a spike. Next to it, a three-foot metal rod with cuffs at each end leaned against the wall. She touched the cool metal and her pulse shot up.

"Sweetheart, you coming to ea—"

She jumped and whirled to face him. Noah's gaze raked over her as he strolled lazily toward her, all lean hips and sleek muscles. At some point he'd rolled up his sleeves so his forearms glistened gold under the dressing room lights. His hair was a touch disheveled as if he'd run his hands through it a few times.

God, he was beautiful.

He stopped in front of her. "You're wearing my favorite shirt and you're standing in my favorite room. I may never let you leave," he growled.

The combination of rough tone, delicious man, and wall-to-wall sexy toys threatened to fry her synapses. He stepped up to her, turned her around so her back was to his chest, and leaned down.

"Which one would you like to try first?" he whispered.

She touched the metal rod. "What does this do?"

"The straps go around your ankles so you can't close your legs. I like the idea of having you wide open to me for hours while I make you come again and again."

Shivering, she touched the rack.

"That goes on the wall in my bedroom. Same principle. Full and unfettered access. But that comes with complete trust. And we're not quite there yet. Ceding control to me in the bedroom was a first step, but there are several steps to complete trust, baby. I want you there with me when we use this."

He took her hand and led her out.

"Come and eat. If you're good, I'll let you choose something from in here later."

Leia tried not to be hurt about the trust remark. Deep down, she knew he was right. Her first instinct when the shit hit the fan today had been to run and hide the way she'd been doing for the last five years. She'd almost walked away because she'd been too scared.

It was time to shed the fear and take a leap.

She curled her fingers around his, and he sent her a smile as they entered the living room. She hadn't taken the time to check out his condo before, and she now looked around.

"Wow, I love your place."

His smile widened. "Yeah?"

She nodded. The living room was huge with vast amounts of open space. White furniture dominated, contrasted with bold splashes of color that drew the eye to strategic pieces of modern art in the room. Floor-to-ceiling windows met on two sides. At this time of night, she couldn't see the ocean but by day it would be spectacular. "I've never been in a billionaire's pad before."

He caught her to him and smacked her hard on the ass. "And you'll never see another unless it's mine."

His hand soothed her flesh. Then he groaned when he realized she was naked beneath. "Let's eat. It's been nearly twenty-four hours since I last fucked you. You're getting it rough and merciless for what you've put me through today, but you're also getting it fast." His eyes held a shade of vulnerability and hurt. "I also need your vocal cords functioning tomorrow for when we meet my guy."

He started to walk away, but she caught him back and touched her fingers to his cheek. "Noah, I'm sorry I didn't call. I was scared you'd think the baggage was too much."

His hand pressed her fingers into his cheek and he kissed her palm. "Sometimes our nightmares loom larger than they really are. Willoughby is a problem. The videos are a problem. But they're not problems you need to deal with alone. I told you, you're mine and I'll take care of you."

They shared a smile that stung her heart and pierced her to the core. For a moment she didn't recognize the feeling. Then it slammed into her.

Happy. She was happy.

Leaning up, she pressed her mouth against his. A split second later, he took over. Eventually, they stumbled to the bar where he'd set up their meal, and they ploughed through the grilled swordfish and salad he'd prepared. He'd rescued the chocolate fondant from the restaurant delivery, and she gorged and licked her spoon clean.

"Wow, that's some mad cooking skills there, King. I may just keep you."

He grinned, drained the last of his wine and prowled towards her. "You better. Because I intend to keep you." He took her glass and set it down. Electrifying blue eyes hooked into hers, one hand around her throat, caressing her pulse. "Now, Leia."

Her breath caught and she stood. "What do you want me to do?"

"Pick a toy and put it on the bed. Take off my shirt and kneel on the bed, legs apart."

The force of his need and the power of his arousal followed her all the way up the stairs. Even as she crossed the carpet to his closet, Leia knew which item she would choose.

She took it off the hook and curved her fingers around the thick handle. Returning to the bedroom, she undressed and crawled onto the high king-sized bed.

He entered five minutes later, his slow predatory footfalls escalating her helpless exhilaration.

"Fuck, sweetheart, you're wet and swollen. Did seeing my toys make you like this?" he groaned.

"No, it's you. All you. I need you so much."

His breath hissed roughly. She heard a rustle of clothes then the bed dipped behind her. Her stomach clenched on a rush of desperate antic-ipation.

"For the next hour, when I ask you a direct ques-tion, you can answer. Otherwise, the only words I want to hear from you are *please* and *Noah*. I don't care in which order. Just vocalize those two words. You got it?"

"Yes, Noah."

He picked up the toy and trailed it along the top of her thigh. "I suspected you would choose this, but I want you to tell me why you chose it."

"I need to be punished for making the monsters win for a while."

"You know how that made me feel?"

"No."

"Angry. Disappointed. Fucking terrified that the real world had taken you from me."

The first hard lash of the leather whip against her pussy made her scream. She fell forward onto hands that trembled beneath the ecstasy roaring through her. The second hit her ass, fanned pain and pleasure in an outward flare that sent another scream roaring through her.

He took turns lashing her pussy and her ass until she was poised on the brink of cataclysmic release. Then he stopped.

"Please, Noah. *Please... please...*" she sobbed.

He dropped the whip and reared up behind her, one hand cupping her breast, the other her hot, aching sex. "Are you sorry?"

"Yes!"

He shuddered deep. "Kiss me, Leia. Show me how much you want me."

She twisted and kissed him, dirty and deep, just the way he liked it. With her tongue, she told him how much she was enjoying what he was doing to her body, how much she needed him.

* * *

With a groan torn from his soul, Noah poised his cock at her entrance and surged into her.

Her teeth clamped on his lower lip and she screamed. Tasting his blood against her mouth was like a drug shooting through his veins. Desperate to keep control, he tore his mouth away. "Sweet heaven, what are you doing to me?" His voice was raw, much rougher than he'd ever heard it.

"Take me, Noah. Make me yours."

He didn't bother to tell her she'd flouted the rules.

He fucked her with everything he had, every desperate emotion he'd lived through today. He made her scream until the sound saturated his blood.

Then he flipped her over, pulled her knees up to her shoulders and started all over again.

Her nails scored grooves in his biceps. "Yes, Noah. More please. Give me more!"

Her insatiable demand triggered his own.

Sweat poured down his temple, dripping into his mouth before landing in hot splotches on her stomach.

His balls tightened as his pleasure gathered strength. Heaven help him, he was going to come way before he was ready, but there was no help for it. She undid him in ways he was beginning to fear he'd never understand.

"Noah," she groaned, and he lost another layer of reason.

Her inner muscles tightened. "Do I make you feel good, baby? Is that why you're so wet, so tight for me?"

"Yes!"

He braced his hand on either side of her head and planted kisses between her breasts. "You feel so gorgeous."

She shuddered and turned her face to his. Shamelessly, she grazed her cheek against his rough stubble. "Make me come, Noah. Please. I'm dying." Her voice broke.

He shut his eyes against the sound of her pleas. God, she was incredible. He kissed her cheek and caught her lobe between his teeth. "It'll be my pleasure, baby."

Sliding his hand between their bodies, he slid two fingers alongside her clit, squeezing the nerve-engorged nub between his knuckles.

She started to come with a low keen. She turned her face and kissed his hand next to her head on the bed.

Shock slammed through him when he realized her cheek was wet with tears. "Oh, baby."

Her silent tears turned into hoarse sobs and he started to unravel. "God. Leia."

His seed gushed out of him with the force of a power hose, scalding him as he filled her to overflowing. The sensation was so intense, he roared, tipping forward as his body gave way under the torrent of pleasure.

Vaguely, he felt her fingers thread through his, her lips touching his flesh over and over in silent benediction as he came harder than he'd ever come in his life.

He knew he was crushing her, that he needed to move. But the semen gushing out of his cock showed no sign of abating.

"Jesus," he groaned. "I can't stop coming."

She shuddered beneath him, and he sucked in a frantic breath.

Get hold of yourself, dammit.

Wrapping his arms around her, he turned them sideways. Her head flopped weakly onto his arm, her silky hair covering her face. He felt her chest expand as she sucked in a breath and felt a twinge of guilt.

"Are you okay, sweetheart?"

She kissed his forearm. "I'm a little sore but it's a good pain." She fell silent for a moment, but he sensed she had more to say.

"What is it? What's wrong?"

"Nothing's wrong. I just... didn't mean to cry again."

He pushed the hair out of her face. She was flushed with embarrassment and her eyes were slightly red with her tears. She'd never looked more beautiful.

"Do you have any idea what it does to a guy... what it does to *me* to have you cry when I fuck you?"

She grimaced. "Is it a good thing?"

He laughed, and he realized his heart was bursting with emotions he couldn't name. "It's a fantastic thing. Don't ever hold back what you're feeling, especially if it's a first."

"Okay."

Leaning closer, he whispered, "I'd love you to soak the sheets with tears, sweat, and cum every time we fuck."

She reddened even more. "Noah!"

He kissed her shocked mouth and started losing himself again in her bone-deep sweetness. Hell, he needed to dial it down a notch before he lost it completely.

And yet... "Are you happy?" he asked before he could stop himself.

Her hand curled against his chest and she sighed.

"Yes." A simple answer that tore at his insides and left him reeling.

"Good. Go to sleep before I get you to spend another hour proving it."

Long after she'd settled into sleep, he lay wide-awake, his arms around her, listening to her breathe. He pondered how very quickly she'd shot up to the top of everything that was important to him.

And how very determined he was to keep her there.

36

Warren regarded his unexpected visitor from across the wide stone coffee table in his living room.

The early hour meant he'd been caught mid-spar session in the underground gym of his property. Although sparring was a misnomer today because his usual sparring partner was absent.

Leia hadn't come home last night, and she hadn't called.

Another first.

The flare of rage sweeping beneath the surface of his calm wouldn't be contained. He'd been trying since 4 a.m. when he'd given up his vigil and changed into gym clothes.

He'd have to spend another hour with the punch

bag or on the Wing Chun. He propped his elbows on his knees, clasped his blood-spotted bandaged hands together. "Apologies for my state of dress."

"It is I who should apologize for barging in so early." A smile. A drift of eyes over his sweat-covered muscles.

Warren ignored the veiled interest and glanced down at the file before him. "Is this accurate?"

"It's an accurate copy."

He leafed through the file and then closed it. "Why?" His question didn't need elaboration and he didn't offer one.

"Our parallel interests ensure a speedy outcome. You're welcome to refuse, of course."

He'd plotted a different path to achieve his goals. But this could expedite things. If it failed, he could resort to his original course of action.

"I'll have coffee brought in for you. Give me half an hour to get ready."

37

"Brunch is almost here."

Leia swam to blissful consciousness and smiled. "I love that you wake me up with the promise of food."

A kiss landed just above her ear and lingered. "I love that you love that."

She faced him and they grinned at each other before he pulled the sheet from her. Picking up the remote, he aimed it at the curtains and they slid back to reveal a cobalt-blue sky and glistening ocean.

Lifting her hands above her head, she stretched, contentment like she'd never known stealing over her.

She'd awoken in the middle of the night in Noah's arms, and the words she tried hard to suppress had bubbled up to her lips.

I love you. I love you. I love you.

Even mouthing them had seemed like a monumental step, but the emotion was there in her heart, ready for when the time was right.

Because. *Too soon, too soon, too soon.*

Noah turned and cursed. "You're swimming in dangerous waters, baby. You're sore from last night and we need to eat and go meet this guy."

She slowly bent her knee, crossed her wrists above her head and pushed out her chest. "Why, what am I doing?" She blinked innocently.

"God, you're fucking lethal." He started towards her just as the buzzer sounded. His curse turned way filthier as he crossed the room. "Get dressed and come down. If I have to come up and get you, you won't be able to walk for the rest of the week."

"Yes, sir."

She basked in the grin he threw over his shoulder as he left the room.

* * *

Noah was still grinning when he pushed the buzzer. "Come on up."

He poured two mugs of coffee and added cream

and sugar to Leia's. He took a gulp of his brew and grabbed his wallet for a tip as the elevator pinged.

The doors parted and he froze.

Of the two people in the car, Ashley stepped out first.

"You don't need to tip me for bringing up breakfast, Noah. Consider it my good deed of the day." She held out the white and gold bag from his favorite deli two blocks away.

Noah ignored it, his eyes fixed on the other occupant of the elevator. "What the hell are you doing here, Snyder?"

Even on a Saturday, the older man was impeccably turned out in a suit, tie, and pocket handkerchief. "I'm here for what is mine."

Cold fury rolled through Noah's gut. "I think you took a wrong turn somewhere, buddy. There's nothing of yours here."

"Manners, Noah. Honestly," Ashley huffed.

Pins and needles shot up his arms, and he realized his fists were bunched tight. He focused on the pain. "Leave now, both of you, before I throw you out. And you"—his gaze flicked to Ashley—"since you don't seem to understand the words stay-the-fuck-away-from-me, I'm filing a restraining order against you first thing Monday morning."

She gave a mock shiver. "I've always thought there was something so sexy and dangerous about a restraining order. Maybe I should look into it. It's that sort of danger that turns you on, isn't it?"

"The problem with you, Ashley, is that you always thought you had me figured out. But you didn't, which was why you resorted to silly mind games."

Her lips pursed. "Oh, come on, we both know you thrive on the danger. What else would you call wanting to tie me up, gag me until I could barely breathe, and smacking the hell out of me? You got off on dicing with death. Dicing with my life."

Horror dredged through Noah as her words sank into his skin like toxic claws. Had she really seen it like that?

"Noah?" Leia called from the kitchen.

Ashley turned. "Ah, there's your little..." She paused at Noah's warning growl. "Friend. Now we can all have a civilized conversation."

Noah stalked past her as Leia entered the hallway. She was wearing his Vassar T-shirt and her leather shorts. Her sun-kissed hair was still mussed from sleep and she was barefoot. He'd never seen her more beautiful.

She looked past him, and her expression changed. "Warren? What are you doing here?"

"I'm waiting for a lucid answer to that myself." Noah caught her arm and pulled her to his side. A shade of his fury abated when she melted into him.

"Like Miss Maitland suggested, I think we should sit down and talk," Snyder said.

Noah noticed that Leia's eyes hadn't moved from Warren. The urge to physically block him from her view was instinctive.

Her gaze shifted to Ashley then to him. "What's going on, Noah?"

"I don't know but, fine, I'll play."

Gritting his teeth, he led the way into the living room and pushed her into the single armchair. He remained standing with a hand caressing her nape. She glanced up at him, and he smiled stiffly.

He waited till Snyder and Ashley seated themselves on the large sofa.

"You wanted an hour? I'll give you ten minutes. Non-negotiable. After that I'm throwing you out."

"Noah, I really wanted to do this in private—"

"The clock's ticking, Ashley."

Snyder and Ashley exchanged glances. Noah hated the rock-hard dread that rolled into his stomach when Snyder's gaze shifted to Leia.

"Did he tell you about how their relationship ended?" Warren asked.

Leia paled a little, and her gaze searched Noah's before returning to Snyder. She totally ignored Ashley. "Why, what does it matter? It ended. The question here is, why are you interested?"

Shards of ice spiked around the dread. "Yes, I'm curious. Why are you interested?"

"Because after everything you've been through, I'm not prepared to jeopardize your safety—"

"Think carefully about what you say next, Snyder. Or I promise, I will bury you." Noah's voice was a thin blade that sliced across the room.

Ashley flinched. Leia's pulse jumped beneath his hand. He stared down at her.

"Leia?" Her eyes met his. His insides shredded with the wariness and confusion he witnessed. "No excuses," he breathed.

Doubt rolled across her face, and she swallowed hard. Noah's insides hollowed.

"My dear, you need to come home now, before it's too late."

"What does that mean?" Leia snapped at Warren, her arms crossing around her middle. "I'm not in the mood for one of your riddles."

Ashley reached into her purse and pulled out a file. Warren took it from her and placed it on the table.

"This is a copy of the charges Miss Maitland filed against Mr. King in New York two years ago. The report and the pictures are clear enough. It lists her injuries—"

"God, Ashley, are you really this desperate?" Noah felt Leia flinch at his raw disgust, but he was past showing mercy. Not when his world was caving in.

Snyder sat forward. "Leia, I'm not prepared to leave you to his mercy—"

"I understand why *he's* doing this but what the hell do *you* have to gain from this?" Noah snarled at Ashley.

Ashley twirled her diamond bracelet and her eyelids fluttered down, then back to meet his. "You weren't supposed to leave."

"Excuse me?"

"Two years ago. You were supposed to marry me and work things out with me. I would've forgiven you for your nasty little traits."

Leia jerked away from him. He frowned down at her but her head was bent. He reefed a hand through his hair and fought for his sanity. "I left, Ashley. Deal with it."

She shook her head. "I want you back."

"Are you insane?"

"You can't have him back!" Leia surged to her feet. Her fists were balled, and her eyes blazed pure determination. "You had your chance with him and you blew it. So trot back to New York on your little princess heels and leave him alone."

God, yes!

His world began to right itself again and he breathed easier. He took a step toward her, desperate to pull her into his arms, feel her warmth.

"Remember when we talked about children, Noah?" Ashley said.

He froze mid-step.

"I was in the hospital after my kidney infection. We talked about having children one day. You wanted two. I wanted three. Do you remember what happened after we discussed it?"

Dear God. "No."

Leia's gaze swung to his, horror alive in her grey eyes. He wanted to reassure her, but his tongue was frozen. His whole body was frozen, unable to move as his world imploded.

"Yes. I did it, Noah. I'm pregnant." Ashley smiled. "You're going to be a father."

* * *

MORE FROM ZARA COX

Another book from Zara Cox, *Million Dollar High*, is available to order now here:
https://mybook.to/MillionDollarBackAd

ABOUT THE AUTHOR

Zara Cox is the writer of spicy contemporary romance, she writes intense, spicy billionaire romances for Boldwood, including the Indigo Lounge series.

Sign up to Zara Cox's mailing list for news, competitions and updates on future books.

Follow Zara on social media here:

ALSO BY ZARA COX

The Indigo Lounge Series

Mile High Addiction

Sky High Obsession

Seven Night Stopover

Million Dollar High

High Sea Seduction

Boldwood
EVER AFTER

XOXO

JOIN BOLDWOOD'S
**ROMANCE
COMMUNITY**
FOR SWEET AND
SPICY BOOK RECS
WITH ALL YOUR
FAVOURITE
TROPES!

SIGN UP TO OUR
NEWSLETTER

HTTPS://BIT.LY/BOLDWOODEVERAFTER

Boldwood

Boldwood Books is an award-winning fiction publishing company seeking out the best stories from around the world.

Find out more at www.boldwoodbooks.com

Join our reader community for brilliant books, competitions and offers!

Follow us
@BoldwoodBooks
@TheBoldBookClub

Sign up to our weekly deals newsletter

https://bit.ly/BoldwoodBNewsletter

www.ingramcontent.com/pod-product-compliance
Lightning Source LLC
Chambersburg PA
CBHW01065910726
47900CB00010B/2734